DANGEROUS ENCORE

A Dangerous Noise Novel

CRYSTAL KASWELL

This is a work of fiction. Similarities to real people, places, or events are entirely coincidental.

DANGEROUS ENCORE

First edition. July 25, 2017

Written by Crystal Kaswell.

Cover by Okay Creations

Also by Crystal Kaswell

Sinful Serenade

Sing Your Heart Out - Miles

Strum Your Heart Out - Drew

Rock Your Heart Out - Tom

Play Your Heart Out - Pete

Sinful Ever After – series sequel

Just a Taste - *Miles's POV*

Dangerous Noise

Dangerous Kiss - Ethan

Dangerous Crush – Kit

Dangerous Rock – Joel

Dangerous Fling – Mal

Dangerous Encore - series sequel

Inked Hearts

Tempting - Brendon

Hooking Up - Walker

Pretend You're Mine - Ryan

Hating You, Loving You - Dean

Breaking the Rules - Hunter

Losing It - Wes

Accidental Husband - Griffin

The Baby Bargain - Chase

Inked Love

The Best Friend Bargain - Forest

The First Taste - Holden

The Roomie Rulebook - Oliver

Dirty Rich

Dirty Deal - Blake

Dirty Boss - Nick

Dirty Husband - Shep

Dirty Desires - Ian

Dirty Wedding - Ty

Dirty Secret - Cam

Pierce Family

Broken Beast - Adam

Playboy Prince - Liam

Ruthless Rival - Simon - coming soon

Standalones

Broken - Trent & Delilah

Come Undone Trilogy

Come Undone

Come Apart

Come To Me

Sign up for the Crystal Kaswell mailing list

Violet and Ethan

Chapter One

ETHAN

Except for the low hum of the fan, the apartment is silent.

Vi must be asleep.

It's nearly four a.m. Of course she's asleep.

Even though my entire body is begging me to wake her, I stay quiet as I make my way to our bedroom.

She's lying on top of the black comforter, in some gorgeous see through bra and panty set. Her Kindle is resting on her chest. Her eyes and lips are dark with makeup.

It's not exactly unusual seeing Violet asleep in a full face of makeup, but this—

She was waiting up for me.

My chest warms. I'm so fucking lucky to have her. I need to *have* her right away. Well, as soon as she's awake.

I can wait until morning to fuck her.

But I can't wait another fucking minute to get my arms around her. I strip to my boxers then I climb into bed behind Violet.

She stirs as the weight shifts. Her lips part with a soft sigh.

"Ethan," she murmurs. "Is that you?"

"Yeah." I place my body behind hers, my crotch against her ass, my chest against her back. "Go back to sleep, honey."

She shakes her head and nestles into my body.

Fuck, she feels good. Warm. Soft. Mine.

"I should shower." It's an empty threat. There isn't a single part of me that wants to be somewhere else.

"No." She reaches back to grab my wrist, then she's pulling my hand over her waist. "You should stay here. Forever."

"Forever?"

"Mhmm."

"What about breakfast?"

"Overrated."

"What if I'm going to make you a dozen matcha lattes?"

"Hmmm." Her voice is a soft mumble. She's still half asleep. "Maybe for two dozen—"

I pull her closer. "That can be arranged."

She murmurs a yes. Her chest rises with her inhale and falls with her exhale. Her eyelids stay pressed together.

Fuck, it's adorable watching her try to stay awake.

"I…" She talks through a yawn. "I was waiting up."

I trace the outline of her sheer black bra. "I can see that."

"Oh. Yeah. It's new. I, um… Do you like it?" She turns so we're face-to-face. There's a nervousness in her eyes.

It's hard to believe that Vi gets nervous about anyone's opinion, especially mine, especially after all this time. We've been living together a year now.

We've been engaged for months.

Fuck, we're getting married in three fucking days.

And she's nervous I won't like the scraps of fabric barely covering her tits and ass.

God damn, I can't stop staring. The sheer fabric does nothing to hide her hard nipples. And there's this corset lacing between her breasts.

My fingers tug the lacing undone. "I fucking love it." I can't help myself. I push the straps off her shoulders one at a time. "But I still need to get rid of it."

Okay, I can't wait to have her.

Not another fucking minute.

"Ethan..." She arches her back, pressing her crotch against mine.

Fuck, those panties are just as sheer. They have that same lacing going over her hip.

There's barely any fabric between my cock and her cunt.

My hands are greedy. One tosses her bra aside.

The other goes to her ass, and pulls her crotch into mine.

She groans as she rubs herself against my hard-on. "I missed you."

"I missed you too." I cup her breast and play with her nipple with my thumb. Thoughts flee my brain at an alarming rate. I need to get this out now, before the only thing I can do is demand her orgasm. "Fuck, Vi..."

Fuck. Too late.

I let my eyelids flutter closed and I bring my lips to hers.

She tugs at my hair as she slides her tongue into my mouth. Her kiss is hard and hungry. Every bit of her need pours into me.

Ten fucking days.

How was this only ten fucking days...

It felt like an eternity.

And in another ten fucking days, we have to do this all over again.

I'm asking her to squeeze our wedding and honeymoon into a break in our tour schedule.

That's not it, not exactly. There are all sorts of venue details that are way too fuzzy with my cock this hard—

There are life details too.

After everything with Mom, we wanted to do it fast.

Carpe diem. Memento mori. All that fucking shit.

But still.

Ten fucking days.

Then we're apart again.

And again.

It goes on forever.

Violet groans as she pulls back. "Did I already say I missed you?"

"Yeah."

"I really did." She pushes my boxers off my hips. "Tell me it gets easier."

"It doesn't."

"I know. Tell me anyway."

"You know I can't lie to you."

"Tell me something good."

"I love you."

"I love you too." She presses her palm flat against my stomach. "God, Ethan…" Her eyelids flutter closed.

She leans in and kisses me, hard.

Then she's wrapping her hand around my cock.

Fuck—

Need pours from her lips to mine.

From my lips to hers.

I can't explain this. I can't put it into words. At the moment, it's a struggle finding any coherent words.

I love Vi more than anything.

More than the band.

More than touring.

More than fucking music.

She'd never ask me to give it up.

Which is good. 'Cause I'm not sure I could fucking do it.

And here we are, three days from getting married, and she's dealing with the weight of that on her own.

She deserves more than that.

She deserves fucking everything.

But, fuck, I need her.

And right now—

She groans into my mouth.

She rubs my tip with her thumb.

I push her panties off her hips, then help her get them off her feet.

We're naked in *our* bed in *our* apartment. This is our fucking life, and it's a good fucking life.

But I still have to ask myself—

Fuck.

That last coherent thought leaves my brain as she climbs on top of me. She straddles me and presses her palms against my shoulders.

Slowly, she lowers her body onto mine.

My cock strains against her.

Then it's one delicious inch at a time.

"Vi…"

"Fuck, Ethan…" Her green eyes are heavy with desire.

She rocks her hips against me. The friction is divine, and she feels so fucking good.

Knowing that I'm bringing her all that pleasure…

That it's *our* bodies joining…

God damn, I'm so fucking cheesy now.

But I don't care.

I bring one hand to her hair and pull her into a deep, slow kiss.

I bring the other to her hips and use it to guide her.

And we stay locked like that, bodies moving together, tongues dancing, all that need and affection pouring between us.

We stay locked together as she comes on my cock.

As her cunt pulses around me.

As her groans vibrate over my skin, all the way to my fingers and toes.

I flip her over and pin her to the bed.

She wraps her legs around my hips and pulls my body into hers.

She tugs at my hair.

It's like she can't take a single hint of space between us.

Fuck knows I can't.

I thrust into her with soft, slow strokes until I'm there.

I groan against her lips, tugging at her hair as I come.

My cock pulses. Pleasure spreads out to my fingers and toes.

Once I've spilled every drop, I collapse next to her.

We're both a sweaty, sticky mess.

But she still nestles into my body.

She still falls asleep in my arms.

In the morning, we shower together. We stay in the tiny space until we're prunes. I can't get enough of her body against mine. Of her groans. Of her nails on my skin, my hands in her hair, my teeth on her neck.

I can't get enough of her. Period.

Reality is right outside the door. There are only two

days until our wedding, and the thought of a single one of her relatives watching me walk down the aisle, that *why isn't she marrying a nice, stable guy* look on their faces makes my stomach tie up in knots.

I know I want to be with Violet forever. I knew that when I marked my body for her.

Usually, I'm good with an audience…

But not that audience.

It's terrifying.

I want my thoughts gone.

I want the world making sense, the way it does when it's just our bodies aligned.

I make Violet come until she's begging me to stop.

We get out of the shower and wrap ourselves in towels. Violet goes to get dressed. I fix scrambled eggs with avocado, coffee for me, a matcha latte for her.

She steps out of our bedroom in a tight black dress and patterned black tights. She's already all made up, her hair in that perfect straight line.

"Your mom coming today?" I ask.

"Not until our hair and makeup run through. She has work." Her eyes fix on me. "Can I convince you to adopt this wardrobe permanently?"

"You know how to persuade me."

She makes a show of checking out my bare torso as I bring our breakfast to the table.

Her lips curl into a smile as her eyes meet mine. She wraps her hand around my wrist and pulls me into a soft, slow kiss.

"How many times have I said 'I really missed you,' now?" she asks.

"I missed you too." I slide into the seat across from hers. There aren't enough words to explain how much I missed Violet, how much I always miss Violet when I'm away.

Her eyes go to the table. She traces the outline of her mug with her pointer finger.

She's thinking something.

Something she doesn't want to say.

She stares at her drink. Then at her twisting amethyst and diamond ring.

Slowly, she meets my gaze. "Are you as nervous as I am?"

I nod.

"Good." She brings her mug to her lips and takes a sip. Her eyelids flutter closed as she lets out a soft moan. "Fuck Ethan, you're too good at this."

"Never stop saying that."

Her laugh dissolves the tension in the room. "You didn't get enough positive feedback?" She nods to the master bedroom/bathroom. "I definitely lost track of how many times I said 'Fuck, Ethan.'"

"It was at least a dozen."

"Braggart."

My smile spreads over my cheeks. God, it feels so good sitting across from her at breakfast. It feels so good talking about nothing with Violet.

She takes another long sip of her drink. "Thank you. For breakfast. And this."

"Anytime."

She nods, but there's something in her eyes. It's not *anytime*. It's anytime I'm here.

Which is barely half the time.

No, I'm projecting. Right now, the only thing in Violet's eyes is satisfaction.

She downs half her drink then moves to her plate of eggs. She chews, swallows, takes another bite, talks with her mouth full. "These too." She swallows. "You're multi-talented, Ethan Strong."

I cock a brow. "Yeah?"

"Well, if you're right about a dozen..." She takes another bite. Her eyes go to the clock on the wall, the one with guitars for numbers. "Fuck, is that right?"

I check the time on the microwave behind us. "Yeah."

"I better hurry." She takes a quick sip. "Are you coming? I know it's not really the most exciting decision in the world, which cake we're getting, but we were supposed to decide two weeks ago."

"You want me there?"

She nods. "Otherwise, it's just me and Piper."

"You sure you want me there? There won't be much left for me *and* you after Piper has her way."

"She's not that bad."

I nod. "She's worse." My little sister has quite the fondness for desserts. And she has quite the affection for Violet. She was over the moon when Violet asked her to be maid of honor.

No doubt, she's been pulling my weight with wedding planning.

Not that it will stop me from teasing her about her sweet tooth.

"How soon do we have to leave?" I ask.

She looks to the clock then back to me. "Twenty minutes."

I nod. "Done."

"I, uh..." Her eyes flare with something I can't place. "I'm going to find my shoes."

I watch her walk away.

Violet has to go through so much of her life alone. Because of me. Because of my choices.

Maybe her family is right. Maybe she deserves some stable guy, an accountant who's by her side night and day.

Maybe she deserves a guy who won't show up late when she's wearing the hottest lingerie in the history of the world.

It's not like I could help the flight delay.

But it's always something.

Violet and I are the same—we love what we do. We need work. It keeps us going.

It's not like before. She does come first. When she needs me, I'm there. Period.

But what if that isn't enough?

Chapter Two

VIOLET

I try to get comfortable in the cozy chair, but it isn't happening. This is the only bakery in all of Orange County that could squeeze us in this last minute *and* promise as ornate a decoration as our hearts desire.

This is a perfectly normal chair, the same as the rickety white chairs in most of the coffee shops in the area.

But no amount of crossing or uncrossing my legs helps me get comfortable.

Ethan is at the counter, talking to the manager. His wide smile lights up his bright eyes. He looks happy. That's how he's supposed to feel as a groom-to-be.

The manager laughs and presses her palm to her chest. She leans over to Ethan and whispers something. Her hand grazes his forearm.

He's charming her. Of course he is. He's Ethan. The man was born to entertain. In his skinny jeans, leather jacket, t-shirt combo, he looks every bit the rock star. He looks like he belongs on stage.

Charming one person at a time is a waste of his skills. He could be charming ten thousand people.

He could be charming a few hundred thousand people with some TV appearance. Or even a million people. Hell, a few million.

I take a deep breath and exhale slowly. This has to be normal, pre-wedding jitters. It can't be anything else, because I can't survive without Ethan.

He's still the only person who really gets me.

It's normal being stressed before a big occasion. Especially one that falls mostly on my shoulders. Nobody talks about the blushing groom and his beautiful suit and his perfect hair and makeup. Nobody asks him what he thinks of the ribbons on the chairs or the floral arrangements or the seating charts.

Two months sounded like plenty of time to plan a wedding when the date at the Kimberly Crest House and Gardens opened up. It was the only available weekend in the next year and a half. Well, the only one that lined up with Ethan's schedule.

His mom had just passed away, and he was hating that he was hurting, and I was hating that he was hurting. It felt necessary to claim him as my family right away.

Don't get me wrong. I still feel that pull to make things official. I still want to tell the entire world—or at least all my friends and family—that Ethan is my family now and forever.

But I'm tired of hearing about it.

There are still so many details up in the air.

And I still have to deal with everyone's reactions on every one of them.

And then there are the opinions on the one thing that really matters—

Nobody in my family gets why I'm marrying Ethan. Mom and Dad try. They really do. But they still look at him like they want to tell him to cut his hair and cover his tattoos.

"Hey." His voice grabs my attention. He's standing at the counter, holding two cups. "Green tea." He places it on the table in front of me then takes the seat next to mine. "You okay, honey?"

Maybe. "Just stressed."

He takes a long sip of his coffee. "You look exhausted."

"Don't tell me I didn't cover up my under-eye circles."

He laughs. "It's more your posture."

"Good." I smooth my dress. I prefer to think of my makeup and wardrobe as armor, but I can't deny that I want to look good as much as I want to look tough.

"Don't worry. You look fucking hot." He leans in to whisper. "I'm tempted to drag you to the bathroom, push those tights to your knees, and get you coming on my hand."

My cheeks flush.

He drags his fingertips up my thigh, over my tights. "I could probably do it right now. Over the tights."

I shake my head. "We need a cake."

He nods and pulls back to a semi-respectable distance. His blue eyes bore into mine.

God, his eyes are beautiful. Expressive. Full of life.

His lips curl into a half smile. He takes my hand and rubs the spot between my pointer finger and my thumb with his thumb. "Talk to me."

"I'm glad you're here." I scoot closer. "It's a lot. And it's almost here."

His expression is earnest. He's really listening. He always listens. He always does everything he can to make me feel better.

He's the person I want.

I should be happy about our wedding. I shouldn't be

agonizing over what flavor of cake we're going to order and exactly how we're going to decorate it, and how people are going to react to it.

It's a cake.

It's not the thing that defines us as a couple.

But it feels that way.

I'm staring into my fiancé's eyes, and I'm thinking about fucking cake decorations. "I need another morning in the shower with you."

"Right back at you." He leans in to press his forehead against mine. "You can say when, Vi. We can get in my car and drive to Vegas right now and do this just us."

I shake my head. I want everyone to see us getting married. I just… I want it to be easier.

I let my eyelids press together.

And I let my lips find his.

God, Ethan is a good kisser.

My hand goes to his dark, wavy hair. I pull him closer.

I kiss him harder.

If only this was the entire ceremony. I could happily spend the next three days practicing our kiss. Though it's really more like two days. Barely sixty hours. Or maybe less.

There's the click of a camera phone. And footsteps.

A low, deep chuckle echoes around the room.

"Baby, you're going to get arrested one of these days." That's Kit.

Oh.

It's not that I don't like the bassist. I do. Quite a bit, actually. But I don't want any more opinions.

Piper looks as adorable and bubbly as always. Her blond hair is hanging over her pink blouse. Somehow, she makes jeans and wedge boots adorable.

She has those expressive Strong eyes.

They're as filled with joy as Ethan's are.

She smiles as she takes her seat. "I can't help it. You two are so cute. Oh my God, did I show you the one of Mal and Lacey I got at the last show?"

"Do I want to see it?" Kit asks.

She scrunches her face with disgust. "It's sweet. Not gross. God knows the kinds of disgusting things they do together." She slides her phone into her purse and sets it in her lap. "You know what? No adorable pictures for you."

He chuckles. "How will I survive?"

"Don't look at me. You dug your own grave," she teases.

Ethan scoots a little closer to me. He squeezes my hand.

It calms me. It really does.

Piper turns to me. "I'm ready to eat any amount of cake. I didn't have breakfast, and I only put a hint of sugar in my coffee."

"That was a hint?" Kit asks.

"It was barely anything," she says.

"A tablespoon per cup is barely anything?" he asks.

"It was less than that."

"Uh-huh."

She laughs. "It was. And you're just as bad."

"I have an excuse."

"And liking the taste isn't as valid a reason as needing the dopamine rush?"

He nods.

She smiles and flips him off.

He grabs her hand and sucks on her ring finger. Her left ring finger. The one adorned with the engagement ring she's been rocking for nearly a year now.

Piper giggles as she pulls her hand away. "Ethan, you and Violet are making us look like we're bluffing."

"Keep bluffing." Ethan looks to Kit. "No offense."

Kit shrugs. He knows it's not personal. Ethan hates his sister growing up.

"You're waiting to finish school, right?" I ask.

Piper nods. "Only two and half years now." Her eyes light up as she looks to something behind us. "Oh my God. That looks amazing!"

"You have a problem, baby," Kit teases.

Again, she flips him off.

This time, when he takes her hand, he nips at her finger.

Ethan must not notice, because he doesn't let out one of his *that's my sister* growls.

His bright blue eyes are fixed on me. He stares at me like he's looking for cracks.

I try to offer a smile, but I'm not selling it. This whole thing makes me nauseous.

And not *I'm pregnant* nauseous either. I took a test, double checked my birth control, took another test.

No, it's just regular old *fuck, I'm not sure I can handle this* nausea.

I try to bury myself in my tea as the manager drops off our samples, but I can barely taste it.

Piper laughs as she digs into the first sample. It's all white with a curvy, abstract decoration.

She sticks her tongue out. "Vanilla on vanilla. Fine, but boring."

"Like brother, like sister," Kit teases.

She makes that *ew, that's my brother* face. Piper still can't stand hearing about Mal's taste in bondage.

I take a bite of the vanilla cake. It's sweet and plain, with a vague taste of vanilla bean. It's not what I want, but it's safe.

Nobody hates vanilla.

Nobody goes *ew, vanilla.*

God dammit. I'm eating cake here. I'm going to at least enjoy tasting my dessert.

I dig into the second sample. Chocolate on chocolate. It's rich and fudgy and sure to please all the real chocoholics and scare off the people who don't like the dark stuff.

It's a possibility.

But is that what I want?

I like chocolate just fine. Who doesn't? But it doesn't feel right for *my* wedding. For *our* wedding.

"Oh, that is perfection." Piper polishes off her second bite of the chocolate cake. "Have I died? Am I in heaven? Can I only eat this forever?"

"You do have a problem," Ethan says.

"You don't like it?" she asks.

He shrugs. "It's cake."

"What do you mean, 'it's cake?'" she asks.

"It's a pastry dessert. It can only be so good," Ethan says.

"And you'd prefer what?" she asks.

"Skipping cake and going straight to our hotel room." He slides his arm around my waist and pulls me closer.

I nestle into his touch. "Can I vote for that?"

He nods.

Piper shakes her head. "How about you order a cake *and* you two skip eating the cake to go straight to, ahem—"

Kit chuckles. He whispers something in her ear.

She whispers back.

I try to laugh, but I can't. Ethan's right.

It's just dessert.

It shouldn't have this much baggage attached to it.

One party shouldn't have this much baggage attached to it.

I try to get into tasting the samples, but I can't. None of the cakes are sure to please everyone.

None of the cakes make me happy.

The only thing that makes me happy is thinking about the moment where Ethan's lips touch mine.

Where it's just the two of us, forever.

Chapter Three

VIOLET

After an hour of sampling cakes and trying to laugh with my family-to-be, I make an excuse about needing to get to my fitting early.

Piper insists on coming with me. We take my car and Ethan goes off with Kit. I'm not sure if they're going to work or play. Sometimes, the lines blur with the guys in the band.

I let my mind wander until we walk into the bridal boutique. It's a little place in Fullerton with mirrored walls and plush beige carpets. The walls are covered in ivory and white dresses, from big ball gowns to sheer lace numbers.

Piper's blue eyes light up as she takes in the flowy chiffon dress on the mannequin. It's girly and modern and utterly perfect for her.

She looks to me. "Is it too early to try it on?"

I shake my head.

She half-smiles. "I don't want to start wedding planning until I have to."

"Don't try to fit it into two months."

"Noted." Her gaze goes back to the breezy chiffon skirt. "It's a strong case for an elopement in Hawaii."

"That's a genius idea."

Her expression gets soft. Caring. "Are you okay, Vi?"

I clear my throat. "I'm… tired."

"It barely shows." She motions to the counter. "Allow me." She waves hello to the shopgirl then moves forward to introduce herself.

Piper has just as much charm as Ethan does, but hers is different. She's more adorable and sweet and seemingly innocent, while Ethan is more smooth and enthusiastic and… well, he's just damn fuckable.

My cheeks flush as I let my head fill with dirty thoughts. There's nothing wrong with focusing on the post-reception part of my wedding day. There's nothing wrong with wanting a hell of a wedding night.

So what if I'm most excited about fucking Ethan as my husband?

God, that really is a sexy thought.

"Oh my God, Violet. Has it always been this beautiful?" Piper's voice calls my attention. She motions to the shopgirl, who's bringing my gown from the backroom to the dressing room.

It really is something out of a fairy tale. Black bodice. Sweetheart neckline. Silver beading. A big puffy skirt with stacked layers of black and deep purple tulle.

It's perfect.

I follow Piper and the shopgirl into the dressing room. Everything else about the space is traditional. White walls, beige carpets, ornate mirror, spinning podium.

"Let me know if you need help getting into it." The shopgirl smiles at us, but I can't tell if it's forced or sincere. "And make sure you can figure out the bustle. I can't tell you how many maid of honors have called from the reception in a panic."

Piper nods back to her. "Thank you." Once the shopgirl leaves, Piper turns to me. "You need any help?"

There's no way I'm getting into it on my own. "Please."

"Aren't you supposed to wear special underwear?"

"The corset top is plenty."

"But the..." She motions to my crotch. "You're going commando."

I have to laugh. "That's the plan."

"I guess, with the size of that skirt no one would know, but... still..."

"Still?"

She shrugs. "No offense, Vi. I love you, and you're the classiest person I know, but commando at your wedding? That's tacky."

"How about crotchless panties?"

"Much better." She laughs. "You know... as much as I hate thinking about it, you should get something special. That, um, ahem. For your wedding night."

My laugh melts the tension in my chest. God, the look on Piper's face. She could not be more uncomfortable.

"What?" She folds her arms. "It's not like Ethan wants to hear about my sex life."

"He doesn't."

"Even Mal doesn't want to hear it."

"Oh, you wanted to talk about Mal's sex life?" I press my wrists together in a *handcuffs* motion.

Piper clears her throat. "I will not picture it. I will not picture it. I will not—"

"Lacey is almost as adorable and innocent seeming as you are—"

"I hate you."

"You think they ever use Ethan's old room? The mirror is still attached to the ceiling, isn't it?"

Piper's eyes bug out of her head.

I can see why Joel is as obnoxious as he is. This is too much fun.

"You never use a mirror?" I ask.

"Well, um… Yes. But I still don't want to hear about your sex life with my brother." She makes that *ew* face then clears her throat. "Do you want to try on the dress or not?"

"I'll keep my panties on."

"Good." She lets out a much too obvious sigh of relief. "Not that I have a problem with seeing you naked. You should see backstage in the middle of a show. Or before. Or after. Lots of underwear. Lots of naked."

"I hear that." I set my purse on the chair then slide out of my dress. My shoes. My tights. My bra.

"I like the mirror. But I don't need any more details about it."

I hate to torture her, but this is the most at ease I've felt… well, I can't say I have my clothes on. But this is the most at ease I've felt with my panties on in a long time. I try to find a smooth way to tease her, but words won't form.

Okay. Let's go for blunt.

"And no bondage?" I ask.

"You're doing this on purpose."

"Why would I do that?"

"I'm not innocent. I have sex. I fuck my fiancé. I suck him off. He eats me out. We've had sex in public. I'm not naive because I don't want to hear about my brother's riding crop."

God, I really want to sympathize with her, but I just can't. I'm not attracted to Mal in any way, shape, or form, but the thought of him with a riding crop—

It suits him.

And it's fucking hot.

"You're picturing it. You're a pervert." Piper lifts the dress from the hanger and starts undoing the corset backing. "I, um… well, Kit and I haven't, but I've thought about it."

"A riding crop?"

"God no." She holds open the dress so I can step into it.

I do. "Not even once?"

"No. I don't like pain. I know you… ahem… with the biting. I can't remember the last time I saw your neck without a hickey."

I have to laugh. "True."

"I don't want to know if you and Ethan… but I do… I wouldn't mind Kit tying me up." She pulls the dress over my hips, my stomach, my chest.

I turn until the neckline is in place.

"Do you and Ethan really do that regularly? Do I even want to know?"

"Do you?"

"No… Well, now I'm curious."

"I can't explain it without details."

She clears her throat. "If you must."

"It's a once in a while thing. There's something about being at Ethan's mercy. About knowing I have to take as much pleasure as he wants to give me… And the way he stares into my eyes as he holds me down. It's really hot." Okay, now, I'm making myself uncomfortable. Piper is practically my little sister, and this is girl talk, but that's her brother.

I wouldn't have wanted to hear about Asher's sex life.

"You don't think… you don't think it's weird or bad that Kit and I are always vanilla?" Piper asks.

"Are you happy?"

"I could die."

"Are you *satisfied*?"

She nods.

"Then who cares what anyone else thinks?"

"And you with the wedding planning?"

"Sex is much better than wedding planning."

"Well, duh." She tilts her head and looks off into space. "I don't feel like I'm lacking. But everyone acts like I'm this poor, naïve thing. And I'm twenty. I've taken care of myself for years. I'm not a kid."

"That's why everyone teases you. We can't stand to see you growing up."

"I guess I'll accept that." Piper's eyes meet mine through the mirror. "You already look so beautiful, Violet."

"Thank you." I stare back at my reflection.

Piper pulls the corset lacing tighter. "Did you really get this off Etsy?"

"Yeah."

"It's so pretty. And it's custom, so no one else will have it."

"True." I suck in a deep breath and hold it there. I want to be able to breathe with this thing cinched.

She focuses on the lacing. I focus on my reflection.

The dress is gorgeous. It's not in any way traditional. It's black and purple. It's fat with tulle. It's sparkly and shiny and it's everything I want in my wedding dress.

This is what *I* want for *my* wedding.

But when I think about the look on my mom's face—

About my relatives shaking their heads *she never got over that goth phase, huh?*

I exhale slowly then take another deep breath. "I probably shouldn't have done this after cake, huh?"

"You barely touched it." Piper tugs at the lacing. "But I

get it. Family is hard. There's no fucking way I'd be half as stable as you are if anyone in my family was coming to my wedding. Well, besides Ethan and Mal."

"You should elope if that's what you want."

"Maybe. Is that good or do you want it tighter?"

Finally. I let out a heavy exhale. The bodice stays snug around my chests. "Not tighter."

"Your boobs look amazing." Piper smiles. "You look amazing. And with the hair and makeup. Oh my God, I get to see it with the hair and makeup later. We're bringing it with us, right?"

I nod.

She wipes her eye. "I'm going to cry."

I do look amazing. Like a princess. Like a weird, goth princess, but fuck it.

I'm a weird, goth math geek.

This is the dress I want to wear.

This is the look I want for my wedding.

That's the only thing that matters.

Even if I can't shake the weight of everyone else's opinions.

My shoulders fall with my exhale. The other details might be wrong, but this one isn't.

"God, Violet, if I didn't love you, I'd hate you. You're too cool. It's wrong." She pulls out her cell phone and points it at the mirror. "You mind? I won't let Ethan get his hands on it."

"No. Go ahead."

She snaps a photo then slides her cell into her pocket. She motions to the podium in the center of the room. "Will you hate me if I ask you to twirl."

I laugh. "I think I'd love you even more."

"Then let's do it. Twirl for me, angel. Twirl. Twirl.

Twirl." When I don't respond, she tilts her head sideways. "*Phantom of the Opera*. No?"

"No."

"You'd like it. It's dramatic and moody. I think it's playing in Chicago right now. I have to check the tour schedule to see if it lines up, but I'm sure we'll make it work."

Right. We always have to check everything against the tour schedule.

I shake it off as Piper helps me onto the podium.

Then I'm spinning. Well, more rotating slowly.

The dress spins with me. The bodice sparkles as it catches the light. The skirt twirls.

It's perfect.

It really is.

I take Piper's hand to step off the podium

"Ethan is going to die when he sees you. It's so you and it's beautiful. And of course, it's sexy. You really do nail goth sexpot, you know?" When I don't respond, she moves closer. Her eyes bore into mine. "Is there anything you want to talk about? You can tell me if you have doubts. You know I like you more than I like him." She smiles like she's joking, but her eyes are sincere.

I trust Piper to keep my secrets. But—"I don't. Not about Ethan. But everything else…"

"It's hard loving a guy who's away half the year."

"It is."

"How much time do we have before we meet your mom for makeup?"

"A while. Our appointment is at six and she won't get there until seven or eight."

"I have an idea."

"I'm listening."

"Well, you can't go commando at your wedding. You

just can't. So how about we go to one of those horribly overpriced lingerie shops in South Coast Plaza, and we find something special for your wedding night."

"You do realize Ethan's going to rip off whatever I wear."

She sticks out her tongue in disgust. "I do realize that."

My smile spreads to my ears. "As long as you're okay with that?"

"I'll do my best."

I laugh.

Right now, it actually feels like this is possible.

I want to hold onto that feeling as long as I can.

Chapter Four

VIOLET

The knock on the door is loud.

I flinch.

I'm in the makeup chair. I'm not supposed to move, much less flinch.

"Oh, shit." The makeup artist, Kelsey, draws my brow line all the way to my ear. "Let me fix that. Piper, could you get that? It should be Ms. Valentine."

I suck a deep breath through my nose. This is the end of my light afternoon (turns out shopping for honeymoon lingerie is good for the mood).

My mom is almost here. It's not because she's spying or babysitting. She wants makeup, so she looks nice in all our photos. She wants to make sure we'll all look like we belong together.

Piper is my entire bridal party. I'm sure Lacey, Bella, and Athena, my ex-roomie and best friend, would have jumped at the chance to help out, but I only wanted Piper standing with me at the altar.

I love my friends, but Piper is family. Even if it's not official yet.

In theory, with me in my black and purple dress, and Piper and Mom in dresses in any shade of purple, we should look good together.

But, in reality…

God, I feel like I'm in high school again. It's like I'm getting ready for school pictures, and I'm bracing myself to fight with Mom about my eyeliner.

My palms go clammy. I barely manage to get out my exhale. I'm an adult, with an apartment and a job and a fiancé. I shouldn't care if Mom likes my dress or my makeup.

But I do.

Kelsey dips a Q-tip in eye makeup remover then wipes off the smudged pencil. Her eyes stay on her work. "Let me fix this before you decide if you want more or less." She dabs my browbone dry then gets to work fixing my smoky eye.

The front door opens. Piper and Mom exchange some greeting I can't make out. They sound happy.

Their voices get louder as they move closer. This studio is actually Kelsey's apartment, and it's a cozy space.

"Have you seen the dress?" Piper asks. "It's amazing."

"Violet took it to the tailor the day she received it. No one else has seen it." Mom waves hello to me. "Hey, sweetie. I won't ask you to get up."

"Thanks." I start to turn toward her.

Kelsey grabs my face. "One more minute then you can hug."

My laugh is more awkward than anything. "Okay." I try to stare straight in front of me the way I'm supposed to.

Kelsey dabs eyeliner. Then highlight. Then one more coat of mascara for good measure.

She pulls back. "We can go more dramatic. But this is a

good baseline." She motions to my mom. "Hugs first, then tell me what you think."

I turn to Mom and take a deep breath.

She's in her usual work outfit. A smart navy suit. Light makeup. Auburn hair in a bun. She's practically the dictionary entry for *classy business woman*.

"It's very you, sweetie." She holds up her arms and motions *come here*.

I push myself up then make my way to her. I'm moving at half speed. My muscles are stiff and achy.

Even so, I melt into the hug. "How was work?"

"Difficult, but nothing I can't handle." She pulls back and takes a long look at my makeup. "Do you like it."

Maybe. I turn to the mirror for a closer look. It's a normal night look. A little foundation, concealer, grey smoky eye, blush, filled in brows. My lipstick is only two shades darker than my natural color. And no false lashes.

This is a lot of makeup for most people.

But for me this isn't even work makeup.

It feels plain.

Ordinary.

Mom smiles. "It's beautiful, sweetie. You look beautiful." It's in her voice. *Keep it like this. Stay normal. Be normal.*

Maybe.

Or maybe that's in my head.

"You can always try more, Vi. Nothing wrong with seeing how you like the look." Piper motions to my wedding dress, currently wrapped in plastic and hanging on a hook on the wall. "Or try it on with the dress."

"Oh, this it." Mom lifts the plastic covering the bottom of the gown and runs her fingers over the tulle. She lets out a soft chuckle. "I can only imagine what Grandma will say."

Piper shoots me a concerned look.

"And my sister." Mom shakes her head. She's shaking it at her sister, and not at me, but it's hard not to feel the brunt of disapproval.

Piper jumps in. "Why don't you try a little more?"

"Yeah. Okay." I take my seat in the makeup chair and I nod to Kelsey.

"That is a dramatic dress." Kelsey picks up a lipstick and holds it against my skin to check the tone. "You want to try matching it?"

Yes. But I don't want to look at my mom's reaction right now. "Let's try it."

Kelsey motions for Piper to sit. "I'll turn on the curling iron." She grabs said curling iron from one of the drawers of the vanity and pulls it in. "Could you do me a favor, Ms. Valentine?"

"Sure," Mom says.

"Could you grab some water bottles from the fridge?" Kelsey asks.

Mom nods and heads over to the kitchen. Her heels click against the tile.

Kelsey kneels in front of me. She looks up at me in that *I'm examining your features* kind of way. "Don't worry. Brides are always tense when their moms show up."

"Is it that obvious?" I ask.

She nods. "It's a lot of give and take, deciding if it's your wedding or if it's Mom and Dad's wedding, or if it's Grandma's wedding. And if the parents are paying for it—you wouldn't believe how often a trial run turns into a screaming fight."

"Yeah?" I ask.

She nods. "The bride wants an updo. The mom wants curls. All of a sudden, they're screaming about that time in the third grade where the bride lost Mom's necklace. Weddings bring up a lot of feelings." She fills a lipstick brush with color and applies it. "This is certainly your face. I say adorn it however the fuck you want."

"Okay."

"No talking yet." She dabs another coat of lipstick. "I always wait until we're doing lips to give my pep talk. There's no chance for sass."

I can't help but laugh.

"That is the downside."

"That's more like Vi." Piper leans against the wall. She shoots me a thumbs up. "But more."

"More what?" Kelsey asks.

"Just more," Piper says.

I nod. "Just more."

For the entire half an hour it takes for Kelsey to fix my hair and finish my makeup, Piper, Mom, and I talk about teen soaps.

We don't talk about the wedding.

Or my dress.

Or my eyeliner.

We especially don't talk about my deep red lipstick.

When Kelsey is finished, she pulls back to admire her work. Her short platinum hair falls over her ear as she tilts her head to one side. "I hate to brag, but look at it." She smiles. "Kidding. This is a no ego zone. Tell me if you want anything changed."

I catch my reflection in the mirror. That feels more like me. Well, more like me at a grand event. My stomach settles. My shoulders fall from my ears.

Then I catch Mom's expression in the mirror.

She's trying.

She really is.

But it's all over her face.

"Your hair looks beautiful, sweetie." Mom presses her lips together as she admires my messy updo. "Did you want to see it with the dress?"

"You need help getting into it?" Piper asks.

"Yeah, thanks." I get up from my chair and follow Piper to the den where my dress is hanging.

I can hear Kelsey telling Mom to sit and asking how she wants her makeup and hair done. Maybe that will keep Mom from making that displeased facial expression.

It's not like I can ask her to feel differently.

She's holding her tongue.

She's supporting me.

She can't help that she wants a more traditional ceremony. A more traditional daughter even.

Fuck, I hate weddings.

I step out of my shoes and strip to my skivvies.

Piper is quiet as she helps me into my dress. She takes her time doing the lacing and cinching it tightly.

She turns me toward the main room. "You ready?"

"I'm not sure what I'm ready for anymore." Even so, I take a step forward. Without my shoes, my dress drags on the floor. I have to be careful not to step on the lining.

It takes a while to get to the main room. There's a long mirror against the opposite wall. Six tiny footsteps and I'm in front of it.

The room is dim. The dress can't sparkle in the light. The mirror can't catch all the drama of my hair and makeup.

But it catches enough that I know—

This is it.

This is perfect.

Then Mom turns to me with that *wow, that's a lot* look on her face, and I don't have a clue what I want anymore.

She presses her lips into a smile. "You really are going to be a memorable bride."

"Yeah." I press my lips together. Memorable isn't a bad thing. It's good. Unique is good. Hell, weird is good. "Thanks."

"You look like an angel sent from hell. It's perfect," Piper says.

Kelsey nods. "You are going to make an impression."

Mom laughs. "Grandma is not going to stop mentioning this." Her laugh gets harder. "And Grandpa too. They're—"

"Could you not?" Words roll off my tongue. My brain refuses to stop them. It's too tired and everything is too heavy. "I know Grandma wants me doing this in a church. I know she doesn't like the crimson centerpieces or the black ribbons. I know that you'd rather I wear an ivory dress and subtle makeup. I know you'd rather have a normal daughter."

"Violet, sweetie. No." Mom moves toward me. She sets her hand on my shoulder. "I wouldn't trade you for a thousand normal daughters. Normal is boring." She pulls her pendant necklace from under her blouse. "You think this is normal?"

"Well, no…" I blink back a tear. It's definitely not normal to get your late son's ashes crushed into a stone. "But, um—"

"You think your dad and I are normal?" she asks.

"I guess not…"

"You're smart, creative, funny, kind. And you have an amazing style that is all you. I don't want you to be normal."

"But you keep saying… You keep telling me no one is going to like any of my choices."

"You know Grandma and Grandpa. You know

everyone in my family. Anything that isn't an ivory gown in a church is going to displease them. But fuck them."

Huh? Mom doesn't say fuck.

Not that it does anything to help me blink back tears.

Piper laughs. "I'm with that. Fuck anyone who doesn't support you."

Mom nods. "This is your day."

"Stop saying that." I wipe a tear with my thumb. The digit stays clean. At least my makeup isn't smearing. "It's not my day. It's our day. And it's one day. Why is it such a big deal?"

"It's not. All the days that come after matter more. Your marriage is a lot more important than your wedding." Mom wraps me in a tight bear hug. "I'm sorry. It's not your problem that my parents hate everything. I didn't raise you to give up what you want to please other people. I don't want you doing it now."

"Yeah?"

She nods. "Yeah. You love Ethan. That's what matters."

"I do." I wipe another tear. God, I'm a mess.

Kelsey grabs me a tissue and hands it over. She motions to the now empty den. "I'll let you guys talk."

"Thanks." I wipe my eyes with the tissue. No smudges. "This shit is really waterproof."

Kelsey laughs. "I know what I'm doing." She takes her leave.

Piper too.

"You... You don't like Ethan." I wipe my eyes. "I know you try, but I can tell. And that's okay, but—"

"That's not it. I love Ethan. He makes you happy, and that's all I've wanted for you."

"He does."

Mom looks me in the eyes. "I just worry. He's away all

the time. And I see the way that wears on you. Last Sunday, when we met for dinner, you were barely there. You looked like your heart was about to break."

I can't exactly deny that.

"No marriage is perfect. There's always compromise. I can't begin to tell you how many things your father does that drive me out of my mind. But I always know he'll be there. I worry about you not having that."

I nod. I worry too.

"It's your life, sweetie. And it's your marriage. And your wedding. You're the only one who knows what you want. I do love Ethan. And I know you don't need it, but you have every bit of my approval. You couldn't find a better guy."

I nod. "Can you tell him that?" Ethan is still under the impression my parents hate him. Not that I can blame him for worrying the rest of my family disapproves. They do.

"Okay." Mom rubs my shoulder. "You know I only want the world for you."

"I do."

"You want a minute alone?"

I nod.

Mom smiles and motions to the den. "I'll make sure Piper and Kelsey stay entertained." She moves into the other room.

I press my back against the wall and suck in deep breaths. My eyes are getting red, but my makeup is still perfect. My dress is still gorgeous.

I'm still an angel sent from hell.

Which is exactly how I like it.

I appreciate the moment to my thoughts. But I don't want to be alone right now.

I want to be with Ethan.

I find my phone in my purse and I call him.

Chapter Five

ETHAN

There's a sound coming from my pants.

Not the ones I'm wearing, but the jeans crumpled on the dressing room floor.

Shit. That's *I'm Only Happy When It Rains* in glorious cell speaker quality. That's my ringtone for Violet.

I bend to grab my cell. "Hey."

"Hey." Her voice is soft. Tired.

All I want to do is teleport to where she is and wrap my arms around her. It's a common feeling with half my time on the road, but right now, it's heavier.

"I, um… I was talking with my mom, and I just kinda lost it." She lets out a soft sigh. "I know I do a pretty good job convincing people I don't care what they think—"

"But you do." I lean against the dressing room wall. I can't rush out of here wearing *only* slacks. No, I can. And I will if that's what Violet needs.

"Yeah. And Mom, she kept looking at me like she didn't think people would approve. And she's right. They probably won't. I mean, what normal person approves of their niece or cousin or granddaughter's wedding looking like a My Chemical Romance music video."

"They broke up four years ago. You need to update your references."

She laughs. "Fuck you."

"The second you get home."

Her laugh gets louder. "That's cheesy."

"You don't want to?"

"I'm only human."

I shift my weight between my feet. Violet and I are the same in so many ways. We both pretend like we don't give a fuck what anyone thinks, but we do. We both hate how much we need approval from other people. "It's okay to care what people think."

"Yeah, but the thing is… I love my mom and dad. And I do really care about their opinions. And yours. And Mal and Piper and all the band family. But I don't care what Grandma thinks. I don't care what Aunt Jeanie thinks. These are people I never see. I only invited them because I felt like I was supposed to. And I kind of wish I hadn't, but I'm not crying over spilled milk."

"Yeah."

"I… I want to stop thinking about everything besides walking down the aisle and taking your hand and saying those vows—"

"And jamming your tongue down my throat?"

"Or course." She laughs. "Maybe some over the clothes groping too. You know I can't be held responsible for what my hands do when you're in a suit. Tell me your suit is ready."

"I'm trying it on now."

"Mhmm. Picture?"

"You have to wait."

"You're cruel."

"It's tradition."

"Since when?"

"Since now."

"Okay, since now." Her voice softens. "I love you, Ethan, and I want this. I want you. But I can't take any more thinking about it."

"Let me take over."

"There's so much—"

"You have a spreadsheet with names, emails, and phone numbers. I can handle it."

She sighs with relief. "Are you sure?"

"Yeah."

"We haven't even picked a cake."

"I have an idea about that. Do you trust me?"

"About cake? I don't know. You really dismissed it earlier."

I feel my laugh in my toes. "Even so."

"Yeah, I do."

"Let me handle it."

"Okay."

"You still sound exhausted."

"I am."

"I want you in my arms, honey. Fuck, the things I want to do to comfort you."

"I, um… I can't now. Mom and Piper are in the other room." Need fills her voice. "And Mom is going to come home with me. For something. I, um, so… it might be a little while."

"I can wait."

"I can't. But I guess I have to." She takes a slow breath. "How can I miss you when you're ten miles away?"

"I miss you too. You want me to drive over and pick you up right now?"

"Yes, but I need to finish this. I love you. I'll see you soon."

"I love you too."

I can feel how much this is weighing on her.

Maybe I can't do anything about the nagging feeling in my gut.

But I can fix this.

The door creaks open. Violet's voice flows into the room.

"Ethan. My mom is with me, so I hope you're decent."

She steps inside. With her makeup dark and her hair in some elaborate style, she looks ready for a ball.

She looks fucking irresistible.

Her eyes go straight to me. Her lip corners turn down as she notes that I am, in fact, decent. "I missed the suit."

Mary, Violet's mom, laughs. "He does look like a different guy in the suit." She steps inside and nods hello. "It's always nice to see you, Ethan."

"You too." I fight my desire to tense up. Violet loves her parents, even if they drive her crazy sometimes. That means I love them too. Even if they think I'm not good enough for her. I look to Mary. "Any way I can bribe you for a picture of Violet in her dress?"

Mary shakes her head.

"That's what I figured," I say.

Mary smiles. "She looked beautiful in it."

"I can't wait. Though Vi would look beautiful in a potato sack," I say.

Violet sticks out her tongue. "Please don't picture me in a potato sack."

I wink at my fiancée. "I'm picturing you in less."

Her cheeks flush. She motions to her mom.

Mary just laughs. "Don't worry, sweetie. Once you get married, everyone expects you to have sex. It's always *when is the baby coming?*" Her expression softens. "I'm not going to ask."

"Good." Violet smooths her dress. "It will be a while." She gives me a long, slow once over. Her eyes scream *how about we get back to you in a suit. Or you out of a suit.*

Very fucking soon. I stare into Violet's gorgeous green eyes. "Two days and that suit is all yours."

She nods. Her lips curl into a smile. She's not thinking about me in that suit.

I'm not thinking about her in her dress.

Planning a wedding three days after a reunion was a bad idea. We're always like this after a week or two apart. We can barely drag ourselves out of bed.

But this isn't a time to think about making Violet come. Not yet. Thoughts of our upgraded hotel room attempt to distract me. Then thoughts of her in some tiny bikini, running around a Hawaiian beach—

"What's this?" Violet's voice pulls me back to the moment. She's staring at the cake samples sitting on the dining table. She moves closer. Examines the first sample.

It's a small slice of sheet cake, covered in purple icing, decorated with dark brown and black lines in an abstract pattern.

"Try it," I say.

She looks to me and raises a brow. "You want me to eat more cake?"

"Maybe just the one on the right." It's decorated the same as the one on the left—black on purple. The slice in the middle has the opposite color schedule, purple on black. The three flavors should be perfect for a three-tier cake. "You like the look of it?"

"Yeah. It's perfect. I guess you saw my fifty Pinterest boards," she says.

"More like a hundred," Mary teases.

Violet grabs a fork from the kitchen and digs into the slice of cake on the right. Her eyes go wide as she takes in the green color.

She looks to me. "Is this—"

I nod.

She takes a bite. Her eyelids flutter closed. She lets out a soft sigh of pleasure.

Slowly, she chews and swallows. "Matcha with vanilla icing."

My lips curl into a smile. The pleasure spreading over her face is everything. "You like it?"

"Perfect." She looks to me. "But won't other people… not like it?"

"Maybe, but—" I motion to the mock up drawing sitting on the table.

But Violet doesn't pick it up.

Her mom does.

Mary chuckles. "Oh." She turns to Violet with a sly smile. "I can see that."

"What?" Violet shoots me a *what did you do* look.

Mary reads aloud from the note. "Vanilla on the bottom, because it will please the most people and we can dye it purple. Chocolate with mocha frosting in the middle. Because I always think of you as the girl who steals my coffee. And matcha on top. Because you deserve exactly what you want, and I know you like to be on top."

Violet turns bright red. "I, um, I don't, even if that's true. I mean, I like it, but I wouldn't even say… oh God." She swallows hard. "I guess this is what I deserve for teasing Piper."

I go to Violet and wrap my arms around her. "You like it?"

She whispers into my ear, "I love it." She squeezes me tightly. "But I'm going to prove you wrong after Mom leaves."

"Is that a challenge?"

"Yeah."

Fuck yes. I nod.

She steps back and motions to the bathroom. "Excuse me."

Mary waits until Violet closes the door to move closer. "The cake will be perfect."

"I hope so."

She motions to the slice of vanilla on vanilla. "You mind if I steal this one?"

"Go for it."

She takes a seat at the table and takes a tiny bite. She motions to the seat across from hers.

Okay. I take the seat. And, fuck it, I grab the slice of mocha on chocolate.

Mary takes a napkin and dabs her lip corners. "Ethan, I know Dan and I haven't always been as welcoming as we could have been. I'm sorry about that."

Huh? She's staring at me with earnest eyes. Her voice is sincere. And it's Mary. The woman doesn't have an insincere bone in her body.

"Thanks." I run my hand through my hair. I bite my tongue. This is fucking weird.

"When the two of you were younger, I worried Violet would give up what she wanted for you. Even now. She loves you so much. I know she acts tough, but, deep down, she needs love. She needs acceptance. And you're the only person who has ever really given her that. She would do anything for you."

"I'm lucky to have her."

Mary nods. "When you have kids, you'll see. It's a scary world out there. All you want to do is protect them. Especially after Asher… I… I didn't think any of us would be happy again." She blinks back a tear. "What I want to say is, I can see that you make Violet happy. And that's the only thing that matters to me. Even if I worry about your schedule. It's her life. It's your life, both of you."

"Yeah."

"You're a sweet young man, Ethan. Dan and I are happy you're going to be a member of the family. You're always welcome with us. Anytime." She places her palm on the back of my hand. Her green eyes—the same as Violet's—bore into mine. "Just promise you'll take care of her."

"Of course."

She pulls back and wipes a tear with her thumb. I'm not sure how to react. I'm usually good with people, but Violet's mom is a whole other can of worms.

I grab a napkin and hand it to her.

She dabs her eye and nods *thank you*.

Violet steps out of the bathroom and looks to me. Her eyes flare with concern. *Everything okay?*

I nod.

She turns to her mom. "Is it good?"

Mary motions to the cake. "Delicious." She pushes herself to her feet. "I should get going." She moves to Violet and wraps her in a hug. "I'll see you at the rehearsal dinner, sweetie, and not a second sooner."

Violet nods.

Mary whispers something to her.

Violet blushes. "Good night, Mom."

"Good night, sweetie. And you too, Ethan."

Violet walks her mom to the door and says another goodbye. She sighs as she clicks the lock on the door.

She presses her back against the door. Her eyes meet mine. "Let's never get married again."

"What if I die?"

"Don't talk about that."

"Still?"

"You want me to love again?"

"I want you happy."

"So long as I carry you around by my heart like Mom does with Asher?"

I let out a soft laugh. "Well, yeah, your new man has to respect that you'll never love him as much as you loved me." I go to Violet and I wrap my arms around her.

She presses her forehead to my shoulder. "I don't like thinking about something happening to you."

"Me either."

Her eyelids flutter closed. She presses her lips to mine then pulls back with a sigh. "You taste like cake."

"You too."

Her lips curl into a smile. "It's amazing, how much lighter I feel with that one thing decided."

"Everything is decided, honey. I have a few more calls to make tomorrow, but it's all confirmations. Everything is ready."

"Yeah?"

I nod. "It's going to be fucking perfect. Of course, no matter what happens, I'm gonna think it's perfect. I'm marrying you."

Her smile spreads over her lips. "You really think that?"

"Of course."

"Me too." She slides her arms around my shoulders. "What did Mom say?"

"It was fucking crazy." I still can't wrap my head around it. "She wants me in the family."

Violet's eyes light up. "That's good."

I nod. "Really good."

"Did she mean it?"

"Has your mom ever not meant something?"

"True." She stares back at me. "I asked her to say something, but I wasn't sure… I know the rest of my family—"

"Orange County elitists."

"Yeah." She presses her forehead against mine. "My parents really do love you. Not that it would have stopped me, but it's good to hear."

"It is." Weird, but good. Really fucking good. My parents… just my dad now. He loves me. Mom loved me. But they haven't been a part of my life in a meaningful way for a long time. "She said she worries about my schedule."

"Oh." Violet's voice drops. Her shoulders tense. She says nothing, but it's written all over her face.

It's the elephant in the fucking room. It has been for a long time now.

I stare back into her gorgeous green eyes. "I worry about it too."

She stares back at me. "Yeah?"

"I hate being away from you. I want to carry you in my pocket everywhere I go."

"So I can always be in your pants?"

I can't help but laugh. "I love your bad jokes."

Her lips curl into a smile. "Excuse you."

"It's hard for me too, Vi. But I'm the one making that choice. I get that I'm asking a lot of you. I hate that I'm asking so much of you."

"Ethan…"

"I wish I could tell you things will change soon."

She runs her fingers through my hair.

"That things will change, period. You deserve someone who's around all the time."

She shakes her head.

"You never think about it?"

"Of course, but I still—"

"Let me say this."

She nods. "Okay."

"I love you more than anything, Violet. More than music. More than the band. More than the fame and the money and the adoration. I want to be with you every fucking second I can. I would do anything to make you happy. If it was really what you wanted, I'd stop. But I… I wouldn't be me." I struggle to keep my voice steady. This is the truth. I can't deny it. But that doesn't make telling her any easier. "I still have too much to do. Too much to prove. Too much to say."

Her voice is a whisper. "I know."

"I'd hate to be without you, honey, but I'd rather be without you than be the lead weight dragging you down."

"You're not."

"What if things never change?"

"I'd still want to be with you." She looks up at me. Her fingers curl into my hair. Her touch is soft. Her voice is softer. "You're my other half, Ethan. There's no way in hell I'm giving you up."

"I can't stand being away."

"I can't stand you being away."

"If only I could teleport, huh?"

She laughs. "That would solve everything." She leans in to press her lips to mine. It's a soft, slow kiss, and it makes me warm everywhere.

"Vi…"

"I… I wouldn't ask you to give up music, Ethan. It's who you are. Like me with math. But I do… *I* can live like this. Right now. We're young. You're untethered. It's easy for one of us to get on a plane."

"Yeah."

"But I know we've talked about kids. And I don't want that for a long time… but when we do…"

"I know." I stare back into her eyes. "After everything with Mom and Dad, there's no way I'd do that to our kids. I'm not saying I'll quit, but… I'm not going to be away either."

"Isn't it one or the other?"

"I don't know. We won't always go this full speed. Right now, we still have a lot to prove. We still have a lot of money to make. Another few albums and…"

"You'll either be famous enough to only tour three months a year or you'll be has-beens?"

"Hey. Who you calling a future has-been?"

She laughs. "I just…"

"You want numbers?"

She nods.

"I like three months a year." I pull her closer. "I can handle three months a year away."

"I can handle nine months of you here."

"Even once we have kids?"

"Not the first year or two. But after that." Her eyes bore into mine. Her voice is soft. Vulnerable. She's laying down all her cards. "I need you, Ethan. That comes before everything. If you said you'd have to be away eleven months a year, I could live with that. But I don't want to. I want you around. But I want *you* around. I want that guy I fell in love with, the one who gets giddy when he perfects a lick. I know that means compromises."

"I ask too much of you."

"No. It's the same with me, you just don't realize it. I

work a lot of late nights. I always will. You'll be the one missing me one day."

"Yeah?"

She nods. "Yeah."

"I look forward to it."

"Me too."

"I love you so much, honey."

"I love you too." She presses her forehead to mine. "I guess we're really going to need a kick ass nanny, huh?"

"We will."

"But not for a while…"

"A while?" I tease. "A few months?"

"Ethan!"

"You don't want to make a baby?"

"Not yet."

"Give me a time frame," I say.

"Five years."

"Five years is perfect."

She presses her lips together. "Good."

"But it's far away. We need to practice."

"Do we?"

"Yeah." I slide my hands to her hips. "What if we get rusty?"

"Well…" She tugs at my t-shirt. "We wouldn't want that."

Chapter Six

ETHAN

Violet and I spend the entire night, and most of the next day in bed. We don't bother getting into our clothes until we don't have a choice.

Even then, we're nearly late to our rehearsal dinner. We're in the back room of a chain restaurant, toasting with cheap champagne as member after member of Violet's family gets up to say something about the geeky goth girl who… to their amazement is still a geeky goth girl.

She's not wearing that heavy expression. She laughs off every mention of her attire—she's in her usual dark makeup in an especially sexy lace up corset dress and spiky heels. She smiles every time someone jokes about how they thought she'd marry an accountant.

When Mary steps in to shut down Grandma's speech, Violet leans in to whisper.

"I kinda love that the uptight people in my family think you're no good." She nips at my ear. "But I know you… you know they're wrong."

"I know."

Her voice gets low, breathy. "Can we ditch yet?"

I look to the clock. "Yeah, but you know we have somewhere else to be."

"I wouldn't miss it."

An hour later, we're at Logan's place in the hills. The Wicked Beat singer and I got to be pretty close our last shared tour.

I complained I missed Vi a thousand times an hour. He rolled his eyes and told me to get the fuck back to whatever video game we were playing at the time.

Everyone is here—the band, significant others, Vi's best friend slash ex-roommate Athena, plus all the guys in Wicked Beat and a dozen or two other friends.

It's loud with laughter and glasses clinking.

Vi is squeezing my hand the way she always does in big groups—she's still not a fan of attention—but she's also wearing a wide smile.

This is our party.

This is what our life is supposed to look like.

Mal pops open a bottle of champagne. The cork hits the ceiling. Bubbly spills over the bottle.

He looks to his girlfriend Lacey and winks.

She blushes and mouths something I don't want to make out. God only knows what he plans on doing with that bottle of champagne later.

Piper holds out her glass. "Me first."

Mal goes around the room filling flutes with champagne. And damn is it a room. Calling Logan's place a mansion is doing it a disservice.

The packed dining room is the size of my and Violet's apartment. It's new and trendy, with hardwood floors and modern furniture. The sliding glass door behind us opens up to a sprawling backyard with a huge pool, a fire pit, and wet bar, and fuck knows what else.

This place is practically the Playboy Mansion.

Which suits Logan, I guess.

Violet squeezes my hand and rests her head against my shoulder. "You ever want a place like this?"

"I don't want our kids to grow up spoiled."

She lets out a soft sigh. "You're going to use that every time you can, aren't you?"

I nod.

She looks up at me with a soft smile. "Good. I like thinking about it. Ethan Strong, my husband… and one day father of my children."

"That's fucking cheesy."

"I know." She runs her fingers through my hair. "Maybe I just like thinking of fucking you."

"Maybe?"

She shakes her head. "Not maybe."

"You look gorgeous as always, Violet." That's Mal's deep voice. He's standing in front of us with two champagne flutes. He hands one to Vi and one to me. "Piper's first. Then me."

Mal turns to Joel—he's sitting on the couch with his wife in his lap—and motions *come here*.

The drummer whispers something in his wife's ear, then he lifts her into his arms, and makes a show of carrying her toward the dining table.

She giggles as she wraps her arms around his shoulders. "My hero."

He sets her down gently. Then he shoots me a wink. "You gotta practice that wedding night shit, Strong."

"Do we still need to practice?" Bella motions to his ring. "I think we know the drill by now."

"No, we always gotta practice. We can't let Mrs. Coen down. She lives to tell us to shut the fuck up," he says.

Bella blushes. "God, she's such a sweet woman."

"And you're such a dirty girl." he mumbles into her ear.

"Ahem." Piper steps onto a chair. "I believe it's my turn to give a toast. That means no sucking face, Joel."

Everyone in the room laughs.

Joel crosses his arms, faux indignant.

Bella peels his arms apart and slides one around her waist. "We'll be good."

"That gives you thirty seconds." Kit chuckles. He's standing behind Piper, looking at her like he's worried she's going to fall.

"Don't I know it?" Piper bends over to pick up her glass of champagne. "I'll keep this short and sweet. Violet, you taught me about boys, and makeup, and clothes. You taught me how to handle myself. You always helped me with my math homework. When you came back into Ethan's life, I felt like I finally had my sister back. But that was nothing compared to what it did to Ethan. He's a different person around you. He's happy. And as much as I want to tell him not to fuck this up, and I do mean that, Ethan. Don't fuck this up."

She laughs

"What I really want to say, is that I've never seen two people who make each other whole the way you and Ethan do. So, congratulations. I hope you have a long, healthy life together." Piper holds up her glass.

Everyone cheers congratulations, and we all drink.

Violet leans in to press her forehead against mine. I pull her closer. It feels so right holding Violet. Knowing she'll be my wife this time tomorrow.

"Hey, no making out," Joel teases. "We have to torture you more first."

"Yes, more torture." Piper giggles as Kit lifts her into his arms and spins her around.

He sets her on the ground then leans in to whisper in her ear.

She whispers back.

He actually blushes. Fuck, is my sister some master of dirty talk?

I don't want to know.

Mal steps up to the front of the table. He looks around the room then his gaze focuses on Violet. "I remember the first time you came over. I thought, fuck, that girl is way too cool for Ethan."

Everyone laughs.

"I kept wondering when you'd realize it and dump his sorry ass. But you never did. And, after five years, I think it's safe to say you never will." He holds up his glass of champagne. "I know we've had our words, Vi, but I think we have the same goal."

"Make Ethan miserable," Joel teases.

Mal chuckles. "I wouldn't trust anyone else with him. Take care of him, all right?"

Violet nods. "You too. You have him as much as I do."

Mal nods.

Violet holds up her glass.

The two of them drink.

Everyone else follows.

Mal goes around the room offering refills. Slowly, he works his way to us.

"I mean it. Congratulations." He leans in to whisper something in Violet's ear.

She laughs and whispers something back.

"Do I want to know?" I ask.

Violet laughs. "Nothing like that." She smiles back at Mal. "Thanks."

"You too." He nods to her then moves on to refilling.

Violet turns to me. "He's sweet, deep down."

"Incredibly deep," I say.

"I think we're good now." She leans in to press her lips to mine.

Her glass clinks against mine. Champagne pours over the sides and onto the hardwood.

She laughs as she pulls back. "I guess I better finish this." She locks arms with mine.

We tilt our heads back to drink from each other's glasses.

"God, they're so cute it hurts, huh?" Piper squees.

"I know. It's disgusting." That's Athena, Violet's best friend. She moves in to take Violet's hand. "This was really nice, really beautiful. But it's time for more important things."

"Oh no." Violet's eyes go wide. "Don't tell me—"

"I won't tell you, but that won't change the facts." Athena turns to Joel and motions *come here.*

"Not strippers." Violet shakes her head, but she's smiling.

"So many strippers." Athena looks to me. "I promise to bring her home at a respectable time. And not too drunk either. No one likes a hungover bride. And it's not just because the strip club doesn't serve booze."

"I have to do this sober?" Violet shakes her head.

"Sober? You have a time machine to go back to this afternoon?"

She moves out of the way to make room for Joel. He's holding up a plastic tiara. Only it's not a normal tiara.

Each of the peaks is topped with a plastic penis.

He drops to one knee and holds it over his head. "My Liege."

"Allow me." Athena takes the tiara and places it on Violet's head.

Violet turns bright red. "Pray for me."

I kiss her goodbye. "I will."

Athena and Piper drag her away. Bella and Lacey follow a few minutes later.

The brightness in Joel's eyes fades as his wife walks out the door. As much as I hate to admit it, marriage looks good on him.

"Why is Logan's house this huge? And where the fuck is he?" Joel pours two glasses of whiskey and brings one to me. "Trust me, Strong, you're gonna learn the difference between married life and single life really fast."

"You're the expert?"

"Fuck yeah, I'm the expert." He smiles. "It's all about what makes her happy."

"You have ten whole months of relationship experience."

"Almost eleven. And you gotta count the six hours before we got hitched." Joel laughs. "You scared?"

"Were you?"

"No. But I didn't have her father standing at the altar behind me." Joel shudders. "Pretty sure he still thinks I'm a fling she's gonna get over." He motions to Mal, who's moving toward us. "And I didn't fucking have Mal as my best man. That's terrifying."

"Love you too." Mal blows Joel a kiss.

Joel catches it and slides it into his pocket. "You know I'm taken."

"And I'm not?" Mal cocks a brow.

"Don't see a ring," Joel says.

Mal shakes his head. "You don't have to bring that up anytime someone mentions Bella."

Joel shrugs. "I can't help that I want the world to know she's mine."

"That must be it." Mal looks to me then motions to the bar.

He's got something he wants to say with Joel out of earshot.

I nod to Joel then follow Mal over to the bar. Joel scampers off to go talk with Kit. And—there's Logan. He's polishing off a bottle of beer, staring at his phone like it's the source of all happiness in the universe.

Fuck.

He better not—

"He won't." Mal picks up the bottle of champagne and pours two glasses. "Even Logan doesn't want some shady stripping agency knowing his address."

Good.

I've had enough of anonymous naked women staring at me like I'm a trophy slash dollar sign for one lifetime.

Mal hands me one of the glasses.

"You trying to get me drunk too?"

He chuckles. "You're the man of the hour."

"Cheers." I hold up my glass.

We toast, then kick back our glasses.

Fuck, we're not classy enough to be near champagne. Chugging it like this is wrong.

My brother looks me in the eyes. "I got you something."

"Tell me it's not a sex toy."

"Well, Joel and I got you something. But this is just me." His lips curl into a wide smile. It's a rarity for Mal. "Trust me. It's fun."

"I'm terrified."

"Your mirror."

I have to laugh. "You're parting ways with it?"

He nods. "It's getting time to sell the house. Dad wants to, but he can't admit it. But fuck, that's a topic for another day."

"Yeah."

"He's gonna be there tomorrow."

"So he says."

Mal nods *fair enough*. "Joel and I did get you under the bed restraints."

"I knew it."

"And I threw in a riding crop. New, of course."

"Of course."

"Not sure if Vi is into that, but with the constant hickeys—"

I laugh. "Not sure I'm into it."

He raises a brow *your loss*. "Listen, Ethan. I, fuck. Let me get this over with."

Mal is nervous.

That's fucking weird.

He's usually the most composed person in the history of the universe.

He drops his voice to a whisper. "When you and Vi got engaged, I didn't take it well. I kept thinking it was the end of me, you, and Piper as a family. In a way, it was. But I get it now. That's life. It moves forward." He runs his hand through his hair. His posture gets stiff. Awkward. "I'll always miss that time, but I'm glad you're moving forward. I'm glad you and Vi are making it official." He pulls me into a hug. "Take care of her."

I have to laugh. "You asked her to take care of me."

"You saying it's not good advice."

"It is, but…" A million thoughts flit through my head. My brother and I haven't always had the easiest relationship, but I've always known he has my back, and he's always known I have his. "Thanks."

He steps back with a nod.

He motions to the other guys on the couch.

Logan waves hello to me and pats the spot on the couch next to him. "Don't tell me I missed the fight."

"A Strong brothers hug without a fight first. Shocking stuff," Joel says.

Logan winks at Mal. "Where's my muse?"

Mal shoots him a *please* look.

"He's harder to bait than that." Kit chuckles.

Mal stays standing. He takes a long look around the crowded dining room. "What are you trying to prove with this place?"

"That kinda thinking is above my pay grade. I liked the pool." Logan motions to said pool. "Free for skinny dipping for anyone, but that's no fun when it's mostly dudes here."

Joel laughs. "This place is ridiculous, Kingston. I thought I was rich, but damn—"

"Your dad's place is bigger than this," Kit says.

"But that's tech money, not music money. Totally different." Joel turns to me. "Fuck, I left Vi's penis lollipop in the car. You're gonna have to make that up to her."

"I'm still waiting for you to kick his ass," Mal says.

"I still say guitarists hit for shit." Joel winks at me.

"I can always fill in, Ethan." Logan holds up his fists. "Only need my hands for one thing and it doesn't happen on stage."

"Hell no. I don't fight stand-ins. We can dance anytime you want, Strong," Joel teases.

I laugh. "I'm good."

"Me too," Joel says.

"When did you four get so calm?" Logan shakes his head. "Your tour bus used to be screaming twenty-four seven and not the fun kind."

"A lot of the fun kind," Joel says.

"Fifty-fifty," Kit says.

"Ninety-ten," Logan argues. He leans back on the couch and stares at the ceiling. His voice gets far away. "I know you're all enjoying this fab pad, but rich isn't all it's cracked up to be. Dangerous Noise still has artistic integrity. Wicked Beat…"

"You had it once? I don't remember that," Joel teases.

Logan laughs, but he doesn't sell it. He shrugs, but he doesn't sell that either. "I just like to sing."

A knock on the door grabs my attention.

"Fuck, tell me those aren't strippers." Joel shakes his head. "You know I'm not into that shit."

Logan shrugs. He motions to the door. "Go find out."

Joel shoots Logan an incredulous look. He pushes himself off the couch then makes his way across the huge foyer to the door.

It takes thirty fucking seconds just for the man to walk across the room. That's how huge—and crowded—this place is.

He pulls open the door. "Not strippers."

"Fuck, Young. You promised I could take it all off." That's a familiar deep voice.

And it's loud. I can hear it all the way over here.

"Hell. Fucking. No. I never want to hear your grunt again. How the fuck did you convince Miles to let you sing backup on a single track much less three?" That too.

Pete and Tom Steele step inside. The bassist and the drummer are brothers. Foster brothers technically. They look nothing alike. Pete is all dark, mysterious features and Tom is all light hair, light eyes, and oodles of charm. But it's clear they're brothers.

They fight like an old married couple.

Way back in high school, the three of us were in a band together. Along with some singer we replaced several times. We parted ways when Mom and Dad first bailed and I decided to prove I didn't give a fuck about anything, but we've always stayed friends.

"Fuck, Kingston. This place is excessive." Tom steps forward. "What's the point of a giant house if it's got no furniture? It looks like a porn set."

"You're welcome for the invite." Logan shakes his head.

"Not your bachelor party." Tom nods hello to me. "You terrified yet?"

"A little," I admit.

"That's normal," Pete says.

"Where's Miles and Drew?" I ask.

"Fuck, aren't you happy to see me?" Tom feigns being stabbed in the gut. "Where the fuck is Miles?"

"Something about wanting nothing to do with your debauchery," Pete says. "He'll be there tomorrow. Drew too."

"Drew can't be torn away from Alexandria and his once again pregnant wife." Tom rolls his eyes.

"You're so fucking jealous." Pete chuckles.

"Willow's always at their place," Tom complains.

"She's a good aunt," Pete says.

"Did I say otherwise?" Tom folds his arms.

Pete chuckles. "Jealousy isn't an attractive look."

"You think I give a fuck about what you find attractive?" Tom shakes his head. "We're here to congratulate Ethan. And we're just sitting around? Isn't this a party?"

"It's called conversation."

"I know about conversation."

"It's sad. The envy. Really?" Pete looks to us for confirmation.

Tom does seem jealous. It's not like him. I've known the guy since he was fourteen, and I've never seen him jealous.

"Is it wrong to want my wife around?" Tom asks.

"Why don't you play with Alexandria?"

"I do."

"But?"

"She's a natural drummer, and Drew fucking stops me every time I encourage her."

Pete laughs.

"He's banned me from the house until I promise to stop."

Pete laughs harder.

"He says no daughter of his is going to be an idiot who can only hit things with sticks."

That gets Pete doubling over.

"Why do you act like you haven't heard him say that a thousand times?" Tom asks.

"Still funny a thousand and one."

"Guitarists are fucking overrated. No offense, Ethan. Actually… you tired of these assholes yet?" Tom asks.

"Yeah, but I think I'm stuck with them," I say.

Joel flips me off.

Pete teases his brother. "You think threatening to replace Drew is gonna—"

"I need some fucking leverage," Tom says.

"He's not gonna quit. Call him on his bluff."

"With one kid, maybe. With two?"

Pete pulls out his cell and offers it to Tom. "Call him. Tell him how you feel. How you need him."

"Fuck off."

"You can admit you have feelings."

"Fuck off twice."

"You can call your wife and tell her you want to knock her up. You can still adopt later."

Tom actually blushes. Fuck, I don't think I've ever seen the guy blush.

"This is Ethan's fucking party! Why are you talking about me?" Tom takes the cell. He looks to me. "You really want to sit here, hearing my brother berate me?"

"Yeah." I laugh. This is one time where I'm sick of being the center of attention.

"Fuck, why do I keep hanging out with musicians?" Tom shakes his head, but he's smiling.

They're still an old married couple.

And we're still a dysfunctional family.

Some things never change.

But tomorrow…

Well, some things change for the better.

Chapter Seven

VIOLET

I wake up exhausted but, mercifully, not hungover. Thank goodness for California's strict laws about separating nudity and alcohol.

My head is still filled with images of naked men writhing to 80s rock.

I never want to see a naked man again.

Well, besides Ethan.

He's lying in bed next to me, his eyes pressed together, his bare chest rising and falling with his breath.

This is it.

Our wedding day.

Forever.

My fingers go to his bare skin. I trace the lines of his chest-piece tattoo. The broken heart. The lock. The wings. That skeleton key with my name written on the shaft.

Violet.

It's there, on his body, forever.

And his name is tattooed on my ribs.

That's forever.

More forever than a legal ceremony that ends at our deaths.

But that doesn't stop my stomach from doing somersaults.

It's okay.

They're good somersaults.

They're *I'm about to jump off the high dive* somersaults.

I want to get to the part where I rip off Ethan's suit, but I also want the vows, the kiss, the first dance, the cake…

I want everything.

AN HOUR LATER, I'M HAVING BREAKFAST WITH MOM AND Piper. They spend forever talking about… about something. I'm too nervous to really listen. Or to eat anything besides a plain bagel, no toppings. Even green tea has too much taste.

We get to Kelsey's around lunchtime. I force myself to have another snack, but all I can manage is a handful of almonds. This is really happening.

Kelsey is fixing Mom's makeup.

Then Piper's.

Then mine.

Then Piper is helping me into my dress. She laces the back with tender care. She checks that she knows how to hook and unhook the bustle.

She squeals over how beautiful I look.

Mom does too.

Then Mom is putting on my necklace. My earrings. And our limo is arriving. And I'm walking toward it.

My dress is huge. It's a struggle to get it into the limo with me.

Piper slides in. Then Mom.

The driver closes the door for us. He steps into the front of the car.

And he pulls away.

We're driving to my wedding.

How did the day go so fucking fast?

My heartbeat picks up. My stomach rises into my throat. It's not like the other day. These are good nerves. Happy nerves.

But they're a lot of nerves.

I take as deep a breath as I can manage with my corset tight. I exhale slowly.

Piper takes my hand and squeezes tight. "It's going to be perfect."

Mom takes my other hand. "It really is, sweetheart."

I nod. "I think so too." Another deep breath does nothing to push my nerves away. I look to Mom. "Am I supposed to be this nervous?"

Her smile lights up her green eyes. "I was, with your father." She looks proud. Happy. Like she really wouldn't trade me for a thousand normal daughters.

Like she really does love that I'm wearing a black and purple princess dress.

Like she really does love Ethan as much as I do.

Well, almost as much. Nobody loves Ethan as much as I do. That's not even close to possible.

Mom blinks back a tear. She wipes it away with the thumb of her free hand. "Asher would have been proud of you too."

I nod.

"He loved Ethan."

"And hated him."

There's a sadness to Mom's smile. "Only for stealing his twin sister's attention." She blinks and the sadness is gone.

"I'll always miss him. I know you will too. But this… if he is out there somewhere, I know he's watching over us. I know he's happy that Ethan is going to be taking care of you forever."

My chest warms as a tear rolls down my cheeks. It hurts thinking of my late brother, but it has a place in the day. I loved Asher. Then I hated myself for failing to protect him. It drove me and Ethan apart the first time, but then Ethan is the person who helped me put myself back together.

Asher and Ethan fought all the time. Asher thought Ethan was a philistine. Ethan thought Asher was a snob. But they did respect each other. And they both cared most about how the other treated me.

"I wish he was here too." I squeeze Mom's hand. "He would have hated my dress."

Mom laughs. "What did he know about fashion?"

"And the roses. And the altar. And the music." I can't help but laugh. "He'd really hate all the songs I gave to the DJ."

"Who says you can't have your first dance to a Garbage song?" Mom asks.

Piper laughs. "That really is perfect for you."

The car slows to a stop. The engine turns off.

I look up to the sunroof. It's just a glass panel looking up at the deep blue sky. I let my eyes fall closed and I whisper one more goodbye to my baby brother.

The driver pulls the door open. He nods to my mother and offers his hand.

She squeezes me in one last hug. "You look beautiful, sweetheart. This is going to be perfect."

I nod as she releases the hug. She takes the driver's hand and steps out of the limo.

Then it's Piper.

She nearly jumps into my lap to throw her arms around me. "You really do look beautiful."

"You too."

"I'm so glad you're going to officially be my sister." She pulls back with a smile. "And just... I really am happy for you guys."

I nod. It's all I can do. My stomach is too full of butterflies. My mouth is too sticky.

This is really happening.

Piper slides out of the limo.

Then it's me.

But that isn't the driver's hand. It's my dad's.

"Need a little help, princess?" he asks.

I have to laugh. He hasn't called me princess in a million years. Not since my very short Disney princess phase.

I take his hand. "Thanks." It's a struggle to get my dress out of the limo without stepping on it, but I manage. "I do feel like a princess."

His smile is wide. "You look like one. You look beautiful." There are no pretenses on his face. It's not a *you're so unique, Violet* smile. He's just happy.

"Thanks." I wrap my arms around him and squeeze tightly. My parents and I fight, and I worry what they think, and they don't always get me, but I love them, and I know they do want the best for me. And I'm so glad they're here. That they're in my life in a meaningful way.

"Can I be cheesy for a minute?"

"It's my wedding day." God, it's really my wedding day. "It would be weirder if you weren't cheesy."

He smiles. "I'm happy for you and Ethan. He's a wonderful young man, even with the tattoos."

I laugh. "You know I have some now too."

He nods. "This is the start of a new phase of your life.

A lot of things will change. But no matter what, you'll always be my little girl, and I'll always be here when you need me. No matter what."

God, now I'm really crying. I wipe my tears with my thumbs. I hug my dad again.

This is really happening.

The wedding coordinator's voice pulls me back to reality. "You ready to go, Violet?"

"Yeah. I think I really am." I'm ready to do this.

She's in a smart black suit, a headset pressed to her ear. She hands me my bouquet—crimson roses wrapped in black ribbon.

Dad laughs. "Perfect."

"It is."

The coordinator presses her headset to her ear. "We're coming." She motions to the stone steps that lead up to the ceremony location. "As soon as you're ready."

I nod and take Dad's arm.

And I take the first step.

The music starts, the wedding march. I can hear it from here.

With each step up the stone staircase, my heart pounds a little faster. My breath gets a little more shallow.

I get to the top step.

I walk the stone path and turn the corner.

There's the ceremony site. The courtyard of this gorgeous grey stone castle.

The decorations are simple. The deep purple walkway. Black ribbons and crimson roses on the chairs. And the black, wrought iron altar, covered in roses and tulle.

And there's Ethan, in his suit, his hair neat, his blue eyes bright.

He's smiling ear to ear.

It's a goofy smile.

A *this is the best day of my life* kind of smile.

And I'm wearing the same one. I can feel it in the way he's looking at me. I can feel my cheeks at my ears.

I hold his gaze as I walk down the aisle. I don't see our friends. I don't see our family. I don't even see the castle around us.

I only see Ethan.

And all the joy in his eyes.

And the joy in our lives.

Everyone sits and the officiant starts speaking. He's doing our reading, the poem I picked out, but I can't hear anything over how hard my heart is pounding.

I can't feel anything but all that love welling up in my chest.

He finishes reading our story, a very abridged version of it, and he looks to Mal. He's standing behind Ethan. He's tall and he's broad and he's impossible to ignore, but I barely see him.

I can't pry my eyes away from Ethan's.

"May I have the rings?" The officiant asks.

Mal nods as he hands over the ring box. He's smiling that same wide smile.

The officiant hands my wedding ring to Ethan. He turns to me. "Violet Valentine, do you take this man to be your lawfully wedded husband?"

I nod. "I do."

He nods to Ethan.

Ethan slides the ring onto my left ring finger.

The officiant looks to Ethan. "Ethan Strong, do you take this woman to be your lawfully wedded wife?"

Ethan beams. "I do."

The officiant hands me the ring. Somehow, I manage to hold it. Somehow, I manage to slide it onto Ethan's ring finger.

"Violet, please take Ethan's hand and repeat after me."

I do.

"I, Violet, take you Ethan, to be my husband. I wish to share my life with you, to rejoice in times of happiness, and console you through times of trouble. I promise to love, respect, and honor you, through all of the trials and triumphs we'll go through together."

I stare into Ethan's eyes as I repeat the vow.

"Ethan, please repeat after me." The officiant recites the vow for Ethan.

And Ethan stares back at me as he repeats it. His smile spreads even wider.

Mine does too.

The officiant claps. "I now pronounce you man and wife."

Ethan doesn't wait for the announcement.

He slides his arms around my waist, and he pulls me into a deep, slow kiss.

And I feel it everywhere.

I'm kissing my husband.

He's really my husband.

Chapter Eight

VIOLET

The ceremony blurs into pictures. Into family hugs and jokes. Ethan even hugs his dad. He even whispers something about how he forgives the guy for never being around.

Our reception is a fairy tale. Twinkling purple lights. Lush rose centerpieces. Dancing with my dad, to his favorite song. Then in Ethan's arms to mine.

And the cake and champagne and, okay, more cake. The night blurs together into one big mix of sugar and laughter.

Then it's over. And Ethan and I are climbing into the limo.

The driver shuts the door.

It's just us.

Alone.

As husband and wife.

He plants on the bench seat and pulls me onto his lap. My dress swooshes under me, the skirt spilling over his legs.

"Fuck, Vi." He presses his forehead to mine. He cups the back of my neck with his hand. "We're really married."

"You're really my husband." I breathe in the joy in his blue eyes.

"You're really my wife."

"Fuck." I slide my hands over his shoulders. His tie. My palm presses flat against his button up shirt. "Say it again."

"You're my wife." He reaches up to undo my updo, one bobby pin at a time. "I'm your husband."

My hair spills over my cheeks. Over the back of my head. Fuck, it feels good undoing the tight style.

It feels better staring into Ethan's eyes.

He pulls out the last pin and runs his fingers through my hair. He looks up at me, his blue eyes filled with love and trust. "You look like an angel."

"From hell?"

"Of course." His smile spreads wider. He cups my cheek with his palm. "You really are my angel. You know that?"

I shake my head. "You're mine." I press my forehead to his and suck a deep breath through my nose. "You put me back together."

"You put you back together. I just helped."

"I couldn't have done it without you."

"Fuck, Vi..." He looks up at me. "I love you so fucking much."

"I love you too." My eyelids flutter closed as I lean in to kiss him. He tastes like cake and champagne. He tastes like Ethan.

Like home.

I can't wait to rip that suit off him.

But I'm not sure I have a choice. There are far too many layers of tulle between me and him. I can't feel anything under my dress.

I kiss him harder.

I groan into his mouth.

I tug at his hair. Really, it's the only thing I can do to contain all the weight of my desire.

We make out like horny high school students until the limo pulls to a stop.

The driver knocks on the door. "Whenever you're ready, Mr. and Mrs. Strong."

I melt. "I'm Mrs. Strong."

His voice is thick with desire. "It suits you."

"Hotel room. Sex. Now."

He smiles. "You want to stop and pick up more champagne?"

I shake my head.

"Something to eat?"

"No."

"We didn't get a bite to eat at dinner."

"Ethan." I tug at his suit jacket. "Sex now. Food later."

It's hard to believe, but, somehow, he manages to smile wider. He pulls open the door and helps me out.

I take my husband's hand, and I follow him into the hotel. It's a big, modern chain, one where we can scream at the top of our lungs without getting calls from the front desk.

Or maybe not.

I'm not watching the volume either way.

Ethan charms the receptionist in that classic Ethan kind of way.

She smiles at us as she hands over our room keys. "Congratulations."

"Thank you." I smile back. It's the four hundredth *congratulations* of the day, but it feels every bit as good as the first one.

Ethan slides his arm around my waist. The bodice of my dress is so thick I can barely feel the pressure of his hands.

But I can feel the change in his posture. There's something about the way Ethan walks when he's holding me. It's softer. Stronger. Like he's wrapping me in a hug and like he's ready to defend me with his life.

He leads me to the elevator and presses the button.

The silver doors slide open.

I clap my hands together as I step inside. This is it. We're almost to our hotel room. We're almost to the part where we strip each other out of our fancy clothes and fuck like rabbits.

Ethan punches in our floor. He watches the elevator doors slide closed then he turns to me. He slides his hands over my hips and pins me to the mirrored wall.

I stare into his piercing blue eyes. "Say it again."

"You're my wife."

"And you're my husband." I dig my hand into his hair. "I don't think I'll ever get tired of hearing that."

"Yeah?"

"Yeah."

His cheek brushes against mine as he leans in to whisper. "It's too bad I have other plans for my mouth."

Oh. I press my hips against his, but with the dress in the way, I can't feel anything. "That's not a problem."

"Not a problem?"

"Not at all."

"Good, because I want my wife coming on my face until she can't take it anymore."

"Ethan…" I pull him into a kiss. It's hard. Hungry. My tongue claims his mouth. His tongue claims mine.

Finally, the damn elevator dings. Our floor.

Ethan takes my hands and pulls me into the hallway. He's still wearing that goofy smile. He's still looking at me like this is the best day of his life.

We stop in front of the room at the end of the hall.

Ethan pulls his keycard from his slacks and slides it into the door. He pushes the door open.

Then he slides one arm around my waist and the other around my shoulders. "You trust me?"

"Yeah." I really do.

He lifts me into his arms and carries me across the threshold. I squeal as I dig my fingers into the fabric of his suit jacket. This is cheesy and perfect and real.

And he's really my husband.

And we're really married.

Forever and ever.

He kicks the door closed and looks down at me. "You ready for this?"

"For?"

"*This*."

"Oh." *This*. It's in that single word, the promise of a million dirty things. I nod. "Yes."

He carries me to the bed and tosses/sets me down.

I bounce off the mattress and fall back onto my back. I can just barely make out the details of the suite. It's beautiful and sleek with a view of the mountains, a big leather couch, a balcony, and this bed—

It's stripped to only the crisp white sheets.

Ethan climbs onto the bed and pushes my skirt up my legs. He peels off one heel and drops it on the ground. Then the other.

He pushes my skirt up my legs.

"How are you?" I lose track of my words as he dives under the skirt.

His lips brush against my calf. My knee. My inner thigh. Then it's his warm breath melting my panties against me.

"Ethan…" I reach for his hair but grab only tulle.

"Yeah?" He nips at my inner thigh as his fingers curl into the sides of my panties.

"I... I really fucking love you."

"I love you too, honey." He tugs my panties down my thighs.

His lips brush my inner thigh.

My pelvis.

My clit.

Fuck.

I sink into the bed as Ethan licks me up and down.

I pull layer and layer of tulle to my waist, but there's still more. I can't get my hands in that dark, wavy hair of his.

I press my thighs against his cheeks instead.

I buck against his lips.

He's licking me just right.

Exactly where I need him.

My husband is eating me out.

It's so fucking romantic.

"Ethan, fuck." I tug at the sheets instead of his hair.

I rock against him.

The tension in my core knots.

Almost.

Fuck.

With the next flick of his tongue, I go over the edge.

I tug at the sheets.

I press my thighs against his cheeks.

I scream his name again and again.

He licks me through my orgasm. Then through the next. It's intense, painful in that good way. Then I'm there, screaming his name as my sex pulses.

"Ethan. Fuck me. Now."

He drags his lips down my thigh and pops out from

under my skirt. His eyes meet mine. "Fuck yes." He takes my hands and pulls me to my feet.

I turn around so he can undo my dress's corset lacing.

He's quick with it. It's true—guitarists really are good with their hands.

Ethan pushes my dress off my hips. I step out of it one foot at a time, and I turn to face him.

I'm naked in front of my husband.

And he's wearing that perfect black suit, that perfect purple tie.

"It really is criminal how good you look in a suit." I press my palms against his chest and my hips against his. Fuck yes. Without the skirt, I can feel his hard-on through his slacks.

And I need it.

Now.

I tug the knot of his tie loose. "But I need it gone."

He undoes his tie and tosses it aside. Then the suit jacket. Shoes. Socks. Slacks.

I watch him push his boxers to his knees.

That's my husband, naked in front of me.

Fuck, it really is romantic.

He scoops me into his arms and carries me back to the bed. We fall onto the sheets, a messy tangle of limbs. My lips find his. My hands roam over every hard inch of his body. It's like I'm rediscovering his body.

My husband's body.

Fuck, the thought of it makes me dizzy.

I slide my hand down his stomach.

Past that soft tuft of pubic hair.

My palm brushes against his cock. I rub his tip with my thumb until he's groaning into my mouth.

"Vi." He drags his lips down my neck. "Fuck."

I wrap my hand around him. I need him inside me. But I need to feel him shuddering with desire first.

He nips at my neck as I stroke him.

His teeth sink into my neck. I let out a groan, half pain, half pleasure.

"Don't stop." I stroke him harder.

He bites me harder.

Fuck.

I can't take it anymore. I drag my hand up his stomach and chest. Around his side. My palm presses against his back.

I pull his body on top of mine.

I look up at Ethan as I wrap my legs around his waist.

He looks down at me as he pins me to the bed.

His tip strains against me.

Slowly, he slides inside me.

Fuck.

"Ethan." I stare up into his eyes.

He stares back at me. "Vi…"

My eyelids flutter closed. My hands knot in his hair.

He kisses me hard as he drives into me.

I rock my hips to meet him.

He wraps his arms around me.

We stay glued together, bodies moving together, tongues dancing together.

Pleasure wells up inside me. The tension in my core knots tighter and tighter.

I groan against Ethan's lips.

I tug at his hair.

Then I'm there, rocking against him as I come. Pleasure spreads out to my fingers and toes. The pulsing of my sex pulls him closer.

He drives deeper.

Faster.

He kisses me harder.

Then he's there too, groaning into my mouth, digging his nails into my skin as he comes inside me.

Once he's spilled every drop, he collapses next to me.

And he pulls me into his arms. He drags his fingertips down my arm and traces my rings.

I do the same to his.

I stare back at Ethan. Words can't express how much I love him.

So I kiss him hard.

Like I'm never going to get another chance to kiss him again.

We're as close as we can be.

And we're married.

This really is forever.

It really is fucking perfect.

Bella and Joel

Chapter Nine

JOEL

Bella presses her ass against my crotch as she stirs.

She's wearing her work outfit—a tight pencil skirt and a dark blouse. One that shows off her fantastic tits.

I know we're doing something here, but for the life of me, I can't remember what it is.

Thoughts are fleeing my brain at an alarming rate.

The view of her lacy bra isn't doing shit to help me regain my concentration.

Fuck, she has a nice ass.

And she smells so fucking good.

Even if the room is filled with the scent of citrus, sugar, and… cranberries?

Yeah.

That's it.

We're making cranberry sauce.

Tomorrow is Thanksgiving.

But that seems a lot less important than spreading her legs and diving between them.

I press my palm against her pelvis and pull her closer. "You need to come now."

She lets out a soft groan as she grinds her ass against me. Her eyes go to her cell, lying face up on the counter. "We have five more minutes."

"You're trying to kill me, angel."

She laughs. "Why would I want to do something like that?"

I slide my hands over her hips. I'm seriously considering trying to get her off in the next—

Four and a half minutes.

I can do it.

But I want to savor her pleasure.

Fuck it.

I can't wait four and a half minutes.

I can't wait another second.

I drag my lips over her neck. "Panties off. You come now. Then we finish this—what the fuck is it again?"

She sighs with pleasure as she grinds against me. "Cranberry sauce. With pineapple."

It sounds familiar. I really should remember, what with us starting this recipe twenty minutes ago.

Right now, my head is filled with thoughts of Bella's groans.

Everything else seems irrelevant.

My eyes go to the pot of cranberry sauce. "That's a lot of fucking pineapple."

"Only three times the suggested amount."

There's a flash of pride in my chest. When we met, Bella would never go off recipe. But she'll try shit now. And not just with food. "This monstrosity is why I have to wait to make you come?"

"No." She takes my hand and places it between her

breasts, right on the button struggling to hold her shirt together. "That's because I want to torture you."

"I'll get you back for that, angel."

"I know." Her voice drops to that needy, breathy tone.

She's counting on me teasing her back.

Which means it's a reward, not a punishment.

But I can't exactly complain about the state of affairs.

My wife is pressed against me, the flesh of her lush ass against my cock, her tits in my hands.

There's all this stupid fabric in the way.

And there's this fucking weird side dish on the stove.

But otherwise, it's perfect.

Still, I need to make her come.

I undo the top button of her blouse. "Panties. Off. Now."

"Here's the thing." She leans into my touch, shuddering as my fingertips skim the top of her bra cup. "I'm not wearing panties."

Fuck, she makes me incoherent.

I turn her so she's facing the counter, the one where her phone is sitting.

"Joel..." She leans forward, pressing her palms against the counter and her ass against my crotch.

"Yeah?"

"I missed you."

"I missed you too, angel." I got in yesterday and spent the night making her come. But she left for work early this morning. It wasn't enough.

It's been two weeks since we've been in the same place. And we only have a few days before we're back on the road.

I need more of her.

All of her, all the time.

I lean down to plant a kiss on her shoulder.

Her neck.

She turns so I can press my lips against hers.

Fuck, she tastes good.

Like sugar and tea and home.

"Hands on the counter," I demand.

She groans as she places her palms against the tile.

She arches her back, rubbing her ass against me.

Fuck, she's too good at driving me out of my mind.

My cock whines, but it's going to have to wait.

This first.

I bring my hands to the bottom of her skirt and I roll the garment up her thighs. Over her bare ass.

My fingertips skim her flesh. "You walk around like this all day, angel?"

"Yes," she breathes.

I drag my fingertips over the backs of her thighs. Higher. Higher. Higher.

Almost.

"Joel." She arches her back to meet my hands.

My fingers brush against her clit.

Bella lets out a low, heavy groan.

She needs this.

She needs me.

I rub her with my thumb.

She bucks against my hand, needy, impatient.

God damn, the groans falling off her lips…

I slide my free hand into her bra.

She shudders as I toy with her nipple.

She shifts her hips, grinding her ass against my hard-on.

Fuck, that feels good.

I rub her a little harder.

A little faster.

Almost.

There—

"Fuck, Joel." She lets out a low, heavy groan.

She's at the edge.

It's torture pulling my hand to her thigh.

She groans that *you're an evil tease* groan just as the timer beeps.

She pushes herself up and turns around so we're face-to-face. Her eyes search mine. They're asking another question entirely, one that goes deeper than which of us is the more vicious tease.

What is she thinking?

How is she thinking anything right now?

I have no idea.

"We should check on the sauce." She slides her skirt over her ass.

There's something off.

Something wrong.

I keep my voice light. "Angel, you really think I give a fuck about anything but making you come right now?"

Her lips curl into an evil smile. She is torturing me.

Maybe.

It's hard to think in this state.

She turns back to the stove, sets the burner to warm, dips the spoon in the sauce. "You want to do the honors, or should I?"

"Go for it."

She brings the spoon to her lips and makes a show of flicking her tongue against the sauce.

Her nose scrunches in distaste.

"Oh no." She shakes her head. "It's um..." She offers me the spoon.

"Quite the endorsement."

She laughs.

I lean in to lick a bite off the spoon. It's *um* all right. Not that I can concentrate on much besides my wife's tits.

Fuck, I would much rather have those in my mouth.

She takes the spoon back and takes another lick. "It's… unique."

"It's horrible."

"Where did we go wrong?" She sets the spoon back in the pot and turns the burner off.

"Maybe the triple portion of pineapple."

"Maybe." She takes a step toward me and presses her body against mine. "It was what made it special, you know? And I had the strangest craving for it."

"Pineapple shouldn't be everywhere."

"You're from California."

"And?"

"You invented Hawaiian pizza."

"Really? We did? Not Hawaii?"

"Yeah. And you love it." She runs her fingertips over my shoulders. "You know my eyes are up here?"

"You know your tits are right here?" I slip my thumb into her bra and rub her nipple.

She lets out a soft groan as she presses her cheek against my neck. "I… Uh…"

"We have four cans of cranberry sauce in the pantry."

"I know. I just…"

"You want everything to be perfect tomorrow?"

"And that stomach flu keeps kicking my ass. It makes everything feel…" Her eyes light up as she presses her pelvis against my erection. "Well, harder."

"Harder, huh?"

She nods.

Conversation is the last thing I want right now. But I'm not going to let her drown all by herself. "We can talk about it."

She slides her hand down my stomach and cups me over my jeans. "You can talk right now?"

"In theory."

She laughs.

"You'll have to put on panties."

"Awful." She slides her other hand under my t-shirt and presses her palm against my stomach. "I really did miss you."

"I missed you too."

"I already said that, huh?"

"Yeah."

She traces circles over my stomach with her fingertip. "I don't want to talk."

"Good." I need a night with my wife without anything else intruding.

She pulls my t-shirt over my head and tosses it aside. Her hands go to my jeans. She undoes the button.

The zipper.

She pushes them to my knees.

Then the boxers.

I kick them off.

She stares into my eyes as she wraps her hand around my cock.

Fuck. That feels good.

She kisses me hard, her tongue sliding around mine, her thumb rubbing my tip.

I need to be inside her.

I need to feel our bodies connecting.

The two of us as one.

All that cheesy shit.

I bring my hands to her ass and pull her body onto mine. There. I find the zipper of her skirt, undo it, push the garment off her hips.

She steps out of it.

I undo the rest of her buttons and slide her blouse off her shoulders.

She reaches around to undo her bra.

Her eyes meet mine. There's a plea in them. It's *help me stop thinking* as much as it's *make me come*.

For a second, I hesitate. If there's something burning a hole in Bella's brain, I want to know what it is.

But I trust her.

If she needs every thought but *fuck me, Joel* wiped from her mind, I'm more than happy to oblige.

I slide my hands to her hips and I lift her onto the kitchen counter. "Spread your legs."

She does.

"Touch yourself."

She stares back at me as she pushes her knees apart.

Her beautiful brown eyes fill with desire. Her expression gets strong, confident.

Bella holds my gaze as her fingertips skim her clit.

The soft touch makes her shudder.

She goes harder.

Faster.

I watch pleasure spread over her face.

Her lips part with a sigh.

Her shoulders shudder.

Her chest heaves.

Her eyes flutter closed.

I can see her thoughts flying away with every groan.

I watch her lips, her eyes, her hands, her tits, her cunt.

Fuck, I love watching her touch herself.

Even if it's torture.

"Look at me when you come, angel."

Her nod is heavy. Needy. She lets out a sigh as she blinks her eyes open.

She stares back at me, her eyes heavy with desire.

There's no space between us.

No distance.

This is right. How we should be—torturing each other.

She shudders as she rubs herself.

Her teeth sink into her lip.

Her nails sink into her thigh.

"Fuck, Joel." Her hand knots in my hair.

Then she's there, groaning my name and tugging at my hair.

This is what I need.

What we both need.

She wraps her arms around me and she pulls me closer.

Her lips brush mine.

All her love is pouring into me.

All my love is pouring into her.

The universe is the two of us.

I slide my hands to her hips and I pull her body onto mine.

She groans against my lips as my tip brushes against her.

Then it's one delicious inch at a time.

Fuck.

She feels so good.

And the way her hand is knotting in my hair—

The way she's bucking her hips against mine—

She wraps her legs around my waist.

She breaks our kiss enough to lean back and plant her hands behind her.

Her eyes lock with mine as she lifts her hips to meet me.

We stay locked like that, moving together, breathing together.

We stay a sticky, heaving mess, until she's there.

She groans against my chest, tugging at my hair, clawing at my back.

I can feel her come in the way she pulses around me.

It pushes me over the edge.

I pull her closer. Fuck her harder.

I thrust through my orgasm. Pleasure overwhelms my senses. It makes the room warm. It makes the fucking universe warm.

I don't stop until I've spilled every drop.

I set Bella down and I wrap my arms around her.

And she buries her head in my chest with a soft exhale.

Right now, the rest of the world is gone.

Right now, nothing else matters.

After we shower together, Bella goes straight to her phone. Her expression hardens as she picks it up.

"Anything important?" I ask.

"It's Alessandra." She taps her cell and brings it to her ear.

I study her expression like my life depends on it.

Something is wrong.

But what?

Her voice is soft. "I have to take care of this." She sets her phone on the counter and goes to the closet. She flips through her stable of work dresses and picks out a sleek black one.

"You okay?" I ask.

"Yeah." She tosses her dress on the bed, drops her towel, pulls on a bra and panties. "Just tired. And nauseous again."

"The cranberry sauce couldn't have helped."

She presses her lips together. "I guess more isn't always better."

I nod. "You see a doctor yet?"

"No. It's just the flu." Her voice is slightly hollow, like she's trying to convince herself. "I'll make an appointment Tuesday. After you leave. I need all the Joel Young I can get."

"Yeah?"

She nods as she pulls on her dress. "I promise I'll make this quick."

"I promise I'll make you come all fucking night."

She smiles. "I'm counting on it."

Chapter Ten

BELLA

I hate driving.

Joel tried to teach me, but I was a nervous wreck. I had to take a dozen lessons with a driving instructor.

I got my license a few months after I moved in with Joel. It's been a year and a half now, more even.

But I still hate driving.

It makes my stomach twist in knots.

It makes my breath shallow and strained.

It makes me want to throw up.

But I don't know if it's driving doing it right now.

I…

I can't think about this. Not today. Certainly not tomorrow. Maybe Sunday night, after I drop Dad off at the airport.

Maybe I can think about it then.

That's four little days of suppressing the question burning in my brain.

Four days convincing Joel there's nothing on my mind.

I can do four days.

In theory.

I try to breathe deep as I pull into the parking garage. It's empty this late the night before Thanksgiving, but that doesn't make me feel any more comfortable behind the wheel.

Not even Lady Gaga's complaints of her shitty romance can distract me today. This song is usually my go-to pick me up, but, right now, I can barely hear it.

I turn the car off and check my makeup in the rearview mirror. Only I'm no longer wearing any makeup. The shower washed it all away.

Alessandra has seen me like this a million times. I shouldn't care. But I do.

I spend a few minutes covering my under eye circles and touching up my lipstick. There. I don't look tired and nervous. Just…

Distracted, I guess.

Who's focused on work the night before a four-day weekend, anyway?

I grab my purse, lock my car, walk to the elevator. It's empty, but that doesn't stop my head from filling with memories of being in this tiny space with Joel, pressed against the elevator wall, making out like no one was watching.

Or maybe, in our case, like everyone was watching.

The elevator stops at our floor with a ding.

The lobby is empty. All the lights are off, save the one in Alessandra's office.

She's sitting behind her desk, on the phone with someone.

It must be that radio asshole who keeps trying to kick Wicked Beat out of the station's holiday concert. It's personal—apparently, Logan stole his girlfriend a long, long time ago.

I hate when it's personal.

You can't reason someone out of a lust for revenge. Logan doesn't do boyfriend. If this guy's girlfriend wanted to fuck Logan instead of him, he's better off without her.

But the male ego doesn't respond to… well, to anything.

Not that the female ego is any better.

If I've learned one thing in this job, it's that people would rather get their way than their money. At least in this industry.

Alessandra's eyes meet mine. She puts her call on hold and motions *come here*.

I pull her office door open and step inside. She looks exactly like she did this morning—short hair neat, dark makeup perfect, sharp suit without a wrinkle.

"Bella, please, I need my good cop." She motions to the phone, still sitting in the receiver.

"Sure."

"This guy… he wants to hear that Logan will apologize."

"That's not going to happen."

"Of course not. But the guy will buy it, and by the time it doesn't happen it will be too late."

"And after the concert when he hates Logan twice as much?"

"What's he going to do? Keep the biggest band in rock off the radio? No. He's fucked. He knows it. That's why he's pissed."

"It's a pop station."

"Pop, rock, it's all the same now. People want to hear Logan sing. People who listen to this station. That's what matters."

She's right, even if I'm not a fan of lying to people.

Still, this is my job.

I need to do it.

I nod an *okay* to her and I pull the phone from the receiver. "Mr. Winters. It's nice to hear from you."

"Is it?" he snaps.

"Yes, this is Bella. You remember. We talked about your *wife's* charity, and how excited we are to lend our bands to support it."

"Yeah." His voice simmers down a notch.

I'm the good cop. I can't let the guy know how irritating I find him. "Mr. Kingston wants to express his deepest apologies about what happened between the two of you, but unfortunately, he's unavailable."

"He finally in rehab?"

I let out an incredibly fake laugh. I usually sell it better than this. Honestly, I'm not sure where Logan is… or *who* he's doing. "Something like that. He really respects the station, and he can't wait to play the concert. The band is ready to promote the show all over social media. They're really excited to support this charity. Your wife's charity."

"Yeah…" His voice trails off.

I wish I could say it's because he's realizing he's being an ass, but I know better. "He's preparing a formal statement. Mr. Kingston, I mean. He really regrets his past behavior."

Mr. Winters chuckles. "Going through all twelve of those steps, huh?"

God, what an asshole, mocking Logan's hypothetical rehab stint. "We can't wait to see you at the event."

"Yeah. Me either."

"Is there anything else I can help you with?"

"You won't tell Alessandra about our conversation?"

"No. Our secret."

"Good. Nice to talk to you…" He struggles to reach for my name. "Uh, I'll see you then."

"Until then." I let out a heavy breath as I hang up the call. "That guy gives me the creeps."

"He's the worst." Alessandra leans back and puts her feet up on her desk. "Are you going to prepare that statement?"

"Maybe." Absolutely.

"Logan will be pissed."

"Logan will be trashed."

She laughs. "He doesn't drink that much. And he's smarter than he looks. Don't tell me you fall for him as a party boy?"

What's to fall for? Logan is a party boy. A manwhore. Whatever you want to call it, Logan sleeps around and has a lot of fun doing it.

Even so—"I'll run it by him."

"You okay?" She pushes herself up from her desk. "You look like you're about to hurl."

"I'm okay." I feel like I'm about to hurl, but I'm not sure if it's nerves or something else.

"You want a club soda?"

"Sure."

She goes to her mini-bar and pops open a can. Then she's grabbing a bottle of gin and pouring both into a glass.

She hands the drink to me.

"You know I only drink gin and *tonic*."

"I don't do tonic water."

I shake my head. "Just the soda."

She shrugs *suit yourself*, downs half the drink, and hands over the half empty can of club soda.

I take a greedy sip. The bubbles burst on my tongue, the same as always, but they do nothing to refresh me.

They do nothing to ease the nausea in my throat.

"Jayce put in his two weeks' notice," she says. "There

are half a dozen tours he's managing. If we don't find someone to take over, we'll have to divide them, and I'll end up doing fucking everything."

I stare back into my boss's eyes. Is she really suggesting I take over?

Six tours?

Alessandra doesn't even manage six tours at once.

I clear my throat. "I'm sure you and Liv can handle it."

"Yes, we can. But we're getting old. And tired. And we both play bad cop." She stares back at me. "You're ready, Bella. You're ready to do this on your own."

"Maybe."

"I'll hate to lose you as an assistant, but you'll make a great colleague. I won't bullshit you. It will be more hours. More work. More travel, even. But it will also be more money. More responsibility. More chances for you to use your brain instead of your tits."

It's appealing. "Can I think about it?"

She nods. "I'm going to start looking for Jayce's replacement soon." *So don't think too long.* "You're a great assistant, darling. You're welcome to work for me forever."

"Until you quit to screw your boy toys?"

She laughs. "Yes, until then."

It's a lot to think about. In theory, this is a great next step.

It's a better job.

More money.

More room to grow.

But only if it's what I want.

I swallow my last drop of club soda. It does nothing to clear my head. Or ease my breath. "I'll think about it." I nod to the door and take a step backward.

Ugh. That nausea. Again.

"I'll walk you out," Alessandra says.

Which means she has some pep talk to give me.

She doesn't get off her ass if she can help it.

And I mean that in the most loving way possible.

I nod *uh-huh*. We walk out of the office and through the lobby together.

The lights feel brighter. The colors seem more garish. And everything is so—

Ugh.

I motion to the ladies' room and dart for the door.

It's open, thank God, and it's clean and empty. I dash into the handicap stall and throw myself at the tile floor.

Fuck.

I slide my glasses off with one hand and pull my hair back with the other.

And I hurl until there's nothing left to hurl.

Fuck, I hate being sick.

The door opens with a creek. Alessandra's slow, steady footsteps move into the room.

She taps a knock on the door. "You need an Advil?"

"No. That's okay."

"It's late to be hungover, but I get it. Your boy toy got home last night, and he does like to celebrate."

"It's the flu."

"Whatever you say, sweetheart."

Getting married while drunk in Vegas gets you labeled a party animal forever. No one believes me when I tell them I'm not a big drinker. Ever.

Least of all Alessandra.

Even so, I protest. "I wasn't drinking last night."

"Too busy sucking cock?"

I let out a hearty laugh. There are only two people I know who would respond like that, her and Joel. "You could say that."

She pushes the stall door open and gives me a long once over.

Her face lights up with recognition. "I see."

"What?" What the hell does she see?

"I didn't realize you and Joel were trying. Or was it someone else? Don't worry. They never do the math."

"What?"

"You don't have to pretend, sweetheart. I get it. I won't push you about the job or the drinks."

I blink a few dozen times.

"How far along are you?"

"What? I'm not… I mean, I don't think… We're not trying."

"Oh." The smile falls off her face. "It isn't Joel's?"

"It's not anything."

"Oh."

"But if it was something, of course it would be Joel's… I'd never."

Alessandra shrugs. I don't know what to make of it. She talks big talk about only wanting men for one thing, but she always does everything she can to send me when someone needs to check in on Dangerous Noise.

"I…" It's been in the back of my head all day. And yesterday. And the day before that. And the week before that.

"Give me a sec, sweetheart." Alessandra turns on her heels and marches out of the bathroom.

I lean against the tile wall and suck a deep breath through my nose.

I have been skipping drinks.

And sleeping more.

And craving red meat like it's going out of style.

But I'm religious with my pill.

It's not possible.

Even if my symptoms line up perfectly.

Why do I skip the placebo week? If I knew when my last period was, I'd know this isn't possible.

Alessandra pulls open the door and crosses the room to me. She leans down next to me and hands something over.

A pregnancy test.

"You carry this with you?" I ask.

"In my office." She shoots me a curious look. "Does that really surprise you?"

"I guess not." She does manage a number of teenage pop star clients. She plans for contingencies. Just like I do.

I really could do her job.

But all that traveling, the late nights, the stress, Joel being away all the time…

Joel and I have never talked about kids.

You skip a lot of steps when you marry someone six hours after meeting them.

Does he want kids?

Would he slow down if I asked?

"If this isn't what you want, no one has to know." Alessandra's expression is dead serious. "I know an OB who does terminations at her private practice."

I'm sure she does. Alessandra knows how to take care of anything that could possibly pose a problem to a musician who simply can't slow down.

She's a maternal figure to a lot of young women.

Me included.

"I'm not…" I curl my fingers around the test. It's still in its plastic wrapping. I'm not *something*.

Do I want a child?

And now?

I haven't thought about it. Things are good. Being with Joel, working here, living in Venice Beach—it's a dream.

For the first time in my life, I'm enjoying the ride rather than obsessing over what comes next.

"Whatever you decide, sweetheart. If you want this, then that's fucking fantastic. But if you don't, or if you don't want it now—you wouldn't be the first woman to have an abortion. And not the first married woman either."

"Yeah. I don't... Um... I haven't even taken the test yet."

Alessandra smiles *if that's what you want to tell yourself.*

It is.

I slide the test into my purse.

I'm not taking it here.

Or tonight.

Or any time before Dad leaves.

Even if that kills me.

Chapter Eleven

BELLA

Joel is sitting on the couch in his boxers, watching some police procedural. I don't recognize any of the detectives or lawyers.

He pats his lap. "I want to make you come again."

"I think I'm going to hit the sack."

"It's early."

"I'm tired."

"You need to see a doctor, angel. You look fucking awful."

"Hey." I smooth my blouse. "I put effort into this outfit."

"Your tits look amazing. But you look tired. Sick."

I nod. "I will. Tuesday." I motion to the bedroom. "Come to bed with me." I want his arms around me. I want to collapse and soak up his strength and forget about everything else in the world. "It was a long day. That asshole Winters keeps getting petty over stupid shit. I've had to kiss a lot of ass."

Joel nods, but his grey-green eyes stay heavy with concern.

I motion to the bedroom. "I'm going to brush my teeth."

"I'm going to think about making you come."

My lips curl into a smile. "Good to know."

"Thought you'd appreciate it."

I do. I really do appreciate everything I have with Joel.

We're just… happy.

I've never had that before. I've never been satisfied with my life. I've never felt like I was where I'm supposed to be, doing what I'm supposed to do.

I let my mind wander as I brush my teeth and wash my face.

Kids were part of my old life plan—the one curated by my parents.

But now…

It would change everything. Maybe for the better. Maybe for the worse.

I slip into the bedroom and collapse onto the mattress. I really am tired. And nauseous. And now my head is full of all sorts of ideas of what comes next.

It's not an easy question—what the hell do I want out of life?

I'm still not great at taking care of myself. But if I have a kid?

I don't know if I can do it.

If I even want to do it.

Joel would be a good dad. But would I be a good mom? I can see myself reading to a baby, playing peek-aboo with her, fussing over her adorable tiny shoes.

But I'm not sure it's what I want.

My thoughts dissolve as the bedroom door opens then closes.

Joel's footsteps are quiet.

He climbs into bed and places his body behind mine.

He slides his arm around my waist.

His breath is warm against my neck. His chest is hard against my back.

But the way he's holding me is soft. Caring. Loving.

He runs his fingers through my hair. "You sure you're okay?"

Maybe. "A lot on my mind."

He slides his hand over my shoulder. His fingers trace the scars on my upper arm. "Tell me about it."

"Later. I'm exhausted."

His voice gets low, sweet. "You seem anxious."

"Is that different than normal?"

"No, but…" He presses his lips to my shoulders. "I have to ask this, angel."

"Shoot."

"Are you cutting again?"

"No."

"You promise."

"On my Ravenclaw jersey."

His sigh is thick with relief. "You know you can tell me anything."

"I know." I swallow hard. "I will. I just… I need to sleep right now. I love you."

"I love you too."

But it's still burning a hole in my brain—what the hell do I want?

Chapter Twelve

JOEL

Bella is on the balcony, wrapped in a blanket.

She's bringing a mug of tea to her lips.

It's possible she's enjoying a peaceful morning, watching the waves roll in.

But given all that tension in her shoulders last night…

I brush my teeth.

I pull on jeans and a t-shirt.

I fill the coffee maker with grounds and turn it on.

She's still out there, looking for something.

I need in her head.

I need to know what she's thinking.

But I'm patient.

Okay, that's bullshit.

But I can get there. For her.

I force myself to wait until the carafe is full.

I fix a mug.

I take a sip.

She's still sitting there, staring at the sky.

Okay, fuck patience.

I need to know what's going through her mind.

Before her dad gets here.

That doesn't leave much time.

I cross the room. My footsteps slow as I get closer to the balcony.

Gently, I knock on the balcony's sliding glass door. "Hey."

"Hey." She turns toward me. Her brown eyes bore into mine.

She's asking for something.

But I'm not sure what it is.

I pull the door open and take the chair next to hers.

She brings her drink to her lips and takes a slow sip. Her eyes stay on the crashing waves. "This really is a beautiful view."

"Yeah."

"This is a nice apartment."

I nod.

"A little small though."

"You want to find a bigger place?"

"Maybe. It's kind of a waste, with you on the road so often. It's just me most of the time."

"Most?"

"A lot." She traces the outline of her mug with her fingertip. "I'm not complaining."

She's not.

But she's upset about something.

I try to keep my voice even. I'm usually good at rolling with the punches.

No, I am.

Just not when it's about her.

I stare back into her gorgeous brown eyes. "You're worrying me, angel."

Her brow relaxes. Her lips curl into a half smile. "I'm just thinking."

"About?"

"What I want to do with my life."

"That little question," I tease.

"Yeah." She takes another sip of her tea then sets the mug on the balcony railing. "Jayce quit."

"And Alessandra offered you his job?"

She nods.

That's good news.

And it explains why she's been more in her head than usual.

But she doesn't look happy.

"You don't want to take it?" I ask.

"I don't know." Her voice is soft. "Things are good now."

"Things are fucking great now."

"I don't want them to change."

"They always do."

"I know..."

"You want to be Alessandra's assistant forever?"

"No, but..." Her eyes go back to the ocean. "It's a lot of travel. A lot of late nights. A lot of time at shady clubs."

"It can't be worse than now."

"Yeah."

"You'll have your own assistant to boss around. Alessandra sends you to do most of her bidding."

"True. But then, I won't get to visit every time something goes wrong."

"We'll make it work."

"Maybe." Her voice gets soft.

"Bella, we will. Whatever this is, we can figure it out together."

"Yeah." She stares at the sand. At the railing. At her red fingernails. "It's probably nothing. I don't want you to worry. And with my dad coming soon. I should check the time. See if he needs a ride."

I grab her wrist. "Trust me. He'd rather take a cab."

"I'm not that bad a driver."

"No, but you're that nervous." I stare into her eyes, even though she's doing what she can to avoid my gaze.

She pulls her wrist to her side, stands, wraps her blanket around her waist. "I'm getting dressed."

"No."

"Excuse me?" She shakes her head and moves into the apartment.

She tosses the blanket on the couch and makes a beeline for the bedroom.

I grab her harder than I should.

My hands curl around her wrists.

I hold her body against mine.

"Joel…" Her voice is needy, but not in the *fuck me* way. "I need to get dressed."

"You have time." I turn her around and stare into her eyes.

"I…" She shakes her head. "I do."

"You need to talk to me."

"But…" She blinks back a tear. "I don't know what to do."

"About the job?"

"Yeah, but—"

"That's not it?"

She nods and buries her head in my chest. "I'm not sure I'm ready to talk about this yet. That makes it real. And I'm not ready for it to be real."

I wrap my arms around her. I run my fingers through her hair.

Her breath slows as she pulls me tighter.

"Go back a few steps, angel. Whatever it is, we can figure it out together."

"Maybe."

"I promise." I pull her closer. "We can figure out anything together."

"Maybe. But if I tell you, you'll… you'll make me take the test—"

"The test?"

"I…"

"You're pregnant?"

Her shoulders tense. Her breath catches.

It's like time stops.

A million things run through my head.

Some good.

Some bad.

Her voice is soft. "Maybe. I'm late, and… I've been, well, maybe this isn't a stomach flu."

"You bought a pregnancy test?"

"Alessandra gave it to me. I threw up last night, and she assumed." She lets out a quiet laugh. "She asked if it was yours."

"Of course she did."

"It is. If it's something. It's probably nothing. But if it's something. You know I'd never—"

"I know." I take a deep breath and exhale slowly. Bella pregnant. Fuck, I wouldn't have guessed that. Not in a million years. "Is that why you didn't tell me?"

"No. Maybe… I don't know what I want to do." She pulls away enough to look into my eyes. "If I am… I don't know what I want to do."

"It's your body. It's your choice." I cup her cheek with my palm. "Whatever you want to do, I'll support you."

"I know. But what do *you* want?"

"I want you to talk to me."

"But… do you want kids?"

Words fall off my lips without stopping in my brain. "Yeah. One day."

"Today?"

"If that's how it goes. And if it's what you want."

"What if it's not?"

"Then it's not."

"What if I never want them?"

"Then you never want them."

"And you're… you're okay giving that up to be with me?"

I nod. "I'd give up anything to be with you."

Her expression softens. "That's sweet, but…" *I'm not sure I believe you.*

"I mean it, angel. Nobody else makes me feel like you do." I run my fingers through her hair. "I'd fucking love to have a family with you. But only if it's what you want too."

She nods.

"Whatever you decide, I'll love you."

She presses her forehead against my chest. "Things would have to change. A lot. I couldn't work this job. Not with you on the road."

So she's considering it.

She wants it even.

A lot would have to change.

A fucking scary amount of shit would have to change.

No wonder she's torn up over this.

I run my fingertips over the back of her neck. "I don't have to be on the road."

"But drumming is your life. Music is your life."

"There are other ways to make music."

"You'd give that up for me?"

I nod.

She blinks back another round of tears. "I... I don't know what to say."

"You don't even know if you're pregnant. Take the test before you freak out."

She laughs. "Way too late for that."

I pull her closer. "I love you so fucking much. You know that?"

She nods. "I love you too."

"It's okay you're scared."

"Yeah?"

"That you're thinking you might not want this."

"I don't know what I'm thinking." Her voice is soft. "It could be good. I can see us having a family. You playing on the floor with our kid. Me reading to her. The three of us doing all that stupid touristy stuff at Disneyland together. But it would change everything else, and I'm not sure... I'm not sure I'm ready for everything else to change."

I can see it too.

But she's right.

I can't fathom the rest of my life with a kid. I don't want to be like my dad, only showing up when it suits my schedule.

But my job means I'm not around a lot of the time.

Something has to give.

She presses her fingers into my back, over my t-shirt. "I don't know if I'd forgive myself if you quit music for me."

"I won't quit. I'll slow down. And it won't be for you. It will be for all of us. But we're getting ahead of ourselves." I stare back into her eyes. "We can take this one step at a time."

"Okay."

I want to say something to soothe her, but I've got nothing. I don't exactly have a lot of intel on accidental pregnancies. Daphne isn't a good resource on that front. My sister is gay. She doesn't ever think about pregnancy.

Mom would have something to say, but Bella wouldn't want her to know.

There's Drew and Kara. He's changed a lot since I had the displeasure of working with him, but I still don't enjoy spending time with the brooding guitarist.

Even if he is a family man.

I can get over it for Bella.

If it's what she wants.

Given the fear in her expression, I'm pretty sure she doesn't want anyone else knowing. Not yet.

There's a sound coming from the bedroom. Her cell. Some jazz song she set as her dad's ringtone.

"He must have landed." She pulls back. "I should get dressed."

That's fair. "Take the test tonight."

"Sunday, after he leaves."

"Tonight."

"Okay." She stares back into my eyes. "Tonight."

Tonight.

I'm going to find out if my wife is pregnant tonight.

Chapter Thirteen

BELLA

I drown my thoughts in tea.

And cooking.

I *do* want to fix a proper feast. My mom always did, every year, no matter how many hours she'd worked the week before.

Joel helps me prepare the turkey, slide it into the oven, and set a timer.

He gives me room to obsess over mashed sweet potatoes, green bean casserole, and baked rolls.

I focus until there's a knock on the door.

It's steady. Strong. Dad's knock.

"I'll get it." Joel pushes himself off the couch. He runs a hand through his wavy hair and shakes his head.

He's upset about this too.

Because it's not what he wants?

Because it is?

Because I'm locking him out?

I don't know. It could be anything. Everything. It could be that Dad is outside.

Joel pulls the door open. "Vincent." He struggles with

Dad's name, like he's reminding himself to call him *Vincent* and not *Mr. Chase*. "It's great to see you. How was your flight?"

Dad shakes Joel's hand. "The same as it usually is." His eyes move around the apartment. Slowly, they settle on me. "Bella, sweetheart, you don't have to cook all that food for me."

"I know." I set down my mixing bowl and spoon and wipe my hands on my apron. "I wanted to. Like Mom always did."

His smile is as sad as anything. It's been ten years since Mom died. Dad never moved on. Not even to flings.

Well, as far as I know.

I don't really want the details.

"No suitcase?" I force myself to move away from the kitchen. I have to greet my father. And I have to find something to say besides *I might be pregnant and I still don't know how I feel about that.*

"I stopped by the hotel." He looks around the room, assessing it as a potential place to stay.

"You could have stayed here." I take another step toward him. Okay, our place is too small to be comfortable for a guest used to the finer things. Even if the finer things are Manhattan sized.

"It's fine, sweetie. I have a pool." He smiles.

I smile too. Dad at the pool—it's absurd. I move close enough to hug him hello.

My exhale is heavy. My shoulders relax. Dad can be difficult, bossy, and demanding, but he always knows what to do. And he loves me.

I'm glad he's here.

Even if the timing is far from ideal.

"You need any help in the kitchen?" he asks.

"No. I think I've got it." My eyes meet Joel's.

He raises a brow *you okay?*

I nod a yes. "How about coffee? I'll make another pot."

"French roast?" Dad asks.

"Yeah. It's on a high shelf. I'll get it." Joel moves into the kitchen and gets to work fixing coffee. "You want some tea, Bella?"

"Yeah. Please." There's no excitement in my voice. I sound tired. Strained.

But I am happy Dad and Joel are here. Even if they don't always get along.

I try to shake it off as I motion to the couch. "We could boot up *Casablanca*." It was Mom's favorite movie.

"Later, sweetheart. I want to catch up with you and Joel." He takes a seat on the couch.

Dad looks impossibly out of place in our apartment. He's pure New York City in his black slacks and grey sweater.

And we're pure Venice Beach with our bright colors and our ocean view.

Joel leans against the fridge. His eyes meet mine.

They bore into mine.

Talk to me.

I want to. But not right now. This is too overwhelming. "I should check on the yams."

Dad nods.

Joel too.

I move into the kitchen, pick up my bowl, go back to mixing mindlessly.

Joel is right there, three feet away, standing in front of the coffee maker, watching the carafe fill with drops of dark liquid.

Drip.

Drip.

Drip.

It really takes forever.

I grab a baking tray and coat it with canola oil. Then I'm spreading a fine layer of mashed sweet potatoes.

I motion to the top cupboard. "Could you get the marshmallows?"

"Yeah." Joel pulls them from the shelf and sets them on the counter.

His fingers brush against mine as I reach for the bag.

His eyes bore into mine.

I want to promise him a million things, mostly that I'll figure this out, but words don't find their way to my tongue.

"Are you okay?" he whispers.

"Not yet." But I will be. Eventually. In theory.

Joel grabs two mugs and fills them both with coffee. He brings one to my dad and grabs the spot on the couch next to him.

He starts talking about some jazz musician dad loves.

Dad's eyes light up.

My shoulders relax. They can go like this for hours.

Dad and Joel talk all morning.

Through three cups of coffee.

All the way to me burning the green bean casserole and setting off the smoke alarm.

Dad goes to pull the balcony door open.

Joel grabs a DVD case and fans the smoke detector.

I turn off the burner and move away from the kitchen. I'm not a natural chef. I like cooking, and I'm usually pretty good at it, but today I'm distracted.

My cheeks flame red with embarrassment.

Mercifully, the smoke detector's beep ceases. Joel stops fanning.

Dad moves in from the balcony.

My husband's expression stays fraught. "How about I get takeout?"

I press my lips together. "Okay. If that's what you want to do too, Dad."

"Sure." Dad nods. "Whatever you'd recommend."

"You have to have real Mexican food. Street tacos. The truck over by Abbot-Kinney will be open today." Joel moves into the kitchen and wraps his arms around me. "We'll call this a snack. We'll still have that turkey for dinner."

"And mashed sweet potatoes. And rolls. And… frozen broccoli." I hug Joel back. God, he smells good. I want him holding me forever.

Dad nods. He says his own goodbye-for-now to Joel then he moves into the kitchen to pour another cup of coffee. "Another Earl Grey?"

"Okay." I leave my apron on its hook, wash my hands, and take a seat on the couch.

This is a good chance for me and Dad to talk alone.

That's why Joel left. I think. We're not doing a good job communicating with each other.

We're usually better at that.

But then we don't usually have something this big up in the air.

Dad joins me on the couch. He hands me my Earl Grey. His eyes fix on mine. "Are you all right, sweetheart?"

"Yeah." I take a long sip of my tea. "Tired. I've been working a lot."

He nods. "I remember when I was your age. It was always long hours. You have to prove yourself."

I nod. I do have to prove myself, but not the way dad means. Not to anyone but me.

"It's been almost two years now."

"It has."

"Have you thought about your next step?"

It's matter of fact, not accusatory, but it still makes my back tense. Dad expects me to go places in the world.

I set my tea on the coffee table and fold my hands in my lap. "I've learned a lot. It's getting to be time to move on."

His expression brightens. "Are you going to stay at your company?"

"I think so. We're a division of a huge label, so there's a lot of room to grow. But we're doing our own thing. It's mostly Alessandra, Liv, and Jayce. Only Jayce just quit."

"You're up for a promotion?"

"It's a possibility." I bite my tongue. It's more than that. Alessandra offered me the job. But I can't tell Dad I'm thinking of not taking it.

He won't understand.

Or maybe he will. Dad is more than a lawyer with a drive to succeed. He loves jazz, he runs in the park, he reads as much as I do.

He would have done anything for Mom.

For me and Anne.

I take a deep breath and I explain my current role—a mix of kissing ass, negotiation, conflict management, and calming down musicians who are freaking out. It takes empathy and quick thinking as much as it takes a will of steel.

Then I explain Alessandra's job, how it would be different. I'd need more will of steel and less empathy. I'd be the one making the tough calls, doing the math, explaining why musicians need to cave or hold out for a higher percentage of ticket sales.

I can do the extra logistics no problem. I can step in during a blizzard, when all the flights are canceled, and find a bus with snow chains. I can schedule around hospital stays, family events, movie shoots. I can dry out the backstage of a gin soaked venue in no time flat.

It's being a hard-ass that scares me.

Having all that responsibility on my shoulders.

My job already demands a lot of me.

I can't do it *and* raise a child.

Not with Joel on the road.

I clear my throat and finish explaining how I'll have to alternate good cop and bad cop roles to my dad.

"It's not that different than negotiating a settlement." He smiles. "I'm proud of you."

"You are?" I don't mean to sound so surprised, but I can't help it.

"Yes. At first, I thought you'd made a mistake marrying Joel. I didn't want to see you become another one of those women who gave up their career for a man."

I nod.

"You've done well. It takes courage to carve out a path for yourself."

"Thanks, Daddy. That means a lot."

He nods. "Do you have a number in mind?"

I can't help but laugh. He shifts back to business mode so quickly. Affection and honesty doesn't come easily to Chases. "It's not all about money."

"Sweetheart—"

"I'm sure it will be plenty more."

He shakes his head in horror.

"I'll ask for twenty percent more than whatever they offer."

"What if you have to name a number?"

"Then I'm not a good negotiator."

He chuckles. "True, but it's not always avoidable."

Fair. I've learned a lot about negotiating in the last two years, but most of it was under Alessandra. She's shrewd and cutthroat, and I mean that in the best possible way. "I'll ask her to double my salary."

"Ambitious."

"That's me." Maybe.

Or maybe I want to slow down, focus on family.

I let my eyelids flutter together and I try to imagine a baby in this apartment.

We'd have to get rid of Joel's practice room. Turn it into a nursery. Paint the walls pink.

I can see a crib in there.

I can see a little girl crawling around on the carpet.

And Joel sitting with her, helping her build a Lego castle.

"You okay, sweetheart?" Dad asks.

I nod. "Thinking." I can see a little girl running around the beach, begging for the waves.

But do I see myself there with her?

I'm not sure.

"Care to share?" Dad's voice is soft. It must be obvious that I'm completely out of it.

"How is Anne doing?"

Dad chuckles. He doesn't buy that I'm thinking about Anne, but he doesn't press me on it. "The same as always."

"And Brian?"

Dad let's out a sigh of distaste. "I still don't know why she married him. All he has going for him is money."

"She loves him."

His dark eyes flare with incredulity.

I have to admit, I wonder it too. My sister and her

husband have almost nothing in common except for their love of status. "Do you talk about Joel like that with her?"

"No."

"Really?"

"I don't bring him up with your sister. I don't need to hear her thoughts about how Dangerous Noise is better than Miles Davis."

I laugh. "Does she really?"

"She knows it irritates me."

"Joel doesn't care if you like the band. But he does… he does want you to like him."

"He's good to you. That's what matters." His gaze goes to the beach view outside the window. "But I hate him for keeping my baby three-thousand miles away."

"I like it here too."

"You only think that because it's been so long since you've had a good bagel."

I smile. "It has been a while." I follow his gaze to the crystal blue ocean. "It's beautiful here, isn't it?"

"It's beautiful in Manhattan."

"That too. But… I like being here. I like being with Joel."

"You *like* your husband?"

"I love him. I wish you loved him too, but—"

"I do." Dad's voice gets serious. "Is there something between you two?"

"No… sorta…"

"Make me a promise, sweetheart."

"Okay." I can do that, in theory.

"Promise you won't quit your job to tour with him."

"I won't. He wouldn't ask."

Dad's expression is pure incredulity.

"Everyone wants their spouse around. You and Mom

were like that too. You always told each other you worked too late."

"We never meant it."

"Joel wouldn't either. He… he's the one who tells me I should work. Well. Sort of. He wants me to take the promotion too."

Dad perks. "Smart man."

"He is."

"You wouldn't know it from looking at him."

"Daddy, you aren't supposed to say that. You're just supposed to think it."

"Anne tells me he's considered very attractive."

I laugh. "You don't think he's good-looking?"

Dad looks to me and raises a brow. It's unusually playful for him. In fact, he's been happy all day.

Well, by his standards.

There must be something going on in his life. Maybe he is seeing someone.

I make a mental note to ask my sister as I take my last sip of tea. "More coffee?"

He nods. "Thanks, sweetheart."

I take Dad's cup and get us both refills then I rejoin him on the couch.

This is like our old Sundays. Before Mom died. Before he closed off and I took on all the weight of keeping up appearances.

My parents always had high expectations—Dad still does. They were strict.

But they were loving too.

They were good parents. Dad still is.

I settle into my seat. "When did you and Mom decide to have kids."

His eyes flare with understanding. "Oh."

"Oh?" Why is everyone reacting like that?

"It would be difficult, having kids with him on the road. If you want to keep working."

"It would."

"I understand why you're thinking about turning down that promotion."

"I... Uh... it's a possibility."

"You can hire help. You loved your nanny, didn't you?"

"I did."

"Your mother would have hated to see you quit your job and stay home, but if that's what you want, if that's what will make you happy... there's nothing wrong with devoting your life to your children. You and Anne were the two best decisions of my life."

"Really?"

"Of course."

I lean a little closer. "When did you know you were ready?"

"You're never ready. Not really."

"But we were... we were planned."

Dad chuckles. "Yes, we were trying for a while before we had Anne."

"When did you decide to start trying?"

His eyes get dreamy as he shifts into memories. It's a rare look for Dad, reserved for thoughts of Mom. "It was your mom's third year at work. She finally felt like she had a handle on working as a lawyer. She finally felt like she had time."

"Did she?"

He laughs. "You know how she was. She gave up sleep before she gave up something she wanted." Regret creeps into his voice. "Nothing would have slowed her down."

Dad and I have gotten a lot closer since I married Joel. It's strange, us talking more now that I live three thousand miles away. But it's easier being honest with him now.

Even so, I rarely see him this vulnerable.

"I miss her too," I say.

He nods. "She would be proud of you. Horrified by your husband, but she'd come around."

"You think?"

"Eventually."

"Did she always want kids?"

"Always."

"And you?"

"I didn't think about it. That was what everyone did. It was inevitable."

That sounds like me and law school.

"At first, I wasn't sure. But once your mother told me she was pregnant with your sister, I knew. I knew I wanted to be a father. I knew it was what was right for both of us."

I follow Dad's gaze out to the beach.

The sky is a bright blue. The sun is a big yellow ball. The waves are crashing into the pristine sand.

I can see us here.

I can see us with a kid.

And I even like the look of it.

Chapter Fourteen

JOEL

Vincent is surprisingly welcoming. It can't just be that I'm now an expert on jazz. Bella must have said *something* to him while I was out picking up tacos, but it couldn't have been her potential pregnancy.

He'd be decking me right now.

Or maybe not. This is how it goes for most people. You get married. Then you have kids. Only most people date, get engaged, and plan a wedding before they get married.

Most people don't marry a stranger in Vegas.

Vincent looks out of place dining on street tacos in his fancy outfit, but he pulls it off. The guy has class. And style.

He's not so bad, really. Even if he still looks at me like he's not sure I'm good enough for Bella.

I get that he wants to protect her.

We both want the best for her.

After lunch, we talk with another round of tea/coffee. We watch one of Bella's mom's favorite movies, then we help Bella fix dinner.

I study every single expression that flickers in my wife's eyes, but I don't call her on any of them.

It's a nice afternoon. A nice dinner. A nice night after we walk Vincent back to his hotel then walk back home on the beach.

The only sound around us is the waves crashing into the beach.

The stars are bright. The air is brisk.

I pull Bella closer to keep her warm.

And I stare back into her eyes.

I'm still not sure what she's thinking.

And I'm still desperate to find out.

But I can tell she needs the break.

When we get back home, I put aside my demand that she take the test right away.

I boot up the first *Harry Potter* movie, I pitch a marathon, I collapse onto the couch next to her, and I hold her until she falls asleep in my arms.

I WAKE BEFORE BELLA.

I fix my coffee. Her tea.

I make eggs and keep them warming in the pan.

I stare out the window, letting my thoughts float along the breeze.

My entire life, the only thing I've really wanted to do is entertain.

I love making people laugh.

I love making music.

Okay, I also want to support my friends and destroy my enemies.

But it's always been about bringing people joy.

Then I met Bella, and I felt this want I'd never felt before.

She's my other half. The thing that fills that emptiness in my gut.

All that cheesy shit.

I could be happy with her, like this, forever.

I've never thought about having a family. Not really.

But I can see it.

I can see her reading our kid *Harry Potter* books and dressing him in some tiny Ravenclaw jersey.

I can see her sitting on the couch with him, watching some kid's show, shooting me *oh my God, how can anyone over the age of three find this entertaining* looks every few minutes.

I can see myself teaching him drums.

And I can see her dragging him away from the kit.

But it's hard to see much outside of this apartment. Outside of the two of us.

Well, the three of us.

I know a million people have juggled work and kids, people who make a lot less money than I do, people who have a much harder life.

Plenty of musicians do it.

But it's hard to envision that future.

Even if everybody would be happy for me.

Even if we're already slowing down.

The bedroom door creeks open. Bella steps into the main room in her tank top and pajama bottoms. She's holding her glasses with one hand, rubbing her eyes with the other.

"Tell me you're only wearing boxers." She slides her glasses on. "You are."

"I was supposed to tell you."

She presses her lips into a smile. "Last night was… it was good. Thanks, Joel."

"Come here."

She does.

I wrap my arms around her. She's still tense. Hell, she's shaking.

She rests her head against my chest as she leans into my touch. Her fingers curl into my upper back.

Her breath warms my skin. "I should probably abandon any plans I had of convincing you I'm doing great."

"Probably." I run my fingers through her hair. Our life together is perfect. It's scary, thinking about changing it. But it's good too.

If I can fucking figure out how to be the kind of parent I want to be.

I try not to get ahead of myself. Bella hasn't taken the test yet. She's been upfront about her uncertainty.

I'm not going to talk her out of an abortion if that's what she wants.

"You're thinking something," she mumbles into my chest.

"*I'm* thinking something."

She nods.

"And you're—"

"Only thinking of you naked."

"Go on…"

"Well, right now you're wearing those awful boxers. This would be a lot more fun if they were gone, and we were on the couch—"

"And you were bouncing in my lap with your tits in my mouth?"

"Exactly." She looks up at me, her brown eyes wide with need. "But I don't think you could fit both at once."

"Is that a challenge?"

"Yes, please." She nods to the couch. "Right now."

"This first." I stare back into her eyes. "It's best to take the test first thing in the morning."

"You were looking it up?"

"You feel asleep early."

"I've been tired... I guess that does suggest..."

"Could be a million things, angel. You work hard as fuck."

She smiles. "You called me angel."

"And?"

"You drop the *angel* when you're upset."

I have to laugh. "Am I that obvious?"

"More."

I pull her body into mine. Fuck, she's warm and she's soft and she's alive. Bella has always been fucking amazing, but these last two years, I've gotten to watch her blossom.

It's a privilege, seeing her this vibrant and happy.

I won't let anything get in the way of that.

"I'm only upset 'cause this hurts you, angel." I breath her in. Fuck, Bella really is everything.

"You don't have feelings one way or another?"

"I do, but it pales in comparison to how much I want to be with you."

"That's cheesy."

"You make me cheesy."

"Yeah?"

"Yeah. This is a great life. We could have a great life raising kids too. It would be different, harder maybe."

"Definitely harder."

"Is that what you want?"

"I'm not sure." Her voice is soft. "I can see it, when I squint, but it would mean giving up so many other things. It would mean a lot of changes."

I nod.

"My dad... I asked him about him and Mom. He said

he didn't know for sure, until she told him she was pregnant."

"You think you'll know when you see the test?"

"No, but I'm praying I will." She stares back into my eyes. "How is it you're always so confident and sure of yourself?"

"You know I'm not."

"But this. You're steady."

Am I? It feels more like I'm shaking. This is big, and it mostly falls on her shoulders, and I can't do shit about that. "I meant what I said yesterday. We can get through anything together."

She nods.

"You ready?"

"No, but I'm not sure I'm ever going to be." She presses her lips together. "Let me brush my teeth first."

I nod and watch her move into the bathroom. She leaves the door half open as she brushes her teeth and washes her face.

There's something different in her posture today. Something softer.

The anxiety isn't swallowing her whole.

I have to let her decide this for herself.

Unfortunately, shutting the fuck up is not one of my strong suits.

I push off the counter and fix another cup of coffee. It buys me enough time with my mouth shut for her to pull the test from her purse and press it between her palms.

"I guess the easiest thing to do is to pee in a cup," she says.

I pull open the cupboard. "Which one is calling you?"

"You want to use the cup after this?"

"I'll wash it first."

"Still."

I laugh. "Okay, we can destroy the cup after this."

She points to the San Francisco Starbucks memorable cup.

"Angel, I'm not sure how to take that."

"It's a coincidence."

"You want to destroy my hometown."

"You're not from the city. You're from the Silicon Valley burbs with all the other rich kids."

"And you, Mrs. Manhattan Penthouse?"

"True. But we have great bagels. You have… strip malls."

"You love strip malls."

"Maybe."

"Bullshit, maybe."

Her smile melts the tension in my chest. "Maybe." She reaches past me for the mug then she leans in to press her lips to mine.

Fuck, she tastes good.

I kiss her back as hard as I can. With everything I have to give her.

She pulls back with a heavy sigh. "Okay. I guess I should leave the mug in the bathroom."

"You can bring it out here."

She scrunches her nose in distaste. "No. Bathroom. I'll pee. Then we'll… we'll wait together." She takes a deep breath. Slowly, she crosses to the bathroom.

She closes the door.

God, this is the longest twenty seconds of my life. I can feel the tension in her shoulders over here.

The toilet flushes. The water runs. A few moments later, she calls me over. "I'm just about ready." She pulls the door open.

I move into the bathroom with her.

She unwraps the test. "Three minutes. Exactly three minutes."

I grab my cell off the kitchen counter and rejoin her. I set the timer to three minutes and show it to her.

She dips the stick for the required five seconds then places it on the counter, face down. "Here goes nothing."

Chapter Fifteen

BELLA

I wrap my arms around Joel's waist.

I rest my head on his chest.

My inhale is shallow.

My exhale is heavy.

I can't look at the time.

I can't look at the test.

I can't do anything but breathe in my husband.

He runs his fingers up and down my spine. The soft fabric of my tank top brushes against my skin.

His touch is thick with affection.

I love Joel more than anything, and I trust him with my life, but I can't help wondering—

Will he feel the same if I'm pregnant?

If I'm not?

If I want to have this kid?

If I don't?

I hold him tighter. I suck in another shallow breath. I'm better at hearing my inner voice now, but it's still a struggle with everyone else.

Joel is still the one person who really gets me.

I don't have to be someone else with him.

I don't have to pretend I'm okay.

I can just be me.

If I lost that…

"You're shaking," he whispers.

"I know."

"You're scared."

"That you'll think differently of me."

"I couldn't, angel. You're fucking everything to me."

I nod into his chest. I slide my hands under his t-shirt and press my palms against his skin. God, he's warm.

And he smells good.

I want him. I want his tongue in my mouth, his body against mine, his touch erasing every thought in my head.

Even if that's how we got into this situation.

If it even is a situation.

I hold Joel tightly and I breathe him in.

Just in case he's wrong.

Just in case this changes everything.

The timer beeps.

I jump backwards and press my ass against the counter. My fingers curl around the test. It's still face-down. I can't see what it says.

I can't bring myself to turn it over.

I look to Joel. "You do it."

He nods and takes the test from my hands. His eyes stay fixed on mine. His gaze stays steady. Reassuring.

He stares back at me. *Are you ready?*

No. I nod anyway.

Slowly, he turns the test over.

His expression stays steady. Reassuring.

I press my lips together. "Well, what does it say? Am I pregnant?"

Chapter Sixteen

JOEL

I blink again.

Again.

The results are still there.

And Bella's eyes are still wide with anxiety.

I want to find some way to convince her things between us won't change.

I can't. This could change everything.

But there's nothing Bella could do to convince me to stop loving her.

There's no way to convince her. We have to get through it and come out the other side together.

I stare back into her eyes. "You're pregnant."

She blinks that same dumbfounded blink. "I… I'm pregnant."

"Yeah." I turn the test to her. It's a clear result—that dark indicator line and the faint one next to it.

She stares at the test. "I'm pregnant." Her voice steadies. "I'm really pregnant."

A million possibilities hit me. Us having a family here,

taking a kid on the road, moving back to New York or the Bay to be closer to family.

Or things staying the same.

I run my fingers through her hair. "You don't have to decide yet."

"No... I think..." She looks up at me, her brown eyes full of wonder. Her lip corners curl up. Her voice brightens. "I'm pregnant."

"You want to—"

"Yeah. Do you?"

"Yeah."

"You're not just saying that?"

"When have I ever?"

"You have."

I shake my head.

She stares back at me. "You really want to have a baby?"

"Not *a* baby. Our baby."

"Our baby." She smiles. "This is fucking crazy."

"Kinda."

"You really want to do this?"

"I do."

She jumps into my arms. "Me too."

Chapter Seventeen

BELLA

Joel pulls strings to get me an appointment with a reputable Ob/Gyn who's willing to come in on a holiday weekend.

It's a normal appointment. Up until the ultrasound.

My heart pounds against my chest. My stomach rises up in my throat. I don't know why, but this is scarier than the pregnancy test.

The doctor smiles. She has a nice smile and a warm disposition, but I can barely notice any of her features. I'm too focused on keeping breakfast down.

She turns the machine to face me. There's something on the screen. It's mostly a grey blur. Or maybe it's a blob.

That little blob is my baby.

Our baby.

I squeeze Joel's hand.

That's our baby. Even if it looks more like an alien than anything right now.

"Your due date should be in May," she says.

I look up at my husband. "That's so soon."

"You scared?" he asks.

I nod. "But excited." I can make out the shape of him. Or her. It's just like Dad said. I have this warmth in my chest.

I'm terrified I'll get something wrong.

I'm terrified everything will change.

But I'm sure this is what I want. I know it the same way I know I love Joel. The same way I know I need to dive into a good book when my nerves are shot.

He looks down at me, his smile ear to ear, his green eyes bright.

And I know.

This is what he wants too.

THE REST OF THE MORNING IS A BLUR.

We meet Dad for lunch.

The second we get there, he knows.

I don't know how—maybe the expression on my face or the way Joel is fussing over me—but that doesn't matter.

Dad knows.

And he's happy for us.

I cry over my bowl of pasta. They're happy tears, and hormone tears, and they're everything.

Because this is the other thing I want, my daddy proud of the direction my life is going.

Accepting my husband, my family.

Joel goes off to do something. I'm not sure what. I'm too lost in all the stories Dad is telling about Mom's pregnancies, about me and Anne as babies.

He's giving me all this advice, and all I can do is nod and take another bite of shrimp scampi and try to soak it in.

The meal goes fast, and the drive back to our apartment goes fast.

The city blurs around us. The sky is blue, the sun is bright, the air is warm and inviting.

This is a beautiful place, southern California. Venice Beach. Our apartment.

It's small for three, but we'll make it work. Or we'll find another place.

I squeeze Joel's hand as we take the elevator up to the third floor. "A lot is going to change."

He nods. "You thinking about moving?"

"How'd you know?"

"You stared at every *For Sale* sign we passed on the way here." He pulls me into the hallway. "We can get a bigger place."

"Maybe. I like this one." I slide my arm around his waist as he unlocks our front door. "It's where we fell in love."

His smile spreads over his cheeks. "True."

"And it's… it just feels like us."

He pushes the door open for me and nods *after you*.

I step inside. Joel would deny it, but he really is a gentleman.

He's a good husband.

He'll be a good dad.

There's something thrilling about thinking of the man I love as a father. About us, raising a family together.

After he locks the door, he wraps his arms around me. Something hits my back. A paper bag.

He smiles. "That's to celebrate." He leans down and presses his lips to mine.

I kiss him hard. The tension of the last few days melts as I slide my tongue into his mouth.

My hands go to his hair. They hold his head against mine.

He pulls back with a needy sigh. "This is fucking amazing, angel."

"You sure?"

"A hundred percent. Are you?"

"Yeah. But it's scary, how everything will change."

He nods.

"What do you think you'll do with the band?"

"I don't know." There's no fear or anxiety in his eyes. Or his voice. "We'll work it out. Everyone will be happy for us."

"I know, but—"

"You're worried?"

"Our jobs aren't exactly kid friendly."

"What do you want to do?"

"I don't know. I like working. But then I don't want to be like my mom. She was an amazing woman, but she worked herself to death. And that—"

"Fucked you up."

I laugh. "You're always poetic, baby."

"Say any more and I'll have to start dirty talking you."

"Any more."

"Angel, that was awful."

"But worth it." I stare back into my husband's gorgeous green eyes. "I think Alessandra will support me. I never know with her."

"She adores you."

"Maybe."

"Neither one of us *has* to work. Not for a while."

"Yeah, with your rich parents."

He laughs. "No, with my rock star money." His expression brightens. "You fucking love reminding me my parents are rich."

"You're cute indignant."

"Am not."

I laugh. "Are too."

"Am not."

"We're going to go in circles. And you have a surprise."

He whisks me to the kitchen, sets the paper bag on the counter, and pulls out a small pastry box.

There are two cupcakes inside. One pink. One blue.

"Since we won't know for a while." He splits the pink cupcake in half and brings it to my lips.

I take a messy bite and wipe the frosting off my lips.

He smiles. "You missed some."

"Did I?" I tease.

"Mhmm." He leans in to plant a soft kiss on the corner of my lip. "Here." Then the other corner. "Here." Then he's dragging his lips down my neck. "Not sure, but I think there's some there."

"Do you?"

He nods and he smooshes the cupcake against my chest. "There is now."

Frosting and cake crumbs stick to my skin.

I'm already sticky.

And eager for him to lick this off.

I laugh as I tug at his hair. "Joel."

"Louder, angel."

"I like this blouse."

"More than you like coming on my face?"

"Well, no..."

God, his grey-green eyes are bright.

With joy.

With desire.

With everything.

We're really doing this together.

And I really need to have him now.

He presses his hips against mine, pinning me to the counter.

He's hard, and fuck how I want that.

Joel snaps my buttons as he tugs my top open. They land on the tile with a clank.

He takes his time sliding my blouse off my shoulders. Letting it fall to the floor.

"Fuck, you really have amazing tits, angel." He plants a kiss on my collarbone. Then lower. Lower. "You're gonna be such a fucking MILF."

"Yeah?"

"Fuck yeah." He pulls my bra cup aside and palms my breast. "I need you so fucking badly right now."

"I need you too."

I need to know he still wants to fuck me as much as he did yesterday.

I need to feel our bodies as one so I can *feel* that he's mine.

Joel laps up every sticky drop of frosting on my chest.

He licks me soft.

Hard.

Slow.

Fast.

He drags his lips over my breast, stopping to take my nipple into his mouth.

Fuck, that soft, wet tongue—

It takes every bit of concentration I have to stay upright. I press my ass against the counter. I dig my hands into his hair and hold him against me.

He reaches around my back to unhook my bra.

Then he's dragging his lips over my other breast, sucking on my other nipple, flicking his tongue against the tender bud until I'm panting with desire.

Every inch of me is awake and alive.

And every inch of me wants Joel.

He slides one hand up my inner thigh and strokes me over my jeans. "This will be easier on the couch."

I nod.

He scoops me into his arms, carries me to the couch, lays me flat on my back.

Joel stares into my eyes as he unbuttons and unzips my jeans. As he rolls them to my ankles and off my feet.

Fuck, all the desire in his green eyes.

I fall back onto the couch.

I spread my legs wider.

I dig my hand into his hair. "Make me come, baby."

He groans against my inner thigh. His teeth scrape against my tender flesh. Hard enough to feel fucking amazing but not hard enough to hurt.

He pulls me to the edge of the couch.

He drags his lips up my thigh.

Almost.

Closer.

There.

His tongue flicks against my clit. He takes his time tasting every inch of me.

Right now, there's nothing between.

No secrets.

No stress.

No apprehension.

Nothing but him bringing me pleasure.

He licks me soft and slow. Hard and fast. Up and down. Left to right.

I buck against his lips. "Fuck, Joel."

"Louder, angel." He nips at my inner thigh. He pulls me closer. Licks me harder.

Harder.

Pleasure wells up inside me. The pleasure he's giving me.

It's sexy as all hell, his face between my legs. But it's more than that.

It's fucking romantic, the way he's groaning against me.

The way he can't get enough of my pleasure.

I tug at his hair, holding his mouth against me. "Fuck, Joel." I scream it louder. Louder.

Loud enough our neighbor bangs on the door.

"I'm almost there, baby." I buck against his hips. My last conscious thought drifts away as Dirty Bella takes over. "Make me come."

The command gets his nails digging into my thighs.

He licks me harder.

Faster.

Almost.

There.

With the next flick of his tongue, I come. I shake. I shudder. I scream his name again and again.

Then I tug at his hair. "Fuck me. Now."

He plants himself on the couch next to me and pulls my body onto his.

I stare into his eyes as I straddle him.

As his hands curl into my hips.

As his tip strains against me.

Fuck, he's staring back at me. His eyes are full of desire, but there's more than that. There's love, need, affection.

Trust.

I tug at his hair as I bring my body onto his.

Fuck, that feels good.

Like it's where we both belong.

He presses his palm against my back, bringing my chest

to his mouth. And he toys with my nipple like his life depends on it.

I have to let my eyelids press together.

I have to tug at his hair.

I have to scream his name.

He still plays me like I'm his favorite instrument.

I'm about to scream for mercy when he moves to my other nipple. Fuck, that feels so good.

I rock my hips, rubbing my clit against his pubic bone, feeling every hard inch of him.

He groans against my chest. He sucks harder. Like it's all he can do to contain his pleasure.

We stay locked like that, grinding and groaning together, taking each other to the edge.

Then I'm there, screaming his name again and again as an orgasm spreads out through my fingers and toes.

And he's there, groaning against my chest and he comes.

Once he's spilled every drop, I collapse on top of him.

And he wraps his arms around me. "I love you so fucking much, angel."

"I love you too."

And I really do believe we can do anything together.

Chapter Eighteen

JOEL

I wake to the sound of laughter. Bella's. And the throaty chuckle of a heavy drinker/smoker.

That Spanish accent that screams *I'd rather be in Madrid than here.*

That's Alessandra.

My wife's boss is in our living room. But then my wife doesn't work a corporate job and her boss isn't the shy type.

I step into the living room in my boxers and shoot the ladies a hello nod.

"Good morning." Bella's lips curl into a smile. Her brown eyes are bright. Her entire expression is bright. The happiness in her eyes shifts to desire as she gives me a long once-over.

"You two can fuck in front of me if you insist," Alessandra says. "Nothing I haven't seen before."

"You've seen Joel?" Bella shoots me a *really* look.

"See one rock star fuck a woman, seen them all." Alessandra exaggerates her eye roll like she can't imagine anything more boring than seeing me pull Bella's dress to her waist, pin her to the counter, and drive deep inside her.

Fuck, I need to think about something else or I might do it.

Bella and I don't exactly mind being watched.

A bored audience won't do shit to spur us on, but it won't stop us either.

Ahem. I nod to the bathroom. "I'll be a minute."

Bella nods.

"And I'll get dressed." I wink at my wife. "To spare you the torture."

Her laugh is full. "You're too good to me."

Alessandra shoots me a look that can only mean *you're lucky to have her.*

Talk about obvious shit.

I slip into the bathroom and go through my usual morning routine. I can't quite hear the details of Alessandra and Bella's conversation, but I can tell it's a pleasant one. They're laughing every few words. There are no harsh tones or whispers or raised voices.

It doesn't take a genius to put two and two together. Alessandra caught Bella hurling into a toilet at work and offered her a pregnancy test. Now, she's here.

She's checking up on the results.

On how we're handling it.

On what Bella is doing with her job.

I wash my hands and step back into the living room. Bella shoots me that same *fuck me now* look. Alessandra shoots me that same *put on clothes, what are you trying to prove?* look.

Fuck, I love the desire in Bella's eyes.

Torturing her is very fucking tempting, but I'm a man of my word. I step into the bedroom and dress in jeans and a t-shirt.

Bella still shoots me a *fuck me now* look when I step into the main room.

Alessandra laughs. "I can see how you two got into this predicament."

"Did you tell her?" I ask.

"No." Bella clears her throat. "But I think you just did."

"It's okay, sweetheart, no one thinks you married Joel for his brains. Not with the way you two go at it like rabbits." Alessandra winks at me then turns to Bella. "It's all over your face."

"Is it?" Bella presses her palm to her cheek like she's trying to feel the inch of skin that's giving her away.

"You have the glow. And the smile. And I know it's not over that fucking asshole Winters bumping the second headliner for Dangerous Noise," Alessandra says.

"But they're due to be in Ohio the day before," Bella says.

I have no fucking idea if that's right. I really don't keep track of that shit. When you tour, everything blurs together. Another path of highway, another crowded club, another average hotel.

Alessandra shrugs *oops*, but she's smiling too. She tries to pretend like she does this shit to annoy me. Okay, she probably does. But it's more that she's looking out for Bella. She makes a point of arranging things so we get all these chances to be together.

"You know, Jayce mostly focused on international tours. Liv has the international contacts. You have the ones in the U.S." Alessandra's eyes spark with that mix of delight and mischief. "You could take over the Dangerous Noise tour schedule."

"I could." Bella looks at me and blinks twice. "I could be in charge of making sure you're home when I need you."

"I'll always be home when you need me," I say.

"Yes, you're adorable and in love. It's great. But that won't pay the kid's private school tuition." Alessandra straightens her black blazer. "It's completely fucked, you being in charge of Joel's tour, but that's normal in this industry."

"Technically, that makes him my boss," Bella says.

"He already is your boss, honey. But everyone knows Malcolm is the one in charge." Alessandra lets out another hearty laugh. Okay, maybe she does do a lot of this to fuck with me.

"I… I don't know what to say." Bella plays with the hem of her dress. She looks to me and raises a brow. *Okay?*

I nod. Way okay.

She turns back to Alessandra. "I've been thinking a lot. I love my job. I don't want to give it up. But I don't want to be like my mother either—"

"Sweetie, I don't need your life story," Alessandra teases. "Tell me where and when you need to cut back and we'll make it happen."

"I want to be part-time. Well, as part-time as I can be with this job. Starting in April. And I want Joel to be around for the first three or four months. Then he can go back to touring. I checked the schedule. We don't have to cancel any shows if we find someone who can fill in for him in July," Bella says.

"You'll give up that outdoor summer tour?" Alessandra looks to me and raises a brow.

"Let someone else melt in the hundred-degree sun and stage lights? How the fuck will I deal with that?" I keep my voice light, even though nobody is buying it. I love performing. Even when it's a hundred degrees and humid. Even when it's raining. Even during a full on summer storm when the tech guy is screaming *get the fuck off the stage; it's basically a lightning rod.*

It will be tough, giving up a chunk of that. Working less. Losing that freedom.

But there isn't a doubt in my head that it's what I want.

And, fuck, the way Bella is smiling. She knows I'm full of shit, but she knows that this is what I want.

And it's what she wants.

Alessandra shoots me a knowing look. "Have you told Malcolm?"

"Why do I have to fucking tell Mal everything?" I ask.

"He's the one in charge, sweetheart. You know it. I know it. Bella knows it," she says.

"Actually. I'm the one in charge now." Bella smiles. "I… I couldn't sleep last night. I worked up a schedule for the next two years. For Dangerous Noise. It assumes your next album will be as big a hit as this one, but I think even if it flops, I can get you into big venues."

"I like you confident, angel," I say. "But that casual mention of our album flopping was brutal."

"You like me brutal." She smiles.

"Yeah, I do." I smile back.

Alessandra rolls her eyes, even though she's smiling. "I have my own contingency, sweetheart."

"Oh?" Bella smooths her dress and straightens her posture. Her expression hardens. She's shifting into badass negotiator mode.

"You have to play up the pregnancy. And the single mom thing—"

"But I'm not. I have Joel."

"You think Alessandra cares about lying?" I ask.

"Not a lie. A careful phrasing of the facts. Your husband is always on the road. It's hard. You need this break, so you can have more time for your son to spend with his dad. Trust me, men can't say no to a single mother," Alessandra says.

"Is that really true?" Bella asks.

Alessandra shrugs. "Maybe not men, but the assholes we deal with, yes. They have all this guilt about the women they fucked and threw away. You have any idea what happens to groupies who get knocked up? It's not pretty."

"I guess that makes sense." Bella nods, studying Alessandra's expression to see if she's teasing or not.

It's impossible to tell with her. There's truth to her story. A lot of the men who run clubs are great guys who just fucking love music. But a lot of them are assholes who cut corners and use the proximity to fame to fuck the women musicians discard. Those guys get quiet really fast when you mention things like *child support.*

"And your tits. Fuck, they're going to be massive. You have to promise to wear low cut dresses every day until… no, just every day you have to see someone in person. I want those on display. I want them screaming *if you get me this deal, maybe you can get a better look.*" Alessandra looks to me and winks.

Bella laughs. "I can do guilt trips and low cut blouses." She looks to me. "As long as you won't get too jealous, baby."

"I might have to show up to threaten to break some legs," I say.

She smiles.

I smile back at her.

Alessandra clears her throat. "Really, you two are disgusting. You'd think you were the first two people to ever have a baby."

Bella laughs. She leans in to hug her boss. "Thank you."

"Thank you, sweetheart. I'm happy for you." Her voice is earnest, a rarity for Alessandra.

"We haven't talked salary yet," Bella says.

Alessandra laughs. She looks to me. "You married a smart woman."

"No shit, Sherlock," I say.

"Less compliments, more numbers," Bella says.

Alessandra pulls a notebook from her purse and scribbles a number on it. She flashes the paper to Bella.

Bella's eyes bulge out of her head. "Even when I'm part-time?" She clears her throat. "I mean, is that starting now or in May."

"Now, but I'll keep you there when you go part-time," Alessandra says.

"Oh. Excellent. What about maternity leave?" Bella asks.

Alessandra laughs. "That's out of my hands. Corporate policy. But it's generous. Twelve weeks at fifty percent your salary."

"That is generous." Bella smooths her dress. She offers her hand to Alessandra.

They shake.

My wife pushes up from her chair and throws her arms around me. "And it's amazing."

"You're amazing, angel."

She nods against my chest. "No. We're amazing."

"Save it for after you tell the band. Trust me, the congratulations sex is always better when you have everything out of the way," Alessandra teases. She shakes her head at our embrace. "I'll let myself out."

"I'll see you Monday," Bella calls.

"With your tits on display," Alessandra reminds.

Bella laughs.

I pull her closer. "She's got some great ideas."

"Yeah." Bella looks up at me. "I know we have to tell everyone, and I'm sure you're as scared as I am—"

I nod.

"But I think she's wrong about the celebration sex. I think we should have it now and after we get everything else out of the way."

"I ever tell you you're a fucking genius?"

"Yes, but not today."

Chapter Nineteen

JOEL

It takes some coaxing, but I manage to convince everyone to meet for dinner. Kit insists on doing it at his place. Piper insists on ordering Vietnamese take-out. No amount of arguing that there are no Vietnamese places near their house can convince them to make alternate plans.

Especially not once Ethan volunteers to pick something up on the way.

Bella and I head over early. It's close enough, and parking in this neighborhood is annoying enough, that it's easier to walk than drive.

Bella squeezes my palm as we walk along the beach. The dark sky is already dotted with stars. The air is already chilly.

I pull her closer and soak in all the warmth of her body.

All the joy in her smile.

There are nerves in her eyes, but that joy is so fucking obvious.

Fuck, there are nerves in my stomach too. Asking for

help isn't my strong suit. I *know* everyone will be happy for me, but I'm not exactly jazzed to ask my friends to make sacrifices for us.

We turn and walk the last few blocks on the streets. Kit and Piper's new place is one of those modern houses on the beach. It's all sleek lines and big glass windows that scream *I want you to watch me fuck my fiancée.*

Bella knocks on the excessively blue front door.

A moment later, Piper pulls the door open. She's in jeans and a sweater, but she manages to make the outfit look adorably innocent. I don't know how she does it. She's twenty-one now, but she still looks like the fifteen-year-old I met the first day I showed up at Mal and Ethan's place to practice.

She throws her arms around Bella. "It's been forever."

It's been a week, max, but neither one of us remind her of that.

She hugs me hello. "How are you, Joel?"

"Good. You welcome your fiancé home properly?" I tease.

"You know I don't do details." She turns to Bella. "Can I borrow your wife?"

"You gonna gossip about me?" I ask.

"Maybe." Her smile lights up her blue eyes. "The universe doesn't revolve around you."

"I'm pretty sure it does." I plant a kiss on Bella's lips. "Go. Gossip."

Bella nods. She's still wearing her nerves in her shoulders, but her expression is pure joy.

She adores Piper and Piper adores her.

I'm not sure if it's me and Kit being close or if it's Piper being Piper, but I'm eternally grateful that she's done so much to make Bella feel at home.

Piper drags Bella off to the kitchen and starts fixing her

a cup of tea. They lean up against the counter, laughing over something. It's probably at my expense, but I don't care.

Seeing Bella happy is fucking everything.

Kit pushes himself off the couch. They really have a hell of a living room. It's as sleek and modern and *we have plenty of spots where we can fuck* as the exterior of the house.

He crosses the room and leans against the wall next to me. "You've got a look."

"Do I?"

He nods. "And not the usual *why's my wife wearing clothes* one."

I shrug like I'm not incredibly aware of how much this is showing in my expression.

"You insisted on this dinner."

"I did."

"Three days after you got home."

"Your point?"

"Usually, it takes a week for you to drag yourself out of bed."

"Maybe." Absolutely.

"You've got news."

"Shut the fuck up. I've got nothing."

He chuckles. "Big news."

I don't even bother shrugging. I can't pull it off.

He stares into my eyes like he's staring into my soul. Fuck, he really is too good at this shit.

"Big news. But you have to fucking wait." My gaze shifts to Bella. She and Piper are still talking about something, still laughing, still smiling. She's happy right now, even if she's anxious. And that pushes my nerves aside enough that I can fucking think.

Kit chuckles. "You're so full of shit."

"Am I?"

"Yeah." He pushes a mass of curly hair from his eyes. "You want to tell me."

"Do I?"

"Yeah. You're fucking dying to tell me. It's killing you, not telling me."

"You flatter yourself."

"Even so."

"I…" I stare back into his eyes. They really are earnest. Piper always accuses him of having sad, pretty eyes. I can't say I disagree. There's something about that expression of his that begs you to confess everything you're holding onto.

"You…"

"Bella is pregnant."

His eyes light up. "And you're gonna—"

"Yeah."

"Fuck, that's great." Kit pulls me into a hug and pats me on the back. "Congrats. Really."

"Thanks."

He pulls back. "Joel Young, family man."

I nod.

"Father to be."

Again, I nod.

"It looks good on you."

"Does it?"

"Yeah. That glow of responsibility. You scared?"

"It never occurred to me before, how many fucking horrible things could happen to a kid."

He chuckles. "You sound like a parent already."

"I know. It's fucking scary how fast my mindset is shifting. It's already the three of us in my head."

"You know if it's a boy or a girl?"

"Not yet. It's early. Too early to tell people probably, but you know Bella."

"She have a plan written up?"

"You want to know something really fucking scary?"

"Scarier than you stinking of responsibility?"

"A hundred times."

"Hit me."

"She's taking over for Alessandra."

Kit chuckles. "That is scary." His smile lights up his dark eyes. "But fucking great. I'm happy for both of you."

"Thanks."

"You're gonna be a good dad, Joel. I owe you a fucking lot. I couldn't have done that shit without you."

"I know."

"That poor kid isn't gonna know shit about humility."

I laugh. That's probably true. Our kid isn't exactly going to have a normal life, but it will be a good life. Our fucking life.

"I've got one question."

"Yeah?"

"What if he hates *Harry Potter*?"

I can't help but laugh. "That will break Bella's heart."

"Let's hope it doesn't come to that."

I nod.

"You're fucking scared to tell Mal, huh?"

"And Ethan. But yeah."

"They'll be happy for you."

"Even so."

Kit leans back against the wall. "First Ethan wants to slow down. Now you. We're dropping like flies."

I study his expression. There's no sign he wishes things were different, but then Kit likes to keep shit to himself. "And you and Piper?"

His gaze goes to her. His smile spreads over his cheeks as he watches her and Bella laugh over something. "This is already her family, our family."

"True." With her older brothers in the band, Piper always has reasons to be around.

"But I wouldn't mind more time at home." He looks back to me and runs a hand through his curly hair. "I guess we're getting old."

"Happens to everyone."

"You'll look good grey."

"Fuck off."

"You will."

"I know." I stare back at his dark features. "You won't."

Kit chuckles. "Probably true."

"And you better hope you don't go bald. She loves your hair."

"She mocks every one of my greys."

"You are a million years older than her."

"I guess eight rounds up to a million."

"Is it obvious I'm fucking terrified?"

"Yeah. But it's cute."

"I don't need you saying that."

He shrugs. "Too bad. It's the truth."

MAL AND LACEY ARRIVE NEXT. THEY TOTALLY IGNORE ME and Kit to go straight to Piper.

It's fucking weird seeing Mal all happy and in love, but it suits him. Lacey is smart, funny, and earnest in that ingénue way he likes. She's even into being tied up and spanked.

She's pretty much perfect for him.

Twenty minutes of shooting the shit with Kit later, Violet and Ethan arrive. She's in one of her *look at my tits* corset dresses, her strawberry blond hair pinned back, her makeup dark.

He's all casual and effortless and *yeah, we did fuck right before we came here, what's it to you?*

They've been married a year now. I'm happy for them, even if I miss how much it used to annoy Ethan when I called Bella my wife.

After they make the rounds with hellos, they bring the food to the table and start unpacking.

Everyone helps get plates, drinks, silverware. I take the seat next to Bella's at the long dining table. Of course, the only thing I can think is *I wonder when they last fucked on this table?*

Then Bella squeezes my hand and all I can think is *fuck, this is happening.*

Piper starts tearing into her container of pho broth.

I rub the space between Bella's pointer finger and thumb with my thumb.

I stare into my wife's eyes. *Now?*

She nods. *Now.*

I push myself to my feet. "We have an announcement to make." I try to keep my voice bouncy, but it's clunky. Awkward.

Bella rises with me. She keeps her hand glued to mine. "It's good news."

I stare back into her gorgeous eyes. "You want to?"

She nods. "I do." She looks at our friends. Her grip on my hand tightens, but she holds strong. "I'm pregnant."

I study expressions like my life depends on it. Kit shoots me a *you've got this* look. Piper's eyes light up. Violet claps her hands together, her usual reserved expression falling into something more giddy.

"Congrats. That's fucking amazing." Ethan nods to me then he leans in to whisper something to Violet.

She blushes then turns back to us. "It really is."

Mal nods at me. It's hard to describe his expression. It's

just so fucking Mal, all paternal, and *I know best and I know that you can do this*.

"That's amazing, Bella. I'm so excited for you. And you too, Joel." Lacey smiles at us, all earnest and sweet the way she always is.

She and Bella share a knowing look. A girl thing, I guess. They're pretty close, what with both of them working in the music industry. They're always trading gossip or *oh my God, he's the worst* complaints about difficult musicians.

"It's early," Bella says. "The due date is in May. And, we... we don't know the sex yet. We don't know a lot. But, um, I planned out your next two years. The tour schedules, with plenty of room for time off and difficulties recording." She winks at Mal.

He shakes his head *I'd never*, but he smiles back at her. "You didn't have to do that."

"I did, actually. I'm taking over for Alessandra." Bella smiles. "I dropped four dates and found about ten where Joel needs someone to fill in, but otherwise it shouldn't affect too much."

"You don't have to do *that*," Mal says. "We can slow down."

"No. You can't. You're the hot thing now. You think this lasts forever?" Bella shifts right back into work mode then she catches herself and shifts out of it. "I mean... I appreciate that. You all accepted me as soon as I got back from Vegas with Joel. You've always made me feel like family. It means a lot to me."

Everyone nods.

Another round of congratulations blurs into teasing about how Bella will be every bit as ruthless as Alessandra.

She's right.

We have a great fucking family here.

We have the support we need.

And we have each other.

I pull Bella into a tight hug.

She whispers in my ear. "We're really doing this."

"We're really gonna have a baby."

And we're really gonna give him all the love in the fucking world.

Not just the two of us. Not just our parents and our siblings.

We have the entire Dangerous Noise family.

Lacey and Mal

Chapter Twenty

MAL

"Mal," Lacey squeals as she takes my hand. "You know I can't walk in these heels."

She can't, and I fucking love that about her.

I love every one of her quirks.

I have it bad. I've had it bad for a year and a half now.

She looks divine in that tight cocktail dress. And knowing she's dressing up for me, because I told her we're going someplace special…

I slide my arm around her waist. "Don't worry, baby. I've got you." I help her traverse the rocky path that leads to the beach.

She holds me tightly, trying to walk on her tiptoes so her heels don't sink into the sand. "You're cruel. You know that?"

"Go on…"

She giggles. "I don't mean—"

"Don't you?" I arch a brow.

"Hmm. Well… is it really cruel if I beg you for it?"

Her eyes are on fire with confidence.

She doesn't doubt it anymore. She knows how badly I want her.

"You tell me." I let my voice drop to something low and demanding. I shouldn't shift the topic to sex. Not with what I'm about to do.

But I can't help myself.

She slides her arms around my waist. Her voice is bright. Happy. "You should have warned me this was a cross-country expedition."

"You don't like the view?" I nod to the ocean.

The dark blue water laps at the pristine sand.

It bleeds into the sky. It reflects the moon. The shining stars. We're far enough into Malibu that we can actually see stars.

Lacey's brown eyes light up. Her lips curl into a smile. "It's beautiful."

She still has every drop of that lust for life.

It's intoxicating.

Contagious.

My smile spreads over my cheeks. I could watch her take in the view all night.

Part of me wants to.

A lot of me.

I'm actually fucking scared.

It's not something I'm used to.

She digs her fingers into my sides, pressing my stiff button-up shirt into my skin. "It's just… it's cold."

"It's cold?"

She nods. "It's fucking freezing. And I'm wearing nothing. And a thong, by the way—"

"Go on."

She bites her lip. "Uh-uh. You have to wait for that."

"Do I?" I slide my hand over the curve of her ass.

She lets out a soft sigh. "You do." Her voice gets breathy. Needy. "It's sexy as hell."

I drag my fingertips over the side of her hip, feeling for the strap.

Her eyelids flutter together.

Her expression softens into *please, Mal, make me come, now.*

I want to.

But she's right.

I need to wait.

Maybe not until after dinner.

But until after this.

"Just..." She clears her throat, struggling to get ahold of herself. "It's not actually cold anymore. Somehow."

"Somehow."

She stares up into my eyes. "But I am hungry." She bites her lip. "God, I sound so whiny, don't I?"

"I like making you whine, baby."

Her cheeks flush. "I missed you, you know that?"

"I missed you too." I've been on the road most of the last month. But—"We have two weeks together."

She nods and nestles into my chest. Her gaze shifts to the ocean. "Really, Mal. This is beautiful. Romantic. Sweet." She lets out a soft sigh. "It's perfect."

It is.

And this is the perfect moment.

Only my mouth is sticky.

And my chest is light.

Fuck, it's a good thing she's holding me. I'm about to float into the sky.

This is what I want.

I have no doubts about that.

The last year and half has been a fucking dream.

And it's all because of her.

I turn toward her. I run my fingers over her cheek. I stare into her gorgeous brown eyes.

I take in all the joy in her expression.

Slowly, I lower myself to one knee.

Her eyes go wide. "Mal..."

"Let me get this out, baby."

"Okay." She stares back at me, her eyes wide, her smile wider. "Are you... I mean. Okay. Go on."

"The last year has been the best year of my life. You wake up this part of me, this happy, playful, enthusiastic part of me. I had no idea that guy existed until I met you. I had no idea I could feel this satisfied." I reach into my pocket, pull out the ring box, and pop it open. "Lacey Waltz, will you marry me?"

Chapter Twenty-One

LACEY

I blink twice.

Mal is still on one knee.

He's still looking up at me like I have his heart in my hands.

I stare back into Mal's piercing blue eyes.

And I nod. "Of course."

He takes the ring—the massive, beautiful, classy solitaire diamond—and slides it onto my left ring finger.

His fingertips brush the back of my hand. The top of my wrist.

He looks up at me with all the love and affection in the world. "I love you so much, baby."

"I love you too."

He pushes himself to his feet.

He pulls my body into his.

Then he leans in to kiss me.

All his love and affection pours into me.

All my love and affection pours into him.

We're engaged now.

He's my fiancé now.

It's just…

It's fucking amazing.

I dig my hands into his hair. I kiss him harder. Deeper.

I buck my hips against his.

My hunger no longer matters.

The cool temperature no longer matters.

This is the only thing that matters.

My ring catches the moonlight. It's glowing. It's luminous. "It's perfect. How did you know?"

"I know you."

He does. He knows me better than anyone does.

I barely manage to rise to my tiptoes. These shoes—my only nice pair of shoes—are not made for walks on the beach.

Or make out sessions on the beach.

Or fucks on the beach.

But I'm not letting that stop me.

Mal leans down to press his lips to mine.

His kiss is sweet as much as it's sexual.

He loves me.

And he wants me.

And it's really possible to have both things.

It's really possible for the man I love to want me.

It's still hard to believe sometimes.

His lips curl into a smile as our kiss breaks. "We better head to dinner."

I shake my head.

"But you're hungry," he teases.

"Mal…"

"And cold." He rubs my shoulders. "I wouldn't want to torture you."

I motion to the car, parked way up the street. "Now."

"You want to head to dinner now?"

"You need to fuck me. Now."

His smile spreads over his cheeks. "This first."

He drags his fingertips to the hem of my dress. Slowly, he pulls the garment up my thighs, over my ass, all the way to my waist.

He holds it there with one hand. With the other, he grips my thong.

He takes his sweet, sweet time pushing it off my hips.

The thing falls to my ankles.

Mal bends to pick it up. He slides it into his pocket as he rises.

He has that demanding look in his eyes. The one that screams *you're mine and I'll do whatever I want with you.*

Yes. Please. Now.

If I can figure out how to walk.

I'm not sure I can even move right now.

Mal slides his arm around me and pulls my body into his. His fingers skim my side. My hip. The outside of my thigh.

He presses his palm against my ass.

Fuck, I need his hands on my bare skin.

I need all of him.

Now.

I struggle to take a step forward. My sex aches as my thigh press together. My heels sink into the sand.

Somehow, I manage a second step. A third.

Mal looks down at me with a smile. "Need a little help?"

I nod.

He slides his hand under my ass and scoops me into his arms.

And carries me all the way to the car.

My balance is shaky.

But I am standing.

We're standing.

We're not kissing. Touching. Fucking.

That's unacceptable.

I slide my hand into his front pocket and grab the key fob. There.

Mal pulls the door open, pushes the seat all the way back, and climbs in. He shoots me a panty melting gaze as he pats his lap. "Come here, baby."

Yes please.

It's difficult climbing into the car—it's really not big enough for this—but I manage.

My knee smacks into the gearshift as I straddle him.

My head bumps into the roof.

Then he pulls the passenger door closed and my other leg is pressed up against it.

This is a tight fit.

A tiny space.

But I don't care.

I stare down at my fiancé.

And I kiss him hard.

His tongue slides into my mouth.

His hands slide into my hair.

Mal reads me like I'm his favorite book. He pushes my dress to my waist. Slides his hands to my hips.

One guides my movements.

The other plants on my pelvis.

He rubs my clit with his thumb.

And he kisses me harder.

Deeper.

He tastes good. And he's mine. Forever. We're going to make that official.

I get him for two weeks before he's on the road again.

It's not enough time.

It's never enough time.

But then—

My sex clenches. I'm close.

I let go of every thought in my head that isn't *need. Mal. Now.*

His fingers dig into the flesh of my ass. His groans vibrate down my throat. His cock nudges against my sex.

God, I want that.

Want him.

I want everything with Mal.

Even marriage.

I pull back from our kiss enough to stare into his piercing blue eyes.

With the next brush of his thumb, I go over the edge. Pleasure spreads through my pelvis.

Fuck, that feels good.

I tug at his nice shirt.

He brings both hands to my hips and lifts me. "Help me with this zipper, baby."

Hell yes. I reach down to undo his belt. His button. His zipper.

He lifts his hips to push his pants to his knees.

Then the boxers.

That's Mal, hard and ready for me.

He keeps one hand glued to my hip. He brings the other to my sex and teases me with one finger.

Then two.

He teases me again and again.

He teases me until I'm dizzy.

"Please," I breathe. I take in all the desire in his beautiful blue eyes. "Please fuck me."

"Beg me," he teases me again.

Again.

"Please."

Again.

"Mal..."

"Yeah, baby?"

"I… You…"

In one swift motion, he slides both fingers inside me. It's intense.

But it's not enough.

I need his cock.

He pushes his fingers deeper.

Deeper.

He stares back at me, daring me to ask for more.

Daring me to beg.

"Please fuck me. Now." I shift my hips to push his fingers deeper.

God, his fingers feel good.

His thumb brushes against my clit.

"I… now." I tug at his hair. "Please."

"You want to come on my cock, baby?"

My *yes* doesn't even vaguely resemble a word.

"Come here." With his hands on my hips, he brings my body onto his.

His tip strains against me.

He teases.

Again.

Again.

Again.

"Mal." My voice is a whine, but I don't care. It's what he does to me. He makes me needy and desperate in the best possible way.

My entire body is buzzing with anticipation.

The only thing in the universe that matters is how much I need his cock inside me.

I'm a sex maniac now.

He does that to me.

He does so many amazing things to me.

Even if they're torture as much as they're bliss.

He teases.

And teases.

And teases.

I let my eyelids flutter together.

I let anticipation flood my senses. I can taste how much I need him. Smell it. Hear it.

"Mal…"

"Yeah, baby?"

"Please."

"Please?"

"Fuck me. Please."

He nods.

He stares back at me as he slides inside me.

Fuck.

Now I'm whole.

He feels so good. Warm. Hard. Mine.

It's intense in the best possible way.

The car is small. I have to hold him close to keep from bumping into the roof. I have to keep my thighs pressed to his, my chest pressed to his, my lips—

I have to kiss him.

He claims my mouth with his tongue as he claims my sex with his cock.

We move together, hips shifting, tongues dancing, fingernails digging into skin.

We stay locked together until I'm there.

I pull back to groan his name.

My sex pulses with an orgasm. Pleasure spreads through my limbs, all the way to my fingers and toes.

I come so hard I see white.

Then Mal is there, digging his nails into my skin, pulsing inside me.

He groans my name.

He holds me close.

He spills every drop he has to give.

When he's done, I collapse on top of him. I press my lips to his.

I kiss him like I can't get enough of his lips.

Because I can't.

I can never get enough of him.

Chapter Twenty-Two

LACEY

Dinner is an amazing, decadent mix of sushi and ocean views. I watch the stars shine over the ocean on our drive home.

And I stare at my ring.

A lot.

As we cuddle up on the couch and watch *The Fortune Cookie*, as I brush my teeth, even as I climb into bed, I stare at my ring.

It still feels like a dream, being with Mal, being an actual director, living in this big beautiful house.

Mal climbs into bed shortly after I do. He slides his arm around my waist and pulls my body into his.

His lips brush my neck. "You're adorable all contemplative."

"Am I?"

He murmurs a yes into my skin. "I'm gonna have to make you come."

"That's not a very good threat."

His laugh is hearty. Full. "What is it you're thinking?"

"What happened to sex?"

"Tell me first."

"Sexual blackmail?"

"What else?"

A million things are running through my head. It's hard to explain it. I want to marry Mal, but after seeing what planning a wedding in two months did to Violet…

I'm not exactly psyched to organize a giant party.

Especially not one so much about family.

But then…

I want to do this.

And soon. Before it gets big and overwhelming.

"Talk to me, baby." Mal's voice is soft. Caring. He has so much love to give. And I get most of it.

"You're here for two weeks."

"Yeah."

"And I am too. I don't have any shoots booked until the second week of January."

He nods.

"Violet… she didn't take planning that big, dramatic wedding well."

"You want to go to Vegas, say the word. I'll book a flight right now. Hell, give me twenty minutes and I'll drive."

I press my lips together. There's something romantic about eloping, but it doesn't feel quite right. "Not Vegas."

"Hawaii?" He leans in to brush his lips against my neck. "I can take care of everything."

I'm sure he can. Mal gets shit done. And a wedding on the beach in paradise—what's not to like? "Maybe."

"We don't have to start planning right now."

"I know, but what if we… what if we did it now?"

"At this very minute?"

"Yes, let's rush to the courthouse in our pajamas. While it's closed."

"Sure." He makes a show of reaching for his cell on the bedside table. "You want to take your car or mine?"

"Haha." I do my best mock laugh. "Then we'll wait in front like we're lining up for concert admission."

"What band?"

"You want me to say Dangerous Noise?"

He shrugs.

"Why would I need to line up when my boyfriend—"

He rubs my ring with his thumb. "Fiancé."

"I have a shitty fiancé if he won't let me in to the venue early."

Mal chuckles. "We can go to the courthouse first thing in the morning."

I shake my head. "I want something special."

"In the next two weeks?"

"Unless you can't pull it together."

He chuckles. "You baiting me?"

I nod.

"Not gonna work. The woman I love just agreed to marry me. I'm over the fucking moon."

"Me too." Well, except for the one thing nagging at my gut.

"I can work with two weeks."

"Yeah?"

"But I need help."

"*You* need help. Are you sure? It doesn't sound like you."

He runs his fingers through my hair. "It's something I've learned. Asking for help."

"Hmm…"

"What's up, baby. You're quiet."

"This is a normal level of conversation."

"Not for you."

"Asshole!"

"Even so."

I lean into his touch. "I'm just thinking…"

"About…"

I turn around so we're face-to-face.

His blue eyes fix on me. They fill with concern. "Something's wrong."

I guess it is.

I guess I'm not as okay with the Waltz family state of affairs as I want to be.

"Lacey…" He runs his fingers through my hair. "Don't worry. We'll figure out this wedding stuff together."

I nod.

"The details don't matter so long as I make you my wife."

"None of them?"

He drags his fingertips over my cheek. "So long as I get to stare into your eyes as I say *I do*, I'm happy."

My lips curl into a smile. "What if I want you to dress like Elvis?"

"The King? Hell yeah. He had style."

"If I want you to wear a T-rex onesie?"

"Only if I can keep it on *after*."

"Oh my God, Mal. No!"

"Come on, baby. We both know how much you love *Jurassic Park*."

"Not like that!"

"You don't have to pretend with me." His smile spreads out to his cheeks. His eyes brighten.

I shake my head.

He nods.

"What if I want you naked?"

He pulls up the covers to show off his current threads —a thin t-shirt and a pair of boxers. "Say the word."

"At the ceremony."

"That too."

"That's a bluff."

"Then call it."

I should. Really, I should. But there's something about his playful smile. I actually believe he'll do it.

"How would you do it? If it could be anything?" I ask.

He stares back into my eyes as he drags his fingertips along my jaw. "Anything?"

"Anything."

"Even you naked?"

"Even that."

His voice gets contemplative. "You and me and a dozen close friends on the beach."

"Your dad?"

"No."

"He showed up at Ethan's wedding."

"Still…" He turns so he's facing the ceiling. "I don't want to be disappointed on my wedding day."

That's fair. Though it's not what I expect from him. "Who else would come?"

"Ethan, Vi, Pipes, Kit, Joel, Bella… nobody else matters." He turns back to me. "We'd do it in the morning, have an afternoon reception, then I'd spend the night making you come."

"A morning wedding on the beach?"

He laughs. "Yeah, before noon."

"I get up before noon."

"Do you?"

"I got up at four a.m. to shoot that commercial."

"And you're still complaining about it." He smiles as he runs his fingers through my hair. "It's cute."

"It's not cute."

"It's adorable."

"Before noon? Really?"

He chuckles.

"You have any idea how much time a bride has to spend in hair and makeup? A noon wedding will mean I'm getting up at four a.m."

His smile spreads over his cheeks. "Not that you'd complain about that."

"Yeah. Never. I never whine. Especially not when my fiancé is torturing me with sexual blackmail."

"We can do sunset. We can party with our friends all fucking night. But I'm going to make you come at least five times before midnight, even if we're at the reception."

That isn't a bluff.

I'm sure of it.

He slides one hand to my lower back and pulls my body into his. "What about you?"

"Huh?"

He chuckles. "Thinking about me bending you over a table at the reception and peeling your dress to your waist?"

I nod.

"Tying you to the cake table?"

"No, that's a new thought."

"Licking cake off your tits?"

"That sounds unnecessarily messy."

His next laugh is louder, lower. "I'd rather tie you to the bed in our hotel room."

"Here or in Hawaii?"

"It doesn't matter, so long as the ocean is our backdrop."

"You're romantic."

"That's news?"

"Sorta." I sling my leg over his hip and nestle closer. "That sounds perfect."

"Every bit of it?"

"Yeah." But my voice is lacking certainty. I let my eyelids press together and I imagine myself standing under some beautiful flower-decked altar with Mal. He's in a grey suit. I'm in a breezy chiffon dress. The beach is behind us. The sun is high in the sky. "Let's do it."

"In the next two weeks?"

"Everyone is here. Why not?" I want Ethan, Violet, Kit, Piper, Joel, and Bella there.

But I also want Carrie there.

And Wren, my go-to producer.

And my dad.

I want him there.

I want him to walk me down the aisle.

But he'll tell Mom and then... I haven't talked to her in two years now.

I like it that way. Even if I can't shake the guilt in my gut every time Mother's Day, Christmas, and her birthday roll around.

I gave her a million chances.

She wasted them all.

I shouldn't feel guilty about cutting Mom out of my life.

So what if I'm getting married?

That doesn't mean—

"What are you thinking, baby?" he asks.

"I think I want to invite my dad." I swallow hard. "And my mom."

His voice is apprehensive. "Your mom?"

"Yeah. I... I think I want her there."

"You sure?"

"No." I force myself to stare into his eyes. They're still full of concern. It's a bad idea. We both know it. But I can't talk myself out of it. "I think I should call them tomorrow."

"Lacey…"

"I should at least talk to her. See if she's different."

That apprehension spreads into every one of his features. It's not like Mal. He's usually stoic.

"It's a big deal, getting married."

He nods.

"If I don't invite her to this, that's it. She'll never forgive me."

"Do you want her in your life?"

"Maybe, but… this is the first step to us officially being a family. I want to know if that's going to include my parents."

He bites his lip. "It's fair, but—"

"I'll sleep on it."

He nods, but his expression stays wary.

I can't sleep with him upset next to me.

Or with these thoughts running through my head.

I need the two of us distracted.

This is a cheap move.

But I don't care.

I slide my hand under his t-shirt and press it against his chest. "I believe I held up my end of the bargain."

He arches a brow.

"The sexual bribery. It won't work in the future if you don't deliver now."

His smile gets wry. "It won't?"

I nod.

"I should test you on that."

"And possibly lose some of your power?"

"I have plenty."

"I'm not sure about that."

He drags his fingertips over my shoulders. "You're baiting me."

I nod. "Is it working?"

"Take your pants off if you want to find out."

I WAKE TO MAL MAKING BREAKFAST IN THE KITCHEN. HE'S still in his boxers and t-shirt. The thin cotton is straining to cover his broad shoulders.

Damn, that's a nice view of his ass.

The man is sculpted perfection.

And the tattoos covering his arms—

I never get used to how hot he is.

He turns to me with an *I know you're checking me out* smile.

I can't help but smile back. He's here, in our kitchen, making breakfast. It's normal. Domestic.

I go through my morning routine then make my way to the dining table. There's a steaming cup of green tea waiting for me. And scrambled eggs, with spinach and avocado, of course.

Mal slides into the seat across from mine. He motions to our plates. "Say it."

"Say what?"

"Bullshit what?"

"You mean something about how no normal person chooses to eat spinach?"

He smiles. "About that."

I wrap my hands around my mug and take a long sip of my tea. "Oh, that." Mmmm, this is perfect Jasmine Pearl. It's floral and delicate and sweet. "Why's that matter? We both know you're not normal."

"You wound me, baby."

"You like it."

He tries to play coy, but his smile betrays him.

I soak in the feeling of being in the same place at the same time as him.

Why give up even a second of this to deal with my parents?

They're not nearly as compelling as Mal's piercing blue eyes.

Or his sly half-smile.

Or his chest piece tattoo, the one he got for me.

They're not as compelling as anything about Mal.

I play with my fork. I've been telling myself I'm happy with Mom out of my life. But at the end of the day, I'm still the fourteen-year-old who wants to tell Mommy about her boyfriend.

I look back to Mal. "I think I need to do it. I think I need to call my parents."

His expression screws with concern. "You really want to open yourself up to all that pain?"

No…

Maybe.

I nod. "I have to be sure."

"I don't want to see you get hurt."

"Me either, but—"

"You need closure?"

I nod.

He nods. "And if opening this can of worms only makes you feel worse?"

"It won't."

In theory.

Maybe.

It's possible something good will come of this.

Mal looks at me like he doesn't believe me.

I want to argue, but I don't believe me either.

Chapter Twenty-Three

MAL

After breakfast, Lacey takes a seat on the couch with her cell. She stares at the screen, her gaze fuzzy.

I'm tempted to hide her phone, to offer sexual favors, whatever it takes to keep her from walking into this fire.

She's going to get hurt.

And I don't want that.

Lacey doesn't talk much about her mom. But it's enough I know Mrs. Waltz isn't someone I want in her life. In our lives.

But I don't want this regret hanging over her head either.

If she has to be sure, she has to be sure.

All I can do is stay by her side.

I move to the couch and place my body behind hers. "You're tense."

"I know." Her voice is as heavy as her posture.

"You want to talk about it?"

"No." She shifts into my lap. "I don't think there's much to say until I actually call her."

I lean in to brush my lips against her neck. "It's sweet you want to resolve this."

"Or stupid. Is it stupid?"

"You're asking me if holding out hope your mom will change is stupid?"

"Good point."

"Hey!"

"Was that a trap? You're better than that."

I chuckle as I pull her closer. "I understand, baby. I understand wanting your parents to be there for the big moments."

She nods.

"But what if she hasn't changed?"

Lacey presses her lips together. "That's most likely, I guess."

"Don't tell her we're doing it now. Don't invite her until you're sure you want her there."

"You think I'm an idiot? I was already planning that."

Fuck, I love when she gets sassy.

I rub her shoulders. "Put it on speaker, so I can pull you out if you get sucked in."

"I don't know…"

"You trust me?"

"Of course, but—"

"Then do it."

She lets out a heavy sigh as she holds up her cell. "Okay, I'll put it on speaker. But not because you demanded it."

"No?"

"Because I think it's actually a good idea. Dad doesn't see Mom the way I do. What if I'm the crazy one?"

"You're not."

"We'll see, I guess." She takes a deep breath and

exhales slowly. "Mal." Her voice hitches. "No funny business during my call."

"Funny business?" I play dumb.

"Funny business." She drags her fingertips up my thigh, stopping to trace the outline of my boxers over my quad.

"What do you call this?"

"A demonstration."

"And this?" I bring my hands to her hips and pull her onto my lap.

"It could go either way."

I can hear the smile in her voice. She's relaxing. That's something.

I slide my left hand over her shoulder and down her arm. Slowly, I trace the outline of her engagement ring.

It's perfect for her.

I enlisted a lot of help making sure it was perfect—Piper, Violet, Bella. I even called Lacey's East Coast BFF Carrie.

It's a beautiful ring, but it pales in comparison to her. Nothing is as bright and vibrant as Lacey.

This isn't going to take away her sparkle.

I won't let it.

I intertwine my fingers with hers. "No funny business." I make a show of placing my right hand under hers. "Unless it's what you want."

"Uh-huh."

"Scout's honor," I promise.

She laughs. "Are you offering to tie a knot?"

"Are you asking?"

"Hmm." She shifts her hips, grinding against me. "I could be interested."

"Could?"

"You're distracting me on purpose."

"Why would I do that?"

"Mhmm." She presses her cell phone into her thigh. Her posture shifts. She's curling into herself. Away from me.

I need to ease up. "Do you know what you're going to say?"

Her voice is soft, uncertain. "I think just the news, that we're engaged. Then I'll see how I feel. Then, we can tell everyone."

I chuckle.

She attempts to imitate my deep laugh. "Explain yourself."

"It's a surprise."

"Oh! Is it a surprise party?" She turns enough to look me in the eyes. Her expression is bright. Her lips are curled into a smile.

I try to hold a poker face, but I can't help but smile back. Her enthusiasm is fucking contagious.

"Is there going to be cake?"

"You're not supposed to ask that."

"Is there?"

"Of course."

"Chocolate?"

"Carrot."

She laughs. "Only carrot? Why not go all the way to spinach cake?"

"I asked, but the bakery refused."

Her smile spreads wider. "I like carrot." She leans in and brushes her lips against mine.

I can still feel that buzz of electricity. That thrill of her kiss. Of knowing she's mine.

She pulls back with a sigh. "And I love you."

"I love you too." I reach up to run my fingers through her hair. She's stalling. If she stalls enough, she might talk herself out of it.

Her lips part with a sigh as she leans into my touch. Slowly, she brings herself upright and turns back around. "Okay. I'm going to call. On three."

She holds up her phone and navigates to the contact *Dad Cell*. "One." She squeezes my fingers. "Two." She takes a deep breath and exhales slowly. "Three."

She taps the *call* button. Then *speaker*.

The dial sound flows through the cell's speakers.

I squeeze her hand back. She needs me to be strong here. I can't let her know how terrified I am for her.

Someone on the other end picks up.

"Lacey, hey." Her dad's voice is affectionate and husky. A smoker's voice. "How are you, baby girl?"

"I'm good." Her voice is even. Still. "How are you?"

"A little tired. It's early. What are you doing up?"

"Oh, is it?" She looks to the widow and takes in the bright sky. "I've been getting up early all week. We were shooting this awesome commercial on the beach at sunrise. It was a pain because we only had two hours at a time, the one before sunrise and the one after. But it's worth it. The final version looks beautiful. Even if everyone was cold and tired and cranky every minute we worked."

"Oh, what was it for?" he asks.

"It's for a clothing site. For their website. I guess it's more of a teaser. It won't be on National TV or anything. Or regional TV. Or any TV, actually."

"Still, it sounds like good work." There's a smile in his voice. He's proud of her.

"Thanks, Dad. It is."

"You've been busy?"

"Yeah, really busy. I'm in demand. I've been meaning to call for a while."

"I'm glad you did. It's good to hear from you. And your mom will be happy to hear your voice."

Lacey's shoulders tense. She digs her fingers into the slick cell screen. "Yeah, that will be good."

Her dad perks. "She misses you. I miss you too. Why has it been so long?"

She taps her fingers against her leg.

He continues. "You should come by for dinner. Maybe tomorrow night. We still do the same thing, every Sunday night."

"Oh yeah?" There's nostalgia in her voice. "What are you making this time?"

"Spaghetti and meatballs."

"With garlic bread?" Her posture softens.

"Of course. I can make an extra loaf for you."

"Maybe." She presses her back against my chest. She squeezes my fingers. But she's not really here with me. She's in her head.

I squeeze her back. I'm tempted to break my promise to play nice, but I resist. This conversation is going about as well as it could.

"How's your car?" he asks. "Still with the Camry?"

"Yeah, it's still holding together," she says.

"Come early Sunday. I'll take a look. When was your last oil change?" he asks.

"Uh…" She squints, racking her brain. "I'm sure it was—"

"Every three months!"

"It was probably September."

"Probably? That's an old car. You need to take care of it."

"I know. I do." Lacey sucks a breath between her teeth. "Listen, Dad, I want to tell you something."

"You're pregnant?"

"What? No?" She shakes her head *what the hell?* "No,

I… well, I guess it's not that far off. Mal asked me to marry him."

His voice is bright. "You're engaged?"

"Yeah." She fidgets the fingers of her left hand. "He asked me last night."

I trace the outline of her engagement ring. I lean in to whisper. "You okay?"

She nods then speaks into the phone. "He's here actually. Did you want to talk to him?"

"Sure, sweetie."

She turns so she can look me in the eyes. "Go ahead."

"Hey, Mr. Waltz. It's nice to finally speak with you," I say.

"It's Malcolm, isn't it?" he asks.

"It is," I say.

"Lacey only has great things to say about you. But we have different concerns. When do you think you'll tie the knot?"

"I'm trying to talk her into Vegas," I tease.

Her dad lets out a hearty laugh. "You don't want to give her a chance to change her mind?"

I stare back into my fiancée's eyes. "I know a good thing when I have it."

"Are you going to keep providing for her?" he asks.

"Daddy! Don't." Lacey's cheeks flame red. "I can provide for myself."

"What about when you have kids?" he asks.

"You can work and have kids." She folds her arms. "We're not having kids soon."

"But you are having kids." It's a statement, not a question.

"Let's talk about this later." She turns to me and mouths *sorry*. "Can you put Mom on the phone. I want to tell her."

"Of course. But she may still be asleep. You should come to dinner Sunday. Surprise her," he says.

"Maybe." She stares back into my eyes, searching them for her answer.

"Give me a sec, sweetheart," her dad says. The phone goes silent. On hold.

He's checking if her mom is up.

"He's ridiculous. Sorry." She sets her cell on her thigh and traces its outline.

"I'm just glad your dad answered that question for us," I say.

Her blush deepens. "I do want to have kids. One day. And you must."

"I must?" I ask.

She nods. "Don't you?"

"Well, I must…"

"Don't even. You're the most paternal person I've ever met."

She has a point. And she's right. But I'm not admitting that just yet. It's too much fun teasing her.

I run my fingers through her hair. Over her cheek. Along her jaw. "Well, anything Lacey Waltz says I must do…"

"You must make me come nine times today."

"Done." I play with the hem of her sleep shorts. "Starting now?"

"Starting after this." She takes my hand and places it on the couch. "And don't bullshit me. We've talked about having kids. You want them."

"I do." I cup the back of her head with my hand and I pull her into a soft kiss. She tastes good. And the way she's groaning against my lips is making me forget we're on hold with her dad.

"Lacey, sweetie, is that really you." There's a woman's

voice flowing from the cell speaker. It's as husky as her father's voice, but it's decidedly less cheerful.

Lacey yelps as she pulls back. "Hey, Mom. How are you?"

"Good. It's been so long. Why haven't you called?" her mom asks. "I miss you."

"I miss you too." My fiancée's voice is sincere. She wants her mom in her life. Some version of her mom. One who doesn't fuck with her again and again. "Did dad tell you?"

"Only that you're on the phone," her mom says.

"Okay, well I will." She takes a deep breath. Her words are slow. Punctuated. "I'm engaged. My boyfriend asked me to marry him. Last night." Lacey takes my hand and squeezes tightly. "We wanted you to know."

"Your boyfriend?" Her mom's voice is impossible to read.

"Yeah. Mal. He's sweet. You'd like him."

"Why haven't I met him?" her mom asks.

Lacey's posture stiffens.

She's been intentionally out of touch with her mom for years. Is her mom in denial about that or is she starting a guilt trip?

Either way, I don't like it.

Lacey ignores the question. "We're busy, but um… Dad told me about dinner Sunday."

"Yes, spaghetti and meatballs this week. You have to come. And you have to bring him. Mal, was it?"

"Yeah."

"You can look through my old wedding albums. I can help you plan. You'd never plan your wedding without my input. I know that."

Lacey tenses. "I guess we can go."

I bite my tongue. Every molecule in my body screams *stop this.*

Lacey needs closure.

But like this? I don't know.

"Still Sunday at seven?" she asks.

"Of course," her mom replies. "I'll bring out the good wine. You can try on my dress."

"Yeah?" Lacey's voice gets soft. "It's beautiful."

"It will need alterations, of course. And it's really meant for a curvier figure. You might need something that plays down your small chest."

"Yeah…" Lacey presses her lips together. "I guess that's true."

"And we'll have to find a hairstyle to play down the roundness of your face," her mom says.

What the hell is that?

I know women look at their bodies completely differently than men do. Every commercial and women's magazine in existence sells the message *something is wrong with you.*

It's always *slim your thighs* or *tone your ass* or *lose those saggy arms*. Or it's about the wrong haircut or the wrong makeup or having too many wrinkles.

It's always something.

Maybe her mom is trying to help.

I don't fucking care.

Nobody is saying shit to Lacey that makes her feel less than.

Not on my watch.

I study her like my life depends on it. Her voice is catching. Her shoulders are up at her ears.

But she's okay. She doesn't need me pulling her out. Not yet.

"Dad says he'd fit right into the neighborhood," her mom says. "With all his tattoos."

Lacey's laugh breaks up the tension in her shoulders. She whispers to me, "You're Riverside material." She turns back to the speaker. "Maybe. He's more of an Orange County rich boy."

"Oh." Her mom's voice perks. "He does well?"

"Jesus," she whispers. "Yes. He does well. And I do well. We won't need any help paying for the wedding. And, actually, we need to get going. We have some plans."

"I love you, sweetheart." There's this hint of desperation in her mom's voice. Like she's trying extra hard to convince Lacey she's worth an *I love you too.*

"Thanks Mom. I um. I have to go. I'll see you Sunday." She hangs up before her mom can reply.

I wrap my arms around her and pull her body onto mine. "You okay?"

She nods.

Then it's time to say this.

I run my fingers through her hair. "You're not going to like this."

She stares back at me. "Then don't say it."

"I have to."

She bites her tongue.

"I don't think you should do this."

Chapter Twenty-Four

LACEY

I don't think you should do this.

Where does he get the nerve?

I bite my tongue. I want to tell him to go fuck himself.

But I can't argue.

This goes against every logical thought in my head.

My mom has pulled so much shit. She doesn't deserve a second chance. A third chance. A whatever number this chance is.

This is a woman who isn't afraid to turn a cancer scare into an *I'm dying; do you really want your mother dying alone?*

She does whatever it takes to get her way.

Her intentions are good. Mostly.

She wants attention. Affection. Love.

But that doesn't excuse her behavior.

"Maybe, but I'm doing it." I fold my arms. "With or without you."

"She insulted your tits."

"They are small."

He tugs at the strap of my tank top. "They're fucking perfect."

"I'm not sure—"

"I am." He traces my top's neckline. "One more word and I'll have to prove it."

"One more word."

He pushes the strap over my shoulder. "You think I won't?"

I stare into his eyes. "You're really bad at this whole threat thing."

He chuckles. "True." He digs his hand through my hair and pulls me into a low, deep kiss. "I'm going to give your tits every bit of attention they deserve."

"I like the plan so far."

"After we finish this conversation."

"You're evil."

He smiles.

"She's right, you know. I would look better in a dress more suited for my figure."

"And you look really fucking happy about hearing that too."

"I have broad shoulders, and narrow hips, and a small chest. I will look best in a strapless or a halter dress with a lot of skirt—"

"You look best naked."

I can't help but smile. "You know what I mean."

He shakes his head. "You're perfect the way you are."

"I guess you wouldn't understand this, what with your effortless rock star hair."

"Rock star hair?"

I run my fingers through his messy hair. "Yeah. It's the perfect shade of brown, and it's just long enough, and it has a slight wave."

"That makes it rock star?"

"Okay, it's not really rock star hair… just effortless."

"And?"

"And this—" I slide my hand under his t-shirt and press my palm against his stomach. "You're built like a tank."

"I spend ten hours a week at the gym."

"Okay, true. But it's because you enjoy it."

"And you don't like working out?"

"Yeah, but I started because I thought Adam would want me if I wasn't chubby."

"And you want to poke at those insecurities because…"

"Not all of us are irresistible sex gods. Some of us need to use makeup, hair, and style tricks to emulate the kind of divine beauty that comes naturally to you."

"Uh-huh."

"Yeah-huh."

"Does it actually make you happy, your mom's commentary about your body?"

"No, but she's right."

He shakes his head.

"Why do you care? Do you have some fetish for long hair I don't know about?"

"Baby, I don't care what you do with your hair. As long as I have enough to pull."

I can't help but smile.

"I don't care what you wear. I only care you feel good about it."

"What if I look hideous at our wedding?"

"Not possible."

"Humor me."

He shrugs. "You'll look fucking beautiful naked, coming on my cock in our wedding suite."

My cheeks flush. "And if my makeup is ugly, there's always doggy style."

"Or I could pin you to the bed."

God damn, the man is giving me all kinds of ideas.

He pulls me closer. "You're irresistible. I'm not going to let anyone make you feel less than. Not about anything."

"Okay, but…"

"You won't cancel?"

"I'm sorry, Mal, but I have to be sure." I look up at him. "You think I'm an idiot, don't you?"

"No."

"I guess you enjoy my masochistic side."

He chuckles. "I do."

"But you're the only one who gets to hurt me?"

"You asking other guys to spank you?"

"You know I'd never."

"I know." He places his palm against my cheek. "I don't want to see you hurt, baby. But if this is what you need, I'll be there."

I nod.

This *is* what I need.

I wish it wasn't.

I thought I was over this. I thought I was happy with my decision to cut ties with my mom. To cut out my dad if he refused to stop the *oh, you didn't want your mom to come to dinner with us* bullshit.

I guess not.

"You're not stupid, baby. Don't think that shit about yourself." He strokes my temple with his thumb. "You're brave."

"Yeah?"

"The bravest person I know." He pulls me onto his lap. One hand slides under my t-shirt and plants on my lower back. The other cups the back of my head. "That's what I admire most about you."

"Not my obsession with movies?"

"That's second place." He leans in to brush his lips against mine.

God, he tastes good.

And his kiss turns off the voice screaming *why are you doing this? Are you an idiot?*

I wrap my legs around his waist.

I dig my hands into his hair.

And I kiss him like the ship is going down.

My body turns on, bit by bit.

The tension in my shoulders eases.

The nerves in my stomach fade.

Desire pushes everything else away.

Mal pulls back with a heavy sigh. "Let me tell you how today is gonna go, baby."

I nod.

"I'm going to carry you to the bed and fuck your brains out."

"Okay."

"Then I'm going to take you to the shower, clean you up, and fuck you again."

My cheeks flush.

"At some point, we'll have lunch. I'm going to spend the afternoon breaking my record. And we're going to spend tonight celebrating, drinking champagne with our friends."

"Champagne?" I lick my lips. "Does that mean—"

His lips curl into a smile. "What else could it mean?"

By the time we get to Kit and Piper's place in Venice Beach, I'm spent in the best possible way.

Piper pulls the door open and throws her arms around me. "I'm so happy for you guys." She squeezes tightly and leans in to whisper. "Don't let him fuck it up, okay?"

"I'll do my best," I whisper back.

"Uh-uh. You'll accomplish," she teases.

She's bouncy and enthusiastic, just like Ethan. But she has Mal's take-no-shit attitude too. Well, so does Ethan.

The Strongs are a bossy, demanding family.

"You two mocking me?" Mal's voice is light. However tough he plays, he enjoys us mocking him.

Piper releases me and throws her arms around her brother. She whispers something to him. He whispers something back.

The two of them laugh.

The three of them are such a happy family. It's nice to see after everything. It's nice to see, period.

Mom, Dad, and I haven't been functional and happy since I was a kid.

Piper motions to the wide open living room. Everyone—Joel, Bella, Kit, Violet, Ethan—is sitting around the table.

Around the cake box in the center of the table.

God, their house is beautiful. It's modern as all hell, with wall to wall windows and sleek furniture. Everything is in shades of black, grey, and pink.

It's the perfect blend of Kit's *all black, all the time* brooding vibes and her adorable girlishness.

Ethan pushes himself to his feet and moves in to hug me hello. "You sure you want to be stuck with Mal?"

"Pretty sure," I say.

He releases our hug. "You know he's bossy and annoying."

"Pretty sure she appreciates how *bossy* he is," Joel teases. He tries to imitate Mal's low, deep voice. "Get on the bed on your back. I want to tie you up."

Bella makes a show of fanning herself. "What were you saying?"

Joel leans in to whisper something in her ear.

She laughs and places her hand on the top of her stomach. The two of them announced her pregnancy last month. Every time I've seen them since (only twice what with all the touring), they've been glowing.

She's just starting to show. And her boobs are even huger than normal.

Bella turns to me with a smile. "Will you forgive me if we leave early? I have… something to do."

"Your husband." Joel wraps his arms around her. "You need to do your husband."

"I prefer baby daddy," she says.

"It's only baby daddy if you're unmarried." Joel looks around the room for support.

Ethan shrugs. Violet nods. Mal and Kit both shake their heads in that *you're ridiculous* gesture.

"Bella should call you whatever she wants," Piper says.

"How about *your majesty*?" Joel offers.

"How about you make your mouth useful?" Bella smiles, despite her blush.

"Fuck yeah." Joel's eyes light up. He nods to the couch then to the stairs. "Here or up there."

Piper clears her throat.

"That won't stop him." Kit turns to us. "Congrats. Really. You two deserve it." He takes his turn hugging each of us.

Then Joel and Bella take their turns.

Then Violet. "The ring is beautiful."

"She helped pick it out," Mal says.

"It was still your call." She looks to me. "It suits you."

"I think so too." I smile back at her. It's easy to feel outclassed next to Violet, Piper, and Bella. They're all pretty *and* stylish. I dress like a filmmaker. Functional, not necessarily cute.

But the three of them always make me feel like I fit right in.

"I'm glad you finally locked that down." Piper winks at me. "You don't want to let her get away."

"Why do you think we're gonna set a date for just after Christmas?" he asks.

"You are!" Violet claps her hands together. "That's great. Do you need help?"

"Yeah… probably." I play with my skirt. Mal is taking care of the practical details. But I still need to figure out a dress. Hair. Makeup. Shoes. It's an event in itself.

"I know a great Etsy shop that does rush orders," Violet says. "If you're interested in custom."

"Ooooh, like yours?" Piper's voice gets dreamy. "It was amazing."

Violet nods. "Or we can try to get something off the rack. Let's go soon."

"Monday!" Piper insists.

Violet frowns. "I have a meeting I can't cancel. But… you, Piper, and Bella should go. Call me if you need backup. I can come after work."

Piper nods.

Bella too.

"Okay. Yeah." My chest warms. My friends are supportive. I'm lucky.

Even if it feels weird not inviting Mom to this.

Well, I guess I can invite her.

If dinner goes well.

It really needs to go well.

"And you? Showing up naked, I assume?" Joel teases.

"That's the plan," Mal deadpans.

"You must need custom suits." Violet tilts her head, examining Mal. "You should see a tailor right away."

"I've got it under control, but thanks." He smiles back at Violet.

"He can't take advice. Really, it's a sickness," Ethan says.

"And you?" Mal asks.

"I'm perfect. I don't need advice." Ethan pulls Violet into a hug. "Right, honey?"

"Uh…" She smiles. "If that's what you want to believe."

"Don't go soft on him now," Joel says.

"Go soft?" Ethan slides his hands to her ass. "Never."

Violet blushes. "You're pretty great." She runs her fingers through his thick, wavy hair. "But I'm not sure you hit perfect."

"Forget perfect. *Pretty* great?" Ethan feigns offense. "That's all I rate?"

I can't help but laugh. I love this group. They're always fun and supportive and sweet.

Joel takes Bella's left hand. He studies her ring then looks to my left hand. "We should compare, angel."

She stares back into his green eyes. "What would that accomplish?"

"You might as well just whip 'em out," Ethan says. "Get down to brass tacks."

Joel stands up and reaches for the button of his jeans. "Sure. Let's go."

"Oh God." Bella hides behind her hands. "He'll do it."

"Tell me something I don't know." Mal slides his arm around my waist. "Keep your pants on, Young. Save it for your wife."

"Is that really what you want, angel?" Joel nips at his wife's ear.

"Tonight." She nods.

"You sure? Could be fun, making you come on this nice glass table." He sucks on her earlobe like no one is watching.

Or maybe like everyone is watching.

I've heard rumors.

Rumors about them putting on shows at sex clubs.

But I'm not sure.

Bella looks like such a nice girl. It's hard to believe she's as perverted as Joel is.

Piper clears her throat.

Bella and Joel ignore her.

"They make me look uptight because I don't want their bodily fluids on my furniture," Piper says.

Kit wraps his arms around her. "Baby, you're not uptight. Just…"

"Just…" Her brow furrows. "Just what?"

"It's cute, how much you hate hearing about your brothers' sex lives." He leans in to press his lips to hers. "Even with them settled down."

"It's not cute," she mumbles.

He murmurs something into her ear and kisses her hard.

She sighs as she pulls back. Her cheeks flush. Her chest.

She turns to us and pushes her blonde hair behind her ears. "I was just saying… congrats. And, um, time for cake!" She points to the pink cake box sitting on the table. "We have sparkling cider. And Joel brought champagne. It's in the fridge. Should I get it out?"

"I will," Violet offers. "You want to cut the cake, Piper?"

"Okay!" Piper squeals. She stares at the pink box like it contains all the secrets to happiness. "How about we put on some coffee to go with this. And um, a pot of tea." She looks to me and Mal. "Green tea, right?"

"Chai," Violet insists. "We need something spicy to go with the cake."

"Cake goes with cake," Piper says. "But whatever makes the newly engaged couple happy."

"Chai is perfect," I agree.

Mal nods to Violet. "With almond milk?"

"How else?" She moves into the kitchen and starts fixing tea.

Ethan follows. He wraps his arms around her waist and leans in to whisper in her ear. Eventually, he pries himself away to grab the bottle of champagne.

Piper opens the cake box, grabs the pastry knife, and cuts a giant slice. She's careful about sliding it onto a plate and handing it to me and Mal. "Take the first taste."

Mal picks up a fork. He slides it into the cake and brings it to my mouth. "After you, baby."

I nod and take my first bite. It's perfect carrot cake—rich, spicy, and just a little sweet.

I lick the last drop of frosting from my lips then I take the fork, scoop a bite, and bring it to Mal's lips.

He holds my gaze as he licks it off the fork. How can the man make eating cake look sexy?

It's wrong.

When he's done, he sets the fork and the slice down.

He slides his arms around my waist and he pulls me into a deep, slow kiss.

People clap, cheer, giggle.

The champagne bottle pops open.

And Mal holds me close.

This is the perfect celebration.

The perfect party.
Our friends are amazing.
But what about my family?
Will they be half this supportive?
I really don't know.

Chapter Twenty-Five

LACEY

Sunday, I try to stay busy. I go to the gym. I make breakfast. I devote myself to editing my latest side project—a silly short film about a couple trying and failing to break up.

But the thought screams in my head all day. *You're seeing your mom tonight.*

I try to push it aside. I try to ignore the concerned glances Mal keeps casting my way.

I fail.

All afternoon, he shoots me those same *I'm not sure about this* looks. Even as I dress. As I put on makeup. As we get into my car—Dad will want to look at the engine.

As we pull onto the freeway.

It's a good thing I'm driving with the way Mal keeps looking at me.

Okay. Focusing on all the intensity in his blue eyes isn't going to help me right now. If I want to drive all the way to Riverside without crashing, I need a distraction.

I make conversation about the songs on the radio. He

plays along, but it's infecting the air, the *this is a bad idea* vibes.

The closer we get to Riverside, the more the nerves in my stomach demand my attention. By the time I pull into Mom and Dad's neighborhood, the nerves are in overdrive.

It's been three years since I've been home. Maybe more. It looks the same as it did. All those rows of little houses. All those parched lawns. The thin slice of concrete on the curb. The worn grey streets, packed with older cars. Practical cars.

This neighborhood is nicer than it used to be, but it's still not well to do. Not by southern California standards.

Not that such things stop my mom from spending most of her pay check on clothes. She's worked part-time as an administrative assistant since I was in grade school.

I don't begrudge her the job. In this neighborhood, most of the moms work. That's the only way to make the mortgage when Dad's job doesn't cover all the bills.

But having to forgo air conditioning because Mom wanted a two-hundred-dollar pair of shoes…

I guess I'm not over it.

"You okay, baby?" Mal's voice pulls me out of my thoughts.

"Yeah." I park on the street just in front of my parents' place. Then I notice the empty spot in the driveway. Mom's car, the sleek silver sedan, is on the right. Dad's souped up muscle car is parked across the street.

He cleared the space for me.

Because he wants to check my engine.

But still. It's sweet.

I pull into the driveway.

The front door pulls open as I turn the car off. There's Dad, standing on the front step in jeans and a greasy t-shirt. His grey hair is short. His dark eyes are bright. Happy.

I'm not sure which pleases him more—that I'm here or that I brought my car.

I nod to Mal. "He's obsessed."

"He is a mechanic," Mal says.

"You're already siding with my parents?" I try to sound like I'm teasing, but I don't get quite there.

Mal slides his arm around my shoulders and pulls me into a slow, deep kiss. "Never."

I believe him, but, somehow, it's not comforting.

Mal gets out of the car first. He walks all the way around the hood to open my door and offer me his hand.

"Thank you, sir." I play along. "You're always such a gentleman."

Mal nods. "Anything for you."

He's teasing, but Dad is enjoying the gesture. My parents are traditional. Extremely traditional. They're going to push *church wedding* even though neither of them attends mass regularly.

"Lacey." Dad outstretches his arms and motions *come here*. "I've missed you."

I move in to give him a hug. It's a little strange. It's been a year since I've seen him and I've resisted his affection for longer. It tends to come with *surprise, Mom's here too*.

"I missed you too." I release our hug and motion to my fiancé. "You haven't formally met Mal."

"I haven't." He and Mal shake. "It's nice to meet you, son." He glances at me. "That ring is nice. Real?"

"Dad! What's that matter?" Really, I don't care how much the ring costs. Mal picked it out for me. That's more than enough.

Mal chuckles. "It exists in reality."

Dad tilts his head. His eyes fill with confusion. He's not a metaphor guy.

"It's real." Mal slides his arm around my waist. "A fake ring might have been better. You wouldn't have to worry about losing it on location."

"This one is perfect," I say.

Dad nods. "It's nice." He looks to Mal then to me. "He's so tall. You didn't tell me."

"He is tall," I agree.

"Handsome. And built too. Like he can fight," Dad says.

"Thank you. Should I call you Mr. Waltz or…" Mal trails off to let him finish.

"Johannes." Dad turns toward the car. "I can tell already. Not regular maintenance."

"Regular enough." Maybe. In theory. The thing still runs, okay?

"Let me look at her." Dad doesn't wait for permission. He slides into the driver's seat and pops the hood. Then he's leaning over it, staring at the engine. "You need a tune up, Lacey."

"I'll get one next week. I promise," I say.

"Baby, you don't take care of your auto," Mal teases.

"It's tragic, I know." I fight my desire to roll my eyes. It's a car. Who cares?

"Bring her to the shop. I'll take care of her," Dad bargains.

"I'll think about it." This is a far drive and I'm not sure I'll be ready for more familial bonding anytime soon.

"Every ninety days, Lacey. And you're in LA. Bad streets, you drive all the time. Every two months is better," Dad says.

"I'll make sure she complies." Mal pulls me closer. He

leans in to whisper in my ear. "Or I might have to punish you."

Ahem.

Dad's attention is still fixed on my car. He motions to the door. "Go help your mother with dinner. I'll be there in five minutes."

"Only five minutes?" I ask.

"You think I want to let you eat all those meatballs?" Dad teases.

He has no idea I'm wracked with anxiety.

He's still wearing those rose-tinted glasses. No matter what, he sees the world as a beautiful, happy place.

No matter what Mom does, he sees her as his beautiful, perfect wife. It's almost sweet.

No, it is.

Just not when I need someone to listen. Not when I need someone on my side. Not when I need him to understand.

I squeeze Mal's hand. I'm here for a reason. Maybe that reason is fuzzy, but I know it's not dwelling in all the things Mom did to upset me.

Mal squeezes back. He keeps his body close to mine as he follows me inside.

The house is the same cozy two bedroom. The TV is pressed up against the wall. The couch is covered in floral pillows.

There's Mom, at the table, in a bright blue and teal fit and flare dress. It hugs her ample chest (I did not inherit her curvy figure) and falls just below her knees. It's pretty, fancy, expensive. As are her designer black heels. And her carefully coiffed, immaculately colored chestnut hair.

She turns to us with a wide smile. It's the same as the last time I saw her. Her lips are a bright red. The same red as always.

But her smile…

There's something about it, something I can't explain.

Or maybe I'm imagining things.

If I'm here to give her another chance, I have to do that. I have to wipe the slate clean. Cleanish.

But that's it. One chance. If she pulls any more bullshit, I'm done.

"Lacey, sweetie. You look so pretty." She moves in for a tight hug. "I missed you so much. It's been too long."

I say nothing. I've missed her, but it's been… mostly, it's been good.

She pulls back to hug Mal hello. "It's nice to finally meet you, Malcolm. I guess Lacey doesn't realize that mothers need to meet their daughters' boyfriends. We need to be sure our girls are with good men."

Mal turns to me and cocks a brow. He turns back to Mom. "It's nice to meet you, too."

She looks to my ring then she smiles at him. "Look how gorgeous that ring is. And you surprised her with it?"

He nods.

"That takes a smart man. Did you figure it out yourself or ask for help?" Mom asks.

"I've learned it's a good idea to ask for help when you need it." Mal's eyes meet mine. They scream *like right now. You can tell me if you need out.*

Not yet. It's strange being home. There are a million memories here. Some good. Some bad. Some that invite extreme self-loathing. I put up with a lot of shit from Mom for a long time.

"Lacey, sweetie. Help me with drinks." Mom looks to Mal. "You can help me set the table."

Mal nods and moves into the kitchen.

I follow.

She's trying to charm him. Or maybe he's charming

her. I'm not sure. It's not like Mal has to try to impress. He has that demanding, stoic presence. It's irresistible.

They laugh as they take plates and silverware to the table. I find the red wine, pop it open, and pour four glasses. Mal only drinks on special occasions.

Does this qualify? I'm not sure.

I can finish his glass if he doesn't want it. Then a third. Fourth. Maybe the entire bottle. That might be enough to settle my stomach.

My deep breath steadies my hands enough I can bring the glasses into the main room, two at a time.

Mom places the food in the center of the table.

Dad heads inside, shoots me a thumbs up, then goes to the kitchen to wash his hands.

Mal pulls out my chair for me.

Mom shoots him a nod of approval. "I never thought you'd find anyone nicer than Adam, but you may have."

I take my seat.

Mal follows. "I'm not sure I rate as nice, but thank you, Judith."

She's already asking him to call her by her first name. No, that's normal. Dad did it right away.

I'm too worked up here.

"How is Adam?" Mom twirls pasta around her fork. "It's been a while now."

"Two years. He's good. He's dating someone from work." I take a huge bite of pasta. Mmm. Carbs, red sauce, Parmesan, garlic. This is Mom's spaghetti and meatballs and it's as good as I remember it.

"You don't mind that, Mal?" Mom asks.

"Why would I?" Mal's expression stays pleasant, but there's something in his posture. He doesn't like the question.

Because it's true?

Or because it's the kind of question that drives couples apart?

"Your fiancée still in touch with her ex? You never get jealous?" Mom asks.

"No." Mal's brow furrows. "Why would I?"

"She was with him for years. Four years, right?" Mom asks.

I bite my lip. "Yeah." What's she getting at?

"You loved him. Didn't you?" Mom asks.

"What's that matter?" I play with my pasta. This can't be an accident. Is she actually trying to make Mal jealous of Adam? I don't see another explanation.

"When I was younger, I couldn't stand your father talking to other women much less his exes. It's good you're more… enlightened." She takes a dainty bite and dabs her lips with her napkin.

"It's more that I know I'm Lacey's favorite." Mal taps his knee against mine under the table. "Unless you have something to tell me."

"No. You are. In every way." I take another bite and chew slowly. "Adam is a good guy. We're friends."

"It's good to stay friends. Too much jealousy is bad for your heart," Dad says.

"True. But it can't always be helped." Mom turns to me. "How is work?"

"Good. Busy. I'm doing a ton of different projects. But nothing for the… well, the holidays are a little slower."

"And you're going to slow down after the wedding?" Mom asks.

"No… it's not nineteen twenty. Women get married and work. They have kids and work. They have husbands who are stay at home dads. They do whatever they want." Seriously, how are my parents so trapped in the past?

"A stay at home husband? Really? Is that what you want?" Mom asks.

"If we can afford it and it's what Mal wants, sure. Why not?" I tear at the sides of my napkin. It's not like I actually expect Mom and Dad to be on board with the idea of a stay at home husband, but the judgmental look on Mom's face is still frustrating.

"That's sweet, baby, but I like working. I know you do too." Mal shoots my parents a serene smile. "You know what it's like, Judith. Even when family means everything to you, it's nice to have a job outside that."

"It's good to get out of the house." Mom folds and refolds her napkin. "I'm glad you'll be working, Malcolm." She turns to me. "Especially if you're going to have a big wedding."

"We're going to do something small," I insist.

"And your dress? Have you thought about a style?" she asks. "You're so thin. Are you eating enough?"

I stuff the rest of my garlic bread in my mouth to answer.

"It will be hard flattering such a narrow figure, but I'm sure Loretta has ideas. And there's padded bras. You want to look good in your pictures."

Right.

I want to look good.

But not like Mom's idea of good.

Like mine.

I…

I stuff another piece of garlic bread in my mouth and try to get my thoughts in order.

Chapter Twenty-Six

LACEY

I let Mom opine about my fashion options for ten minutes.

The entire time, Mal shoots me *are you really okay with this* looks.

It feels familiar. Normal.

But he's right.

I don't like hearing it.

I'm not going to put up with hearing it.

After my next glass of wine, I summon up the courage to say something.

"Mom, could we not talk about my body?" I run my fingers over the rim of the glass. "I'm happy with how I look."

"I'm only trying to help." Mom frowns.

"I know. But I'd like to table the conversation." I top off my glass. "Or we can leave."

"Okay." Mom's voice is apprehensive. "Your dress will need to fit your location. Where are you planning the ceremony?"

"At the beach." I take another bite of the buttery garlic

perfection. It's pure comfort food. It's exactly what I need to quell my stomach's flip-flopping.

Even so, I follow it up with a long sip of wine.

"Hmm." Mom's voice lifts to that judgmental tone of hers. "That's modern."

I need to cut her off at the pass here. "No, it's normal."

"I guess people might like it if you plan it right." She lifts her wine glass to her lips and takes a dainty sip. "You don't have to ask for help. I know you're not the kind of girl who would plan a wedding without her mom's help."

"Actually." I stab a meatball with my fork. "We have it under control."

Mom balks.

I stuff the meatball in my mouth, chew, swallow, smile.

"You must mean that you have most of it finished." Mom sets her wine glass on the table. Her lips purse. "You'd never lock me out of your wedding."

My fingers curl into fists. This is how it starts. A few *you'd never hurt me like that* comments.

Then it's the *I'm sorry I ruined your life* crying fits.

Dad is swirling pasta around his fork like everything is normal.

Mal's eyes are narrow. Well. For him. It's almost imperceptible, but I know his expressions.

He's pissed.

So he sees it too.

He doesn't think I'm the crazy one.

"Actually." Mal keeps his voice even. "We appreciate your offer, Judith, but we have it under control. We won't need any of your help."

"None?" Mom presses her hand to her heart. "You really know which of your cousins are willing to sit next to each other?"

"We're doing something small," I say. "Just friends and immediate family."

"You're not going to invite your cousins?" Mom asks.

"No." I stab another meatball. This one is the same tomatoey goodness, but it's lacking taste.

"Grandma?" Mom stares at me like I'm striking a dagger through her heart.

"No, I'm not." My wine is equally void of flavor.

"You don't love your family?" Mom asks.

This is bullshit. Right?

I look to Mal for confirmation.

He stares back at me, his eyes wide with concern.

He arches a brow *are you okay?*

I am. I think so.

I can handle this.

"Mom, it's not like that. I know you're trying to help, but I'd appreciate it if you'd let me and Mal handle it." I unfold and refold my napkin.

"Judith, you know Lacey loves your mother. She still sends her Christmas cards," Dad jumps to my defense.

"Oh." Mom presses her lips together. "You send Grandma Christmas cards but I don't rate a phone call on Mother's Day?"

"Mom, can we not?" I ask.

"I don't know. Can we not? You don't want my help with your wedding. You don't want my input on your wedding dress. You send cards to Grandma but not to me. What can we do?" Anger bleeds into her voice. "Do you love me at all?"

"Mom, don't start. This is why I haven't sent you a card."

"Yes, I know. I'm a horrible mother. I don't even deserve a call on my birthday."

"That's not what I mean."

"I'm that awful." She blinks back a tear. "I'm ruining your life."

"You can't lay on these guilt trips because you don't like what I'm saying." I push my plate away. "If you want to be in my life, you need to respect my boundaries."

"Now I don't respect you?" Mom wipes her eyes with her napkin.

"Stop it!" I push myself to my feet. "Stop trying to guilt me into giving in. This is why I don't spend time with you. Because you always make me feel like shit."

Mal gets up and wraps his arms around me. "Come on, baby, let's go."

"I want you in my life, Mom. But not if you're going to manipulate me every chance you get." Now, I'm blinking back tears. "If you want to be invited to my wedding, you'll apologize. No… even that won't be enough."

"You're not inviting me to your wedding?" Mom scrunches her napkin into a tiny ball. "This is the daughter I raised?"

"It's that kind of thing." My voice is shaky. My hands too. I take a deep breath. I need to get this out. "You can't treat me like this if you want to be in my life."

Mom scoffs.

"I… I don't want it to be this way, Mom. But it will. Until you change." I swallow hard. I'm officially uninviting my mom from my wedding. Which means I'm uninviting Dad. Which means another few years of frost. Maybe more.

Maybe forever.

But do I want my daughter to have to go through this kind of thing one day?

Do I want her to hear that she's too chubby or her boobs are too small?

Do I want my son to learn he's useless unless he's a provider?

Do I want anyone I love to have to walk on eggshells around my mom?

I know this is the right thing to do.

But that does nothing to push the guilt from my gut.

Mal wraps his arms around me. "We're leaving. Now."

Right.

Okay.

I let him lead me out of the house. He presses the door closed calmly. No slamming. No temper.

But there's anger in his piercing blue eyes.

More than I've ever seen.

He reaches for the driver's seat.

"I drove here." I'm not sure why I'm arguing. I have no intention of driving after four glasses of wine.

"And you drank most of a bottle." He motions *get in*. "You know I don't mind if you drink, baby. I like the way you get mouthy."

"I do not."

He drops his voice to that low, demanding tone. "Get in the car. Now."

Fuck. His voice sends heat straight to my core. It pushes away the nerves. The frustration. The *what the hell am I doing* questions floating around my head.

I slide into the car and click my seatbelt.

Mal follows. He turns on the car, pulls out of the driveway, and heads for the freeway.

I turn the radio on and play with the stations until I find something I like. There. The "classic oldies" station is playing an 80s night. The song is pure energy. Exactly what I need.

After he pulls onto the freeway, Mal turns to me. He gives me a quick once over.

He rests his free hand on my knee. "What are you thinking, baby?"

"Too many things."

"You feel guilty?"

"I'm cutting my mom off. Officially. How could I not?"

"She deserves it."

"Still." It's gnawing at my stomach. It's tugging at my chest.

How can I do this?

I know it's the right decision.

But still…

Mal's voice is that mix of caring and demanding. "You need help getting over it." It's more of a statement than a question.

I nod anyway.

"You want to come tonight?"

"Mal—"

"Yes or no?"

"Yes."

"Then do exactly as I say."

My breath catches in my throat. I… um… "We're in the car. My car."

"I won't touch you while I'm driving."

"Oh." My voice is more disappointed than I mean it to be. The man is driving. He's skilled, yeah, but I'm not sure I want to test his ability to drive while getting me off.

He chuckles. "You want me to touch you, baby?"

"Yes."

"This first."

I press my lips together. This first. Whatever *this* is, I want it coming first. I want it pushing all the ugly thoughts out of my head.

"Take off your panties."

"Here?"

"Here."

"Uh…" I reach for the hem of my dress. My eyes catch a passing car. I can see the driver's t-shirt, his jeans, his friend in the passenger seat.

Which means other people will see me.

But I need this.

I lift my hips to slide my panties to my knees. They fall to my ankles and collect at my feet.

"Spread your legs," he orders.

God help me, I do. I can't believe how willing I am to give myself to him when he uses that demanding tone.

No, it's more than willing.

I need it.

Crave it.

Mal drags his fingertips up the inside of my thigh. "Touch yourself."

"What?"

"You heard me."

"I…" Uh… here? Now? In the car where anyone can see us?

"Lacey…" Mal plays with the hem of my dress. "Don't make me ask twice."

Chapter Twenty-Seven

MAL

Lacey's breath catches in the back of her throat. She stares into my eyes.

Damn, that look.

She trusts me to lead her.

She trusts me with anything.

I have to force myself to shift my gaze to the road.

Doing this while driving is not my best idea.

But I need to get her out of her head.

And over this guilt.

Now.

I can't wait the hour until we get back home.

Not sure I can wait the hour for her satisfaction, period, but I'm going to try.

I brush my fingertips against her inner thigh one at a time. First the pinkie. Then the ring finger. Middle. Index.

I rub her skin with my thumb.

She spreads her legs a little wider. Shifts her hips a little higher. She's inviting me to touch her.

I want to.

But this is all I can manage while coasting down the

freeway at seventy miles per hour.

Besides, I need her on the edge. That's the only way I'm going to be able to help her work through this guilt.

I shoot her a demanding look.

She nods as she slides her hand under her dress.

Higher. Higher. Higher.

There.

Her eyelids flutter closed as she rubs herself. I can only see the outline of her hand under the thin fabric of her dress.

But I don't need to see her hand to know.

It's all over her face—in the way her lips are parting, in the way her eyelids are fluttering together, in that soft furrow in her brow.

"Mal, I… this is fucking crazy. You know that?"

"And?"

She nods. It's enough. I am fucking crazy when it comes to Lacey. And I don't care.

That's part of being in love, knowing someone has the power to drive you out of your mind.

Being willing to go out of your mind for someone.

I force myself to turn back to the road. Traffic is quiet on a Sunday night.

Between the wide-open freeway and the dark sky, it's unlikely anyone will see her.

She leans back into her seat, shifting her hips as she strokes herself.

Her eyes blink open. She stares back at me with this expression that begs me to touch her.

Begs me to watch her.

Again, I force myself to look to the road.

I stroke her inner thigh with my right hand.

She needs to know I'm in this with her.

That I want her as badly as she wants me.

"Mal." Her voice breaks into a whine. A *please touch me, you're cruel for not touching me* whine.

"You want to come, baby?"

She nods.

"From my hand?"

She nods.

"On my cock?"

"Please."

"Then stay at the edge."

"What?" She stares at me.

"Keep touching yourself, but don't come."

"I…" She presses her lips together. She tugs at her dress with her free hand. "All the way back to Santa Monica?"

"Until I say when." I'm not going to make it to Santa Monica.

If I want to survive this drive, I need to find a secluded spot to fuck her. In the next ten miles.

The strip mall to our left catches my attention. The next twenty miles are all strip malls and little neighborhoods. There are hills up ahead.

Hills that might work.

Lacey presses her back against the seat. She bites her bottom lip. Digs the nails of her free hand into her skin.

She's close.

And she wants release.

But this—the sweet agony of being on the edge—is what she needs.

I split my attention between her and the road for the next five miles. She's fucking beautiful wracked with pleasure. And the way her groans echo around the car, drowning out the music.

It's poetry.

Distracting poetry.

Fuck, it's not usually this difficult driving with a hard-on.

Or resisting making her come, period.

Don't get me wrong. Making Lacey come is my favorite thing in the entire universe.

That's why I need to torture her. I need every second of her pleasure I can get.

Even if it's agony as much as it's ecstasy.

Especially if it's agony as much as it's ecstasy.

She pulls her hand to her inner thigh and sucks a deep breath between her teeth. "I'm too close. I can't."

I drop my voice back to that demanding tone. "You can."

"I… I'm not sure about that."

"You want me to fuck you?"

"Yes," she breathes.

"What else?"

"Everything."

"You want me to spank you?"

Her reply is a messy collection of vowels that can only mean *yes*.

She needs torture. She needs pain. It centers her. It pushes out everything else. It helps her work through the guilt eating at her.

I can't exactly complain about my fiancée needing me to spank her then fuck her brains out.

But I still wish she didn't feel this guilt about her parents.

They don't deserve it.

I know better than anyone that people don't deserve a second, third, eight millionth chance just because they happen to share half your DNA.

"Mal." It's a curse. A *fuck you, you're evil.*

I am.

And she loves it.

I take her hand—the one she's been using to touch herself—and plant a soft kiss on each of her fingertips.

She always touches herself with her middle finger.

Or middle and index, if she's fucking herself.

I bring her index finger to my mouth and suck on her fingertip. It tastes like her. It tastes fucking good.

But it's nothing compared to her middle finger.

Damn, these jeans are fucking uncomfortable.

I bring my attention back to the road. Well, as much as I can manage. "Now touch yourself, baby."

This time, she complies. She leans back into her seat, moving her hips in tiny circles. Her dress is still covering her hand, but I can tell.

It's in her groans. In her eyes. In the sighs that fall off her lips.

I focus on driving enough to pull off the freeway and take a main street up into the neighborhood in the hills.

There are rows and rows of houses.

But there, at the top, there's a scenic outlook.

It's private enough.

We're halfway to the secluded spot when Lacey's eyes blink open.

She takes in our surroundings then looks to me. Those gorgeous brown eyes of hers fill with anticipation. "You're going to?"

"I'm going to do whatever the fuck I want with you." No one is around. It's safe to take this further. I push her dress to her waist. "Did I tell you to stop?"

"No… I…" She nods as she rubs herself with her middle finger. "Mal, I…"

"What, baby?"

"I need you."

"I know, baby. Show me how much. Show me how you

want me to touch you."

"But I'll... Okay... I..." Her expression is hazy. Needy.

She slows her movements. Makes them light. She's barely touching herself, but her breath is still hitching.

She's close.

And I'm a man of my word. If she comes, I don't fuck her.

But I can't take that possibility. Not tonight. Not when she needs me this badly.

I wrap my fingers around her wrist and bring her hand to my lips. This time, I savor the taste of her middle finger. Every fucking inch of it. Every fucking drop of her.

"Take off your bra and play with your tits," I demand.

She nods as she pushes her sleeves off her shoulders. Off her chest.

She reaches around her back, unhooks her bra, slides it off her shoulders, and drops it on the floor next to her panties.

She's topless in this car for me.

Without her panties for me.

Touching herself where anyone can see for me.

Fuck, the feeling of all her trust.

It does something to me.

It takes thirty seconds to pull onto the secluded street. Another thirty to get to a quiet enough spot. Another thirty to best position the car for privacy.

The entire time, Lacey is leaning against the seat, her back arched, her fingers working her nipples.

Fuck, those should be my fingers.

I turn the car off.

She hustles to undo her seatbelt. Then mine. Then she's back to playing with her tits.

"Good girl." I savor the sight of her for a minute. I can't believe the shit her mom said about her body.

She's perfect.

Especially her perky tits.

Right now, I'm going to show Lacey just how much I appreciate every inch of her.

Later, we can talk about it.

Fuck, I'm going to come in my pants at this rate.

And that's fucking unacceptable.

"Get out of the car, baby," I demand.

She looks around, studying our surroundings. Either she decides it's private or she's tipsy enough she doesn't care.

It doesn't matter. I care enough for both of us.

She pushes the door open and steps outside.

I follow.

It's a cold night, and I'm in my leather jacket. She must be fucking freezing in that thin dress, especially with the top half of it bunched at her waist.

I want to feel my skin against hers.

I want every inch of her.

But I want her comfortable enough to enjoy this.

I slide my leather jacket off my arms and move around the hood.

Her eyes fix on mine. They're wide with that intoxicating mix of need and trust. When she's in this state, she'll do anything I ask.

The responsibility of that fills me with a thrill that goes all the way to my fingers and toes.

First, this.

Then she comes.

I help her into my leather jacket one arm at a time. She arches her back, leaning into my touch.

I slide my arms around her waist and pull her into a slow, deep kiss.

She tastes like red wine and chocolate and Lacey. And

the way she kisses back, hard and hungry…

Like she can't get enough of me.

Like she'll never get enough of me.

I bring my hands to her hips. "Turn around and put your palms on the hood, baby."

She does. Her ass brushes against my crotch. Her back arches.

She sighs with pleasure as she grinds against my hard-on.

Slowly, I drag her dress up her thigh. "You want to come on my hand?"

"Yes."

"You want me to spank you?"

"Yes." Her breath hitches. "Please." She rubs against me as she lifts her ass into the air.

Fuck.

I pull her dress to her waist and get into position at her side.

"Mal…" Her voice is needy. Desperate.

I drag my fingertips over the curve of her ass. "Why do you want this, baby?"

"I don't know."

"Because you feel guilty?"

She nods.

"You shouldn't."

"I… Maybe."

"I'm so fucking proud of you, standing up for yourself like that."

She bites her lip. Uncertainty spreads over her expression.

"I'm going to hurt you. Because that's what you need." I bring my hand into the air. "Because it makes you fucking wet."

"Mal, I…" Her voice is mixed up. Confused. There's a

lot going through her head.

Maybe too much.

"You want this?" I check in.

"Yes. Please."

"Count for me."

"Okay."

I take my time teasing her. Brushing my hand over her ass. Against her cunt.

She's wet.

Ready to come.

Ready for me.

Which means I need to be careful.

She'll think she can take more than she can.

I lift my hand then bring it down on her ass. It's more a tap than anything.

It's not enough for her.

She arches her back. "Harder, please."

I clear my throat. She knows she's supposed to be counting.

"That was nothing. It doesn't deserve a 'one.'"

I should scold her for talking back, but I can't. I fucking love it. "You want hard, baby?"

"Yes."

"You want to hurt?"

"Yes. Please."

I smack her harder.

She lets out a soft groan. A *more* groan. "One."

Again, a little harder.

"Two."

This time, I spank her hard enough to hurt.

Her groan is loud enough to wake the sleeping birds. "Three."

Her fingers dig into the hood of the car.

She arches her back.

Lifts her ass.

She's demanding more.

"I'm doing this because you need it baby." I lift my hand and bring it down hard. It's a proper spanking.

"Four."

Fuck, the way she groans and arches her back.

The way she claws at the fiberglass like she can't take her anticipation…

I can't take much more of this.

"Not because you deserve it. You haven't done anything wrong." I spank her again.

"Five."

"You know that, baby?"

"Uh…"

"I need an answer."

"I… I know. It just… Please, Mal…"

Again.

"Six."

Again.

"Fuck, Mal… Seven."

One more. I bring my hand into the air and bring it down hard.

Her groan is low, heavy. "Eight."

"You're coming on my hand now, baby." This is what she needs—her pain twisting to pleasure. She's too far gone to actually fucking talk about it.

Her yes is a messy string of run-together words.

I don't tease her. I slide one finger into her cunt. Then two.

She's fucking dripping. And she's close. I can hear it in her groan.

This is going to be fast.

I rub her clit with my thumb as I fuck her with my fingers.

She bucks against my hand, groaning my name again and again.

She pulses around me as she comes.

I have to cover her mouth with my hand to muffle her groans.

Fuck, the way she rocks her hips against me…

I need to be inside her.

"Come here." I pull her closer, holding her back against my chest.

Slowly, I drag my hands up and down her sides. I bring one to her chest to play with her nipples. I use the other to unbutton and unzip my jeans and slide them off my ass.

"Please, Mal… Please fuck me."

"Bend over, baby."

She does. She spreads her legs without me asking. Plants her hands on the car for support without me asking.

"You need me to muffle you?"

"Yes, please."

I cover her mouth with one hand. I bring the other to her hips.

Slowly, I pull her body onto mine.

My tip strains against her.

Then it's one delicious inch at a time.

Fuck, she feels good.

Soft.

Wet.

Warm.

Mine.

My hand doesn't do enough to muffle her groan.

As much as I love hearing all that need in her voice, I don't want us arrested.

I better make this fast.

I move us to the left, so she's pressed up against the passenger side door.

She groans as she rocks her hips.

I stroke her with my index finger.

I fill her with a deep thrust.

Another.

Another.

I do it as slowly as I can manage.

I savor every fucking inch of her.

She moans into my hand.

She rocks her hips to meet me.

I move a little faster.

A little harder.

There—

She nips at my fingers.

She groans my name.

I pin her to the car as I fuck her.

As I stroke her.

As I fucking lose myself in her.

God damn, the way she's groaning against my hand—

The way she's shaking—

With my next thrust, she comes.

She makes circles with her hips. She groans my name. She nips at my fingers.

The pulsing of her cunt pushes me over the edge.

I keep her pinned, thrusting through my orgasm.

I tug at her hair.

I nip at her skin.

I groan her name into her ear.

And I spill every drop I have to give her.

Pleasure spreads through my pelvis, my torso, my arms and legs.

Every part of me feels good.

Then I untangle our bodies, turn her around, pin her back to the car, and I kiss her.

And every part of me feels better.

Chapter Twenty-Eight

MAL

At home, we shower together. We cuddle up on the couch and watch Lacey's favorite movie, *Some Like It Hot*. (She always claims she can't pick a favorite from Billy Wilder's "career full of masterpieces," but this is the one she tends to go back to. It's surprisingly feminist given that it's about two guys pretending to be women for a gig).

She spends the run time alternating between talking about all the ways the movie challenged the censorship code of the era and telling me to shush, because we're at the good part.

The tension melts, bit by bit. Even so, when we climb into bed together, she's still off some other place.

I slide my arm around her waist and pull her body into mine. There must be a million thoughts in her head. No matter how badly I want all of them, I need to be patient.

She's dealing with a lot of shit.

I press my lips against her neck. "You're still shaking."

"Mom isn't going to be in the front row."

I nod.

"Dad isn't going to walk me down the aisle."

"It's a big change."

"I know it's the right decision, but… it's a lot."

"You want to talk about it?"

She shakes her head.

"You still in to do it in the next two weeks?"

"I think so."

"You think so?"

She turns to look me in the eyes. Her palm presses against my cheek. Her thumb rubs my temple. "I do. It's just… that's also a lot."

"I've got it under control. All you have to do is show up."

"A dress in a week and a half is no easy feat."

"You can show up in a bikini."

"You'd like that."

"A white bikini."

She laughs. "It's December."

"A wet suit?"

"Now we're talking." She smiles, but she's not selling it. Her eyes meet mine. "I'm sorry, Mal. I am excited. Really. I'm just…"

"I get it, baby. We can wait if you need more time to get okay with this."

She shakes her head. "I need a day or two. The thought of officially making this forever… it's awesome. And the honeymoon."

My smile spreads to my ears. "Your true motivation."

"Of course. Especially after *that.* You're a sex god. Why do you think I'm marrying you?"

"Money?"

"Nah. Money doesn't do you any good when you're fucking."

"Sex toys?"

"I can buy my own."

"Lingerie?"

"Ditto."

"Fancy hotel rooms?"

"A bed is a bed."

"And a balcony?"

"Sounds dangerous with the way you play."

I run my fingers through her hair. "I'm booking us a hotel room in Malibu. We can fly to Hawaii the next day."

She smiles. "Yeah?"

I nod. "I'll have all the details figured out tomorrow. And then Piper and Bella are going to take you dress shopping, like you planned."

"Oh. We did plan that."

"We can delay, but…"

"I've got like seven days?"

"More like ten. But it's not a lot of time. Piper will take you to stores with stuff off the rack. She knows what she's doing."

She nods.

"That's all you need to do, baby. Just show up."

"So you're picking the menu?"

I laugh. "Extra kale."

"All kale, probably."

"You know me too well."

"And carrot cake."

"Unless you object."

"You want to know a secret?"

I nod.

Her lips curl into a smile. "Carrot is my favorite flavor."

"Carrot it is."

Chapter Twenty-Nine

LACEY

Piper's sedan is idling at the curb.

She's in the driver's seat.

Bella's in the passenger seat.

The two of them are laughing about something.

Which is good.

Today is going to be a good day.

Even if *omg, I'm really not inviting my parents to my wedding* won't get out of my head.

I'm finding my dress.

I'm having fun with people who support me.

Period.

I love my friends. Video production is still a male-dominated industry. I don't meet a lot of women through my job.

It's nice having female friends who are nearby.

Especially at a time like this. Bella and Piper know clothes. They don't ascend to Violet levels of personal style (the woman is practically a Pinterest board), but they always look pretty and put-together.

They'll help me find a dress.

Maybe even figure out what to do with my hair.

Piper gets out of the car with a take-out cup in hand. She moves around the trunk, meets me halfway up the steps, and pulls me into a tight hug. "I'm so excited. Are you excited?"

I nod. Excited. And nervous.

Piper releases me then offers me the take-out cup. "Green tea, with a little honey."

"Thanks." I take a sip as I follow Piper to the car. A little honey? Really? This drink is practically honey with a touch of green tea.

Piper has a problem.

Bella laughs as she takes in my expression. "I told you it was too much."

"Maybe a little." Piper pulls on her seatbelt. "I'll drink it if you don't like it. We can stop and get you something else."

"So you can have coffee number five," Bella teases.

"Well, while I'm there…" Piper smiles as she turns back to the steering wheel.

Bella turns to me. "You're the guest of honor. I should give up the passenger seat, but…"

"You're already pulling *I'm a tired pregnant woman*?"

She adjusts her dark frames. "I *am* tired. Hermoine saps every bit of my energy." She rests her hand on her stomach. "She's going to be difficult."

"Well, yeah. She's half Joel." Piper laughs.

"Are you excited?" I ask.

She nods. "And scared… really scared. But I have a while."

"Not even six months." Piper squeezes Bella's hand. "Not to make you nervous."

"Of course not." Bella grabs her takeout cup and takes a long sip. "My only cup of tea for the day."

"You have to limit your caffeine?" I ask.

She nods. "I'm not sure Piper could do it."

Piper laughs. "Maybe."

"Have you and Kit talked about kids?" Bella asks.

Piper presses her lips together. "Well, it's sort of… I don't know. We both have such fucked up families. And… I just can't picture it, me with a child. I'm not sure I want to picture it."

"That's fine, Pipes. Not everyone has to have kids," Bella says.

"You have time to figure it out," I agree.

Piper nods, but there's uncertainty in her expression. "Hey. Why am I not heading to our first boutique?" Piper checks her mirrors then pulls the car onto the street. "It has the broadest selection. But I think this place in Santa Monica is perfect for you."

"Oh?" I ask.

"You might not have time. The dresses are custom made and they take forever. I don't want to get your hopes up," Piper says.

"Try me." After that dinner with my mom, my hopes are sufficiently crushed.

"They make these beautiful raw silk dresses. They're simple and elegant. And sexy too." She motions to Bella's cell. "Show her the picture."

"She showed me this picture thirty times." Bella taps her screen a few times then hands her phone to me.

The sleek silk gown drapes over every curve of the model's body. It's backless, with thin straps and a deep v in the front.

Piper is right. Simple. Classic. Incredibly sexy.

Mom would hate it.

I… I'm not sure how I feel.

"It's beautiful, and it would look perfect on the beach.

But do you really want Lacey stealing your dress?" Bella asks.

"Each is custom made. The one I'll get will be different. If I get one. If we ever actually get married," Piper says.

"You're the one making him wait," Bella says.

"Yeah…" Her voice lifts back to a bouncy tone. "What do you think about the dress? Pretty, huh?"

"Beautiful." It really is.

"Won't it be hot on the beach in all that silk?" Bella asks.

"Not in January," Piper says.

"Have you set a date, officially?" Bella asks.

"Yeah, but I'm not sure what it is. Mal is taking care of everything." My shoulders relax. I trust him with the details. I trust him to get shit done.

"Sounds like my brother." Piper laughs. "Do me a favor, Lacey."

"Yeah?" I ask.

"Make sure you have veto power over the menu," Piper says.

Bella laughs. "You have a problem."

"Carbs are good for you." Piper takes a sip of her coffee. "And sugar… gives you energy."

"Until you crash," Bella says.

"That's why God made coffee," Piper says.

The sun bounces off the bridal shop's white and ivory display. Damn, those are some serious dresses.

Huge, fancy, princess dresses.

The kind of thing Violet would wear (well, if she wanted to wear white). And pull off.

I step out of the car and slide my purse around my arm.

Piper nearly bounces to the street. "Oh my God, isn't that one beautiful?" She points to the gown in the shop's window, a puffy ball gown with miles of tulle.

"It's huge," I say.

"Is it?" Bella arches a brow. "I've always assumed, but…"

"Don't start." Piper scrunches her nose. "The *dress* is huge. Other things… I don't want to know."

Bella laughs.

I do too.

Piper is relaxed in most ways, but she's incredibly uptight when Mal or Ethan's sex lives come up.

The bouncy blonde clears her throat as she leads us into the store.

Damn. The place is swimming with white and ivory fabric, in every design imaginable.

It's all here.

It's all… so bridal.

"Do you know what you want?" Piper asks.

"Something simple and beachy." And more cute than sexy. More fun than formal. More *me* than anything in the display.

Oh yeah, and it has to soothe the *hey, you uninvited your mom* voice in my head.

"I did it all with Violet. I know the drill. You get clothespins and mark the dresses you'd like to try, then the saleswoman will pull them for you." Piper lets out a soft squeal. "Then we get to try them on."

"We?" Bella arches a brow.

"Yes, I'll help. Some of them are complicated. It's a team effort." Piper takes a step backwards. "I'll get them."

"Thanks." I take a long sip of my much too sweet tea. It's not better lukewarm.

"She's really sweet," Bella says. "And you can tell she's on her fourth cup of coffee."

I laugh. "You can."

"I'm jealous. Seething, actually. I want eight million more cups of tea." She shakes her take-out cup. It's empty. "I should toss this." She motions to my cup. "You want the rest of your honey?"

I laugh as I hand her the tea. "Thanks."

Bella goes in search of a trash can.

Which leaves me alone.

Just me and a hundred fancy dresses.

I need to pace myself.

I need to treat this like editing—focus only on strong possibilities, viciously cut out anything okay.

I move to the first rack on the left side of the room. It's packed with beautiful dresses. A smooth ivory A-line satin. A heavy taffeta gown. A snug mermaid.

Piper joins me as I move to the second rack. She hangs back, nodding *uh-huh* to all the gowns she deems flattering, and offering clothespins when I linger on something for more than ten seconds.

We move to the third rack.

The fourth.

The fifth.

The last.

Somehow, I pin half a dozen dresses.

Piper alerts the salesgirl, a tall woman with long waves and a pink dress.

"Please, get comfortable." The salesgirl points to the dressing room in the back.

It's a wide-open space with mirrors in the middle and stalls on the ends.

We take seats on a cream leather couch and watch as a happy bride-to-be models a mermaid gown for an older woman.

Her mother, probably.

The mom hugs her daughter.

They both look to the mirror, their eyes dotted with happy tears.

That guilt nags at my stomach. This is the right decision. I'm sure of that.

But it hurts.

"You okay?" Bella nudges me. "Too busy thinking about your fiancé naked?"

I shrug, playing coy.

Piper shakes her head. "Think about chiffon and lace now. You can think about skin and sweat later."

"You're a shopping machine," Bella teases.

Piper beams, taking it as a compliment.

The saleswoman steps out of the dressing stall and nods to us. "Do you have the undergarments you're going to wear?"

Uh… am I supposed to? "No."

"Let me grab you a bustier. What's your bra size?" she asks

I tell her and she runs off to fetch proper undergarments.

Piper pushes herself to her feet. "Do you want me to help now or would you rather get into your skivvies first?"

"I'd love your help." I look to Bella. "It's a little small for three."

She laughs. "Go. I'm only here for the fashion show."

I nod, follow Piper into the dressing room, and start stripping out of my jeans and t-shirt.

The salesgirl hands the bustier over through the crack in the door. It's a huge white thing that covers most of my stomach. It's cut low in the back, low enough to work under most of these dresses.

Piper helps me latch the last few hooks then motions to the dresses hanging on the wall. Three are sleek shift dresses. Three are breezy chiffon numbers. "Anything calling your name in particular?"

"This one." I point to the simplest dress. It's an ivory sheath without any adornments.

"Okay." She unzips the dress and lifts it off its hanger. "You want to pull it over your head or step into it?"

"Let's try stepping into it."

She nods as she pulls the sides apart.

One foot at a time, I step into the dress.

Piper pulls it up my legs. It catches at my hips. I have to shimmy to get it to my waist.

She pulls it into place, helps me get my arms through the shoulder straps. Cinches the zipper.

It's a size too small. Two even. Possibly fixable with alterations. Possibly not.

Piper gives me a long once over. "It looks good. Plain, but sexy." She reaches for the door. "You ready for the big mirrors?"

I nod.

She pulls them open, steps into the main room, and holds out her arms like she's presenting a queen at her coronation. "The lovely and talented Lacey Waltz."

I step into the main room.

Bella claps.

I catch her gaze and raise a brow. *Is it good?*

She makes the *it's okay* motion. Bella and I are close, closer than Piper and I are, and I trust an honest opinion from her. It's not that I think Piper will lie. More that she's blinded by how much she loves Mal and wants him to be happy.

Piper takes my hand and leads me to the double-mirror in the center of the room. "Well, what do you think?"

It's a pretty dress. Simple.

Classic.

But… boring.

I turn around and check the back of the dress. The tight fit is flattering on my less than ample ass. But there's no spark.

"I'm not in love," I say.

Piper nods. "What is it you don't like?"

"The neckline."

"Boat neck. Not enough cleavage on display. Got it." She smiles. "What else?"

"The fabric looks a little—" I lower my voice. "A little cheap."

"Hmm. Fair." She gives me a long once over. "Do you like the sheath style? It's elegant. And you're tall enough to pull it off. Especially in a nice pair of wedges."

"I don't know. It's pretty, but… a little prim and proper." I wink at Bella. "No offense."

"You can't top my wedding attire. The black shift dress I wore when I had to go into court." She laughs. "Very classy."

"And being drunk on gin and tonics?" I offer.

"Even more classy." She gives me a long once-over. "It looks great, but it's not *you*. You're more spunky. Playful."

"Casual?" I offer.

Bella nods. "But not in a bad way. In a beach girl kind of way."

"Seashells in my hair?" I ask.

"Okay, I know you're kidding, but that would be really cute." Piper tilts her head to one side, assessing my look. "Let's try the chiffon one."

This time, it only takes two minutes to get me into the dress.

It's closer. Chiffon skirt. Empire waist. Thin shoulder straps. It's breezy, all right, but it's not remotely flattering.

Piper helps me out of the dress.

We're in a routine by now. Unzip. Right leg. Left leg. Hip shimmy. Arms over my head—this one is strapless.

She cinches the zipper.

Adjusts the bodice.

Her voice lifts. "Oooh! Don't look until we're at the main mirror."

She pulls me toward said mirror before I can get a proper look. The dress *feels* right. It's a little too big, but the skirt has the right sway. The waist hits at the right part. The sweetheart neckline hugs my chest just so.

Bella's eyes go wider. She claps. "It's so you, Lacey."

I let my gaze go to the mirror in the middle.

It is.

The ruched bodice is the perfect mix of simple and pretty. The chiffon skirt falls over my hips. It sways with each of my movements.

The strapless bodice highlights my toned shoulders.

The sweetheart neckline flatters my less than ample chest.

Between the jeweled waist belt and the slight pouf to the skirt, I actually look curvy.

"It's perfect." And it actually fits. I spin a few times to be sure. I am. This is the dress. I can see it gliding over the sand, whooshing as I dance with my husband.

"Is that it? Are you really sure?" Piper asks.

I nod. "I am."

She throws her arms around me.

Bella gets up to join the hug.

My chest gets warm. My entire body is warm.

I have all this support in my life. All this love.
The dress is perfect.
My fiancé is perfect.
My friends are perfect.
Maybe we can actually make this happen.

Chapter Thirty

LACEY

There's something on our dining room table.

A little pink box.

A cake box.

Mal steps out of the kitchen in jeans and a t-shirt, a mug of tea in his hands. Not his usual steaming sencha.

Something milky and beige.

"A chai?" I ask.

"With almond milk."

"Does that mean—"

He nods to the little pink box. "You want to do the honors?"

"This is going to be the cake? Our cake?"

"It is."

"Okay." This is going to be our cake. And I have my dress. And what with the relaxed, accomplished look on Mal's face, I figure we probably have our date, and our exact venue, and our colors. Everything.

I set my purse on the table and pull open the cake box.

There's a square slice, carrot cake with cream cheese frosting in a modern, swirly pattern.

I break off a piece with my hands and motion *come here* to my fiancé.

He does.

He makes a show of bringing his mouth to my hand, sucking the cake off my fingers, licking every drop of frosting.

His eyes stay glued to mine. "Perfect."

He breaks off a piece and brings it to my mouth.

I'm a lot less graceful about getting my taste.

I swallow and lick my lips. "Perfect."

"You have your dress?"

I nod. "Piper told you?"

"With some commentary about how she won't give me any details."

"How traditional." I scoop another bit of frosting and lick it off my finger. "I'm getting measured for alterations tomorrow."

"Good. We have an official date."

"Yeah?"

He smiles. "Next Saturday."

"Next Saturday as in the day after this Friday?"

He nods.

"That's five days away."

He nods.

"That's… that's soon."

"You want to back out?"

"No."

"Good. I've already got Carrie coming in Friday on a first-class ticket."

"Yeah?"

He nods. "She wants to know if she's your maid of honor."

I laugh. "That's Carrie. But are we… it's only a dozen guests."

"We don't have to appoint anyone officially."

"Ethan won't mind?"

Mal shakes his head. "I asked him."

"Yeah?" Just us in front of our friends. No bridesmaids or groomsmen. Not because no one deserves it. Because everyone deserves it, and how would we ever pick. And —"You need that much attention?"

Mal chuckles. "Of course."

"Egomaniac."

"Thank you, baby." He slides his arms around my waist." "Wren will be at the ceremony. At five."

"At sunset." Oh no. "You're going to hold me to that five orgasms before midnight thing, aren't you?"

He shrugs, playing coy.

But I don't buy that.

He is.

"Saturday at sunset. That's... that's perfect." I throw my arms around my fiancé.

He squeezes me tighter. "I love you so much, Lacey."

"I love you too."

THE NEXT THREE DAYS ARE A BLUR. ALTERATIONS. JEWELRY. Shoes. Second alterations. Hair. Makeup. Lingerie. A swimsuit for our honeymoon. Another. A few dresses, a pair of shorts, some tank tops…

More lingerie.

Another try at makeup, because this is too fucking much for the beach.

Friday afternoon, I pick up my dress. It's still perfect.

With everything in place, I really do feel like I'm going to be a blushing bride.

I'm confident I'm going to look beautiful.

I stick to tradition and take it straight to Piper's place. We're all meeting here to get ready tomorrow morning. It takes so long we have to start in the morning (eleven a.m., but still. It counts as morning!)

But I don't mind the thought of hours in the makeup chair.

There's a pang in my gut when I think about walking down the aisle sans Dad. Looking to my friends to note Mom's absence.

But it's manageable.

This is the right decision.

I don't want to spend my wedding day bracing myself for an insult, a tantrum, a guilt trip.

I want to spend it thinking about forever with my fiancé.

AFTER A FEW ROUNDS OF TEA/COFFEE, PIPER AND I HEAD over to our not exactly a rehearsal dinner.

It's at Joel's place, of course. Piper tried to volunteer hers, but we decided we can't trust the boys not to peek at the dress. And nobody wanted to drive all the way to Orange County to party at Ethan and Violet's apartment.

Which leaves us crammed into Joel's cozy two bedroom. Everyone is here—Piper, Kit, Joel, Bella, Ethan, Violet, Carrie—

Carrie is here!

I run to my best friend and throw my arms around her. "It's been too long."

She nods. "You look beautiful."

"And you?" I take in her trendy haircut and her all black attire. "You look so New York. It's disgusting."

"I know. I'm in love. Not as in love as you, but still."

She smiles as she looks around the apartment. "You couldn't invite any single guys to this?"

I laugh. "Sorry."

"They're just all so fucking hot."

"I think Logan is coming." I look to my fiancé, chatting with his sister in the corner. "Is Logan coming?"

"Baby, that hurts," Mal teases.

"Probably. That's all Logan does." Joel bounces over to us and introduces himself to Carrie. He tilts his head, trying to wait out a fangirl reaction.

But it's not going to happen. Carrie's only knowledge of Dangerous Noise comes from my gushing.

I take Carrie around the party, introducing her to everyone. Her cheeks flush from the attention, but she shows no signs of celebrity-induced nervousness.

Just the regular *why is everyone looking at me when I'm not the one getting married* nervousness.

"You want a drink?" I offer.

She nods and moves into the kitchen. We do our usual thing. Our old usual thing—whiskey sour. Well, sort of. Joel has whiskey and he has lemons. Close enough.

Once our drinks are full, we raise our glasses.

"To you living a freaking dream life." Carrie smiles. "Girl, how the hell did you manage this?"

"I have no idea." We clink glasses. I take a long sip. Not quite a whiskey sour, but not bad.

"Toast time!" Piper squeals. "Yes, I love toast time." She climbs onto the couch. "Can I go first?"

"Can anyone stop you?" Kit teases.

She nods. "If no one brings me a glass." She looks to Joel. "Champagne, please."

"Am I your bitch?" Joel teases, but he still goes straight to the kitchen, pops open a bottle of champagne and starts filling glasses.

Bella grabs me and pulls me into the center of the room.

Next to Mal.

We're now the official guests of honor.

It's more attention than I'm used to. Even if it's only my friends.

I slide my arm around Mal's waist.

He leans down to whisper. "This is all going to be at my expense."

My laugh is more giggle than I mean it to be. "It is."

Joel brings over our glasses of champagne. He hands over Mal's. Then mine. "You sure you can put up with him, Lacey?"

"Don't give her ideas," Mal teases.

"It's the sex," I say. "Worth almost anything."

"Must be with his personality." Joel winks at Mal. "Guess he's beautiful too."

"He is." I laugh. "And tall."

"Freakishly tall, though," Joel says.

Bella laughs. "Baby, leave her alone."

He turns back to his wife. "Well, I could be incentivized." He nods to their bedroom.

She licks her lips.

"It's our place. No one can ask us to stop." He moves toward her. This is a small apartment. It only takes him three steps to wrap his arms around her.

"It's not our party." She runs her fingers through his hair. "It's for Mal and Lacey."

"And you don't think they're as big of perverts as we are?" He leans in to whisper something in her ear.

She nods and presses her lips to his.

Then they're making out.

It *is* their place.

And she is pregnant.

They get extra leeway.

Piper clears her throat. "Anyone who'd like can watch the show." She nods to Joel and Bella.

Bella pulls away and turns to us. She mouths *sorry*, but she keeps her hand in the back pocket of Joel's jeans.

"I'll keep this fast, so we don't miss our showtime." Piper winks at Carrie. Then at Violet. Then Bella. She looks to me. "I assume you like incredibly muscular men taking their clothes off, what with your choice of fiancé."

"I do," I say.

Piper holds up her glass. "I can admit I've been somewhat fixated on my brothers' inability to find something real for a long time. But Ethan and Mal kept screwing things up. I couldn't help it."

Everyone laughs.

She continues. "Mal, I never thought I'd see you this happy. I never thought I'd see you in love. But I don't think there's anyone in the universe more right for you than Lacey." She looks to me. "I don't have to tell Mal to take care of you, because I know he will. Take care of him, okay?"

I nod. "I will."

Piper wipes a tear from her eye. "You two deserve all the happiness in the world." She holds up her glass. "To finding the family you deserve."

Everyone toasts.

I clink my glass against Mal's then take a long sip.

She's right.

This is our family. And it's the best family I could hope for.

I'm lucky. There's a lot of love in my life.

Kit pulls Piper into his arms. She giggles as he spins her. After he steps her down, he steps up to the couch.

"Hey, watch it with the furniture, Lockhart." Joel feigns

indignant. "We need the couch springy so we can fuck on it."

Kit looks down to his motorcycle boots with a look of faux horror.

"We wiped it down." Bella's cheeks flush. She turns to her husband. "You're ludicrous, baby."

"Mmm. I love when you use big words." He pulls her into a deep kiss.

And now they're making out some more.

"It's not a bad idea." Ethan slides his arms around Violet.

"Are we that tacky?" She runs her fingers through his hair.

He nods.

She shakes her head.

Still, they kiss. It's more of a smooch and less of a make out, but it's plenty sweet and hot.

Kit clears his throat. "I better make this fast. Before the orgy breaks out."

Everyone laughs. Even Piper.

Kit looks to us. "Mal and I haven't always had an easy relationship. He did a lot of shitty stuff to me. I did a lot of shitty stuff to him. But I'd like to think we're past that. Mal, I trust you with anything and I love you like a brother."

Mal nods.

Kit turns to the rest of the room. His deep voice stays calm, even. "When Mal found out Piper and I were dating, he pulled me aside after practice. I thought he was gonna kill me right there. I was getting ready to fight."

Mal chuckles. Everyone else laughs.

"But he didn't deck me. Instead, he looked me in the eyes, with that take no shit voice of his, and he said, *Kit, I know you've got your shit together now. But if you slip, and you drag my sister down with you, then I will fucking kill you.* And I knew he meant every word of it." He looks to me. "Mal is a guy who will do whatever it takes to protect the people he loves. So don't make any enemies, Lacey. Or do, if you don't mind your husband risking jail time."

I can't help but laugh. "I'll keep that in mind."

"Here's to women who are willing to put up with difficult men." Kit raises his glass full of sparkling cider.

Everyone laughs.

Toasts.

Drinks.

Then Carrie grabs my hands and shoots Mal an apologetic look. "Our turn with her."

He leans in and plants a soft kiss on my lips. "Enjoy the show, baby."

"You were in on this?" I ask

He shrugs, playing coy.

I blow him a kiss as Carrie pulls me away. I wave goodbye to everyone, then I let her whisk me to our limo downstairs.

And Bella, Violet, and Piper join us.

And they adorn me with a *Bride to Be* sash and that same penis crown they gave Violet.

And we drive off to my last night as a single woman.

Chapter Thirty-One

MAL

My stomach rises up in my throat as I step into the limo.

Ethan follows. He's bouncy with that Ethan-like energy, but there isn't a sign of nervousness on his face.

There's nothing but amusement in his bright blue eyes.

He smiles as he adjusts my tie. "You look queasy."

I feel queasy. We're twenty minutes out from my wedding. Maybe only fifteen. And fuck, we're running late.

And the sky is still grey.

It needs to be that vibrant pink of sunset.

That's what Lacey wants.

That's what she'll get.

Somehow.

I still haven't managed to get Mother Nature to bend to my will.

Maybe one day.

But right now, my energy is more focused on deep breaths.

I'm light again.

Like I'm going to float into the sky.

And we're only on the way to the ceremony site.

Once we actually get there…

Fuck.

I'm still not used to nerves. I'm still not used to the way Lacey owns my heart. Fuck, she owns every piece of me.

It's thrilling.

And terrifying.

And intoxicating.

And everything.

Today needs to be perfect for her.

But there's nothing left to do except experience it.

Ethan leans back into the bench seat. He folds one leg over the other to make a four, that *I'm kicking back* gesture.

"You're mocking me?" I arch a brow.

"Would I do that to you? On your wedding day? That would be cruel."

"Right."

"You'd never have done that to me."

My chuckle melts some of the nerves in my gut. "Never."

"We'd never fuck with each other like that."

"Never."

He pulls his cell from his pocket and points it at me. *Click*.

"Who are you, Piper?" I shake my head. I press my palms into the leather seats. I stare at the tinted windows.

Lacey and I are getting married.

She's going to be my wife.

I can handle that.

Absolutely.

"You want a drink?" My brother points to the mini bar. "Calm your nerves?"

I shake my head.

His eyes get bright. "Need your vocal chords in tip-top shape to issue orders?"

I nod.

Ethan laughs. "And to scream loud enough to wake up the hotel?"

"Gotta make sure you hear me all the way in Newport."

"Kind of you."

"I try."

His smile spreads over his ears. "You never look nervous."

"I know."

"You hate it, don't you?"

I nod.

"Fuck, this is weird. You, nervous." He snaps another picture. "She's good for you, you know?"

I fire up a *no shit* but my mouth is sticky. All I can manage to do is nod.

"Perfect, actually."

"You're trying to make me more nervous, aren't you?"

Ethan shrugs, his expression utterly innocent. "Nah, just want to remind you how important today is."

I groan.

"So you remember it."

"You remember your wedding day?"

He smiles. "Every second."

"Especially the hotel room?"

"Of course." He looks out the tinted window. The limo is slowing. We're almost there.

Fuck. This is about to happen.

I'm as light as I was when I asked her to take me back. Lighter even.

Lacey is everything.

And this, us being together forever, is everything.

The limo pulls into the parking lot and slows.

It parks.

Stops.

The driver's door opens.

Ethan turns to me. "You ready."

I nod. I am.

"I'll give you some advice."

"You're giving me advice?"

"I'm a married man. You should listen."

I arch a brow.

He tries to hold a poker face, but he breaks within seconds. His laugh lights up his eyes. All his features.

He's happy for me.

Everyone is.

"It's good advice," he says.

"Go for it."

"Don't fuck it up."

I can't help but laugh. "How is that our best advice now?"

"It's wise."

"Joel is wise?"

"He's a genius, when you think about it."

"I'll tell him you said it."

"I'll tell him you agree."

The door pulls open and the driver offers his hand.

"After you." Ethan nods.

I slide out of the limo. My feet plant on the concrete. I'm here. Standing. Not floating into the air.

It feels impossible, but it's happening.

Ethan steps out of the limo and pats me on the back. "You're usually the one giving me the pep talk."

"Pep talk?"

He laughs. "Okay, more like." He copies my stoic pre-show posture and shoots me a paternal glance. "If you can't handle this, I can call in a backup."

"Yeah?" It's exactly what I'd say to him if he was nervous before a show. "Everybody here is coupled or married."

"I can call Logan."

"You wouldn't."

He shrugs the way I do. "Try me."

"Fuck, I'm an asshole."

"You're just figuring that out?"

The coordinator interrupts us. She's in a bright suit, her light hair in a bun. She nods as she introduces herself to Ethan then to me.

"Ethan." She points to the ceremony site on the beach.

The limo blocks part of our view. It must block the view from those little plastic chairs too. Violet, Joel, Bella, Kit, and Piper are already there. And a few other friends too.

"It's just you and Carrie walking together. She's on her way. Can you wait here for me?" she asks.

Ethan nods.

The coordinator turns to me. "You ready, Mal?"

Ethan shoots me an enthusiastic smile. "You've got this."

I do.

I nod to the coordinator.

She nods back. "Follow me."

I do.

I follow her around the limo, around the lifeguard stand. The ceremony site is just in front of us.

She nods to the aisle—it's lined with pink rose petals. All the decorations are beautiful. Exactly what Lacey will want.

Not that she cares about that shit.

But hot pink is her favorite color.

And the sky is finally cooperating. The big orange sun is sinking into the ocean, casting a soft glow over everything.

The coordinator taps me on the shoulder. "Whenever you're ready."

I am.

I'm nervous as fuck, but I'm ready.

Fuck, I never thought I'd be this guy.

I never thought I'd be happy with a woman much less desperate to marry her.

But I am.

And all I fucking want is her happiness. Her smile. Her joy.

I want it more than I want music, more than I want respect, more than I want my family together.

No, that's not right.

Lacey is my family.

Dangerous Noise is my family.

This is the fucking culmination of my family being together.

I let out a deep breath and I take my first step forward. The second. The third.

I don't sink into the sand or float into the sky.

I don't dissolve into the clear, blue ocean.

I make it down the aisle, past our friends and family.

All the way to the altar.

The officiant smiles at me.

I turn.

Everyone is smiling at me.

Then Carrie and Ethan are walking down the aisle together. She looks nearly as happy as he is, which is fucking hard to believe. Nobody is as joyful and bouncy as Ethan is.

Nobody but Lacey.

He kisses Carrie's cheek and takes his seat on my side of the aisle, next to Violet.

Carrie takes her seat, next to Piper.

Piper waves and shoots me a thumbs up.

Of course she's sitting on Lacey's side.

That's so fucking Piper.

I take a deep breath and exhale slowly.

There's no more heaviness in my body.

Only nerves.

Then the wedding march starts.

And everyone stands.

And turns.

And there's Lacey, climbing down the stone steps.

Walking across the sand.

Down the aisle.

She looks so fucking beautiful. Her dark hair is pinned in some elegant updo. Her light makeup brings out all the joy in her dark eyes, the smile on her red lips.

Her ivory dress hugs her chest and waist in a way that begs for my hands.

It falls over her hips.

It sways with every step.

It blows in the breeze.

She's a fucking angel.

My angel.

She's been my angel for a long time.

There's nothing left in my body except happiness.

My smile is as wide as it's ever been.

And hers is too.

She gets closer.

Closer.

Then her hands are on mine.

And she's next to me.

And the officiant is speaking.

It's all a blur until I'm saying I do and sliding the ring onto her finger.

And she's doing the same to me.

The officiant nods. "You can now kiss."

I wrap my arms around her.

And I kiss her like I can't get enough of her.

Because I can't.

Lacey is my angel, my best friend, my salvation.

And, now, she's my wife.

Chapter Thirty-Two

MAL

The reception—conveniently at our hotel's restaurant—is the perfect mix of laughter, congratulations, champagne, cake, and dancing with Lacey in my arms.

Even so, I'm very fucking glad to bid our friends and family goodbye and whisk Lacey to the lobby.

We don't have to stop at the front desk. I already have our room key. It's a good thing, because I can't wait an extra few minutes to make her come.

This is official.

It's forever.

She's mine.

I pull her into the open elevator and push the button for our floor.

She looks up at me, her dark eyes filled with joy. "This is… Wait? Why am I talking?" She wraps her arms around my neck. "Kiss me."

"I want to hear what you were gonna say." I place my hands on her hips and pin her to the elevator.

"Mal, this…" She arches her back, rubbing her crotch against mine. "It's perfect."

My smile spreads over my ears. "Yeah?"

"Everything." She presses her palm against my chest. "You, in your suit. And the hot pink flowers, and the salmon and kale, and the carrot cake, and the champagne. And… you look amazing in that suit."

"You look like an angel, baby."

"Really?"

"Incredible." I bring one hand to her chest and trace the neckline of her dress. "Sexy as hell."

Her smile is equal parts *fuck me* and *fuck yeah*. She drags her fingers through my hair as she leans in to my touch. "Wait until you see what's under it."

I tug at her skirt to tease her.

She laughs and pulls me closer. "I like these wedges. I don't have to get to my tiptoes to kiss you." She leans in and presses her lips to mine.

She tastes like cake and like Lacey.

Fuck, I need to be inside her.

I need her groans in my ears.

I can't wait for anything.

I drag my lips down her cheek and over her neck. "You're irresistible. You know that, baby?"

"Yeah?"

"Fuck yes."

The elevator dings. The doors pull open. A good thing. She deserves better than a fuck in the elevator.

I slide my arm around her waist and whisk her into the hallway.

She giggles as she leans in to my touch. "You're in a rush, Mr. Strong."

"And you, Mrs. Strong?"

"I'm a misses." She squeezes my hand. "It's unreal."

"Get used to it." I stop in front of our hotel room, pull our key from my pocket, unlock the door, push it open.

Here goes nothing.

I slide one arm under Lacey's ass, the other under her armpits, and I lift her.

She squeals as I hold her against my chest.

Her arms go around my neck.

Her eyes fix on mine.

She has that same goofy look I do.

The *I can't fucking believe my luck you're mine* look.

I can't.

I'm not sure I ever will.

Or that I want to.

This is a cozy room. It's only a few steps to the bed. I lean over to set Lacey down on her back.

She stares up at me with all the affection in the world. "Is that all we're doing tonight? Lying here?"

"You don't have to bait me. You've already sealed the deal." I motion to my ring finger.

"What if you stop putting out now that we're married."

"You'll divorce me."

"True." She laughs, but there's an undercurrent in it. Her ex rejected her for years. She still has those wounds, buried deep.

"I won't." I sit on the bed, push her dress to her ankles, bring her leg into my lap. "I go out of my mind over how much I want you."

"Still?"

"Always." Slowly, I unbuckle her wedge sandal and peel it off her foot. I drag my fingertips over her ankle, up her leg, to her other leg, down her ankle. I peel off the other shoe.

"You promise?"

"Cross my heart and hope to die."

"Do you really?"

I stare into her dark eyes. "I do, baby. I do."

Her shoulders soften. Her lips curl into a smile. Fuck, she always looks gorgeous, but with her hair in that fancy style, and her makeup bringing out her features, and that dress...

"You look so fucking beautiful, baby." I lean down to take her hand and pull her to a seated position. "I almost hate to ask you to lose the dress."

"You do?"

I nod. I really do. She looks like an angel. My angel.

But I need her naked.

I need all of her flesh against all of mine.

She turns so I can get her zipper.

I trace its line back up her back.

She stands up, lets her dress fall off her hips, and steps out of it.

She's wearing this lacy white bra and a matching thong. The set is sheer. It does nothing to hide her hard nipples.

Or her wet cunt.

Fuck, it's perfect.

Sweet, innocent, lacy.

It's irresistible, just like her.

She grabs me by the tie and pulls me to my feet. "Your turn to get naked."

"Whatever my wife wants."

Her smile spreads over her cheeks. "Say it again."

I undo my tie and toss it aside. "Whatever my wife wants."

She pushes my suit jacket off my shoulders. "I want my husband naked."

"I want my wife coming on my face."

She undoes my top button. The next. The next. "I

want my husband in my mouth." She gets the last button and slides the shirt off my shoulders.

"You know what that means?"

Her teeth sink into her lower lip. She nods. "It means you need to get naked faster."

"It's called a seduction."

She wiggles her left ring finger. "You've sealed the deal too."

"But I live to torture you."

"You do." She presses her palm against my hard-on, over my slacks. "Fuck, Mal… Why do you look so good in a suit?"

"I look good in everything."

She smiles. "Or nothing."

"Best in nothing."

"True." She undoes my belt and tosses it aside. Then she's rubbing me over my slacks. "But you also look damn good in that suit." She undoes the button and zipper and slides my pants off my hips. "Or jeans."

"Just jeans?"

"Of course."

"How about this?" I kick off my dress shoes and step out of my pants. I'm in boxers and dress socks.

"Oh, baby. This might be my new favorite." She wraps her arms around my waist and pulls me into a deep kiss.

Her hands go to my hair.

Mine go to her waist.

I pull her onto the bed.

Peel off my socks.

She pushes my boxers to my knees.

I rub her over her sheer bra.

She groans into my mouth as I press the soft fabric against her nipples.

She plants her palms against my shoulders and climbs on top of me. Her leg swings over my hip.

She straddles me, rubbing me as I rub her.

Fuck, the friction of her sheer panties against my cock. That lingerie is perfect but it's between me and her skin.

I need it gone.

I undo her bra and toss it aside.

Then I slide her panties off her ankles.

She leans down to press her lips to mine.

She kisses me hard and deep. Like she's claiming me. She is. She has. I'm all hers already, but I always find more of myself to give her. More love, more trust, more affection.

I want her to have it all.

And I want all of hers.

Lacey drags her lips over my cheek, my chin, my chest. She swings her body around, bringing her cunt to my mouth, kissing her way down my torso.

I dig my fingers into her hips and bring her to my lips.

I tease her with the lightest lick imaginable.

Her thighs shudder as she groans.

She nips at the skin just below my belly button.

I tease her again.

Again.

Again.

She flicks her tongue against my cock.

Again.

Again.

She teases me as expertly as I tease her.

When I can't take it anymore, I bring my mouth to her clit, and I lick her just how she needs me.

And she takes me into her mouth.

Fuck, that feels good.

I hold her in place as I work her. She groans and shakes and presses her thighs against my cheeks.

When I lick her harder, she sucks on me harder.

It's fucking thrilling, the feeling of giving her pleasure as she's giving it to me.

She's too fucking good at this.

I need her coming first.

Because I need to come inside her.

I press my lips against her thigh. "On your back, baby."

She releases me and drags her lips along my thigh, across my hip, over my torso.

I flip her over so she's on her back.

I plant myself between her thighs and pin her legs to the bed.

And I lick her.

Soft. Hard. Slow. Fast. Circles. Zigzags. Back and forth. Left to right. Up and down.

I lick her until she's tugging at my hair.

Until her groans are echoing around the room.

"Mal." She bucks against my mouth. "Please. Fuck."

A few more flicks of my tongue and she's there. She groans my name again and again as she comes.

I watch the pleasure spread over her face. Her lips part with a sigh. Her eyelids press together.

Her cheeks flush.

Her chest heaves.

Fuck, she looks beautiful coming.

It's my favorite sight in the entire fucking world.

My wife coming.

It's fucking romantic.

She blinks her eyes open and looks up at me. Her hands go to my shoulders. She wrestles me onto the bed, on my back.

And she straddles me, bringing her body onto mine.

I stare up at her.

She stares down at me.

Slowly, she lowers herself onto me.

Fuck, that feels good.

I stare into Lacey's eyes as she takes me.

She swivels her hips in that perfect figure eight.

I bring my hands to her chest and play with her nipples.

She presses her palms into my shoulders, rocking her hips, driving me out of my fucking mind.

I get lost in the feel of her skin, the sounds of her groans, the divine friction of her around me.

Pleasure spreads out through my body.

I bring one hand to her head and pull her closer.

And kiss her harder.

She kisses back, pressing her chest against mine, groaning against my lips.

Torturing me with those perfect figure eights.

We stay locked like that, kissing, touching, fucking, until she's there.

She tugs at my hair.

Her groans vibrate down my neck.

Her cunt pulses around me.

Then I'm there, holding her closer.

Kissing her hard.

Digging my fingers into the flesh of her ass.

Once I spill every drop, I wrap my arms around her and I bring her next to me.

Lacey collapses onto my chest.

Her palm presses against my stomach.

Her head rests against my shoulder.

We hold each other as we catch our breath.

She looks up at me. "That was two." She motions to

the clock. It's 11:40 p.m. "You have twenty minutes to hit five."

"You think I'm not good for it?"

She shrugs, coy. "Who knows?"

"You really want to come until you pass out?"

She nods.

"I'm going to test you on that."

She presses her lips to mine. "Perfect."

Piper and Kit

Chapter Thirty-Three

PIPER

I steal the spoon from Kit and take a taste.

The broth is sweet, floral perfection.

Warm.

Salty.

Rich.

And it's ours.

We made it. Just the two of us, a dozen ingredients, and a recipe.

It's a long recipe. It takes forever.

But we're not exactly strangers to slow.

"How is it?" Kit's deep voice pulls me from my thoughts. His soft lips press into a smile. It lights up his dark eyes.

God, those eyes are full of love, affection, raw desire…

Why are we making pho broth?

Why are we in the kitchen?

Why are we talking at all?

"You try it." I scoop a bit of broth and bring the spoon to his lips.

His eyes lock with mine. He stares back at me as he takes a taste.

His tongue slides over his lips.

His eyes scream *I'd rather have my mouth on you.*

"Perfect." There's pride in his voice. "You have a new skill for your résumé, baby."

My laugh eases the tension in my chest. "How is this going to help me get acting gigs?"

"There may be one other person in the universe who craves pho as much as you do."

"Doubtful."

"Almost as much then."

I take another taste of the broth. It really is perfect.

Kit is giving me credit, but we made it together.

We can do anything together.

Anything except actually get married.

I know. I'm impatient. I'm the one who asked him to wait until I graduated from college.

But now that I only have a week of classes left, and neither one of us is setting a date, it's starting to feel like I'm going to wait forever.

It's not that I doubt he loves me.

Or that he's committed.

It's just… I want things to be official.

Soon.

I want to stand at the altar with the man I love and say *I do.*

Kit's eyes fix on mine. He stares at me like he's staring into my soul.

He has this way of examining me that makes me feel like the most fascinating person in the world.

Like he wants to know every little thought in my head.

"Talk to me." Kit's voice is even, soft. He wants in my head.

I can't blame him. I certainly want in his head.

Or to shake him and ask him what the hell he's waiting for.

But I'm pretty sure that's not going to work.

Still… I need to say something.

We've been engaged for two and a half years now.

That's an eternity.

I stare back into Kit's dark eyes. God, his eyes are beautiful. All of him is beautiful. "School's almost over."

He nods. His expression stays inscrutable. "Excited?"

"More nervous. I still need to get through finals."

"You'll ace them."

"Ace them?"

His smile spreads over his cheeks. "Yeah, you work hard. You should give yourself credit."

"There's credit and there's being delusional."

"Call me delusional."

"You really think I'm going to get an A in chemistry?"

"Is it that hard to believe?"

Yes. Does he really think it's possible? I stare back at him as I nod. "It's the least likely thing to happen in the history of the universe."

"The history of the universe?"

"Yes."

"That's what, a few billion years?"

"If I knew that, I'd be more confident about my chemistry grade."

"Isn't that physics?"

"You really think I know the answer to that?"

He lets out a deep, sexy chuckle. It lights up his dark eyes.

God, his eyes are bright and they're focused on me.

He's happy.

To be with me.

To tease me.

To do absolutely nothing important with me.

This is my favorite time of day.

This is my favorite time, period.

My fiancé and I, doing nothing of particular importance.

But it would be better if it was my husband and me.

Ahem. "I'll be happy with a C. Really. As long as I graduate, and never need to use math again, I'll be happy."

"You'll need to use math at some point in your life."

"You're no fun."

He nods. "I try."

"Do you?"

"Why do you think I was so pedantic about the recipe?"

"Because you're bossy."

He smiles.

"You fucked up. I had a lot of fun." My teeth sink into my lower lip. Teasing him makes me warm everywhere. God, it really is heaven just being in the same place as he is.

"You're breaking my heart."

"Truth hurts sometimes." It's a struggle to keep up my poker face. Thank God, I've been studying acting for the last four years. Thank God, I've been spending my summers going up for auditions and doing small roles in films.

I went full-throttle this year. Spent most of my free time working on indie features and student films.

I even applied for big roles. Real roles. Roles that could actually launch a career.

I got callbacks for half of them.

And two are still up in the air.

I might be the lead in a feature.

The lead.

In a feature.

It's hard to believe.

Harder than an A in chemistry,

I run my fingers through his dark hair. "I hate to be the one to tell you this, but you're the most fun person I know."

"How could you say that?" he teases.

My lips curl into a smile. I can't keep up a poker face. I can't keep thinking about all the things I don't have, not when Kit's teasing me.

Not when he's staring at me like he's desperate to rip my clothes off.

I stare back into his dark eyes. "I'll keep it our secret."

"You're too good to me, baby."

"I know."

He smiles.

I can't help but smile back. I can't help but slide my arm around his neck.

And press my lips to his.

He tastes good.

Salty.

Sweet.

Mine.

My tongue slides into his mouth.

His hands dig into my hips.

He pulls my body against his.

God, he feels good. It's been too long. He's been here for a while, but I've been busy. And too stressed about finals and auditions to really *enjoy* our time together.

I tug at his hair and I kiss him harder.

He pushes my dress up my thigh, over my ass. His fingers brush the edges of my panties.

Yes. Please. Now.

I arch my back, pressing my crotch against his.

He's hard.

And I want that.

Now.

I grab his t-shirt and tug it over his head. My palm presses against his chest.

God, his skin feels good against my palm.

I shimmy my panties to my ankles and kick them off.

My breath catches in my throat as I turn, and press my ass against his crotch.

He presses his palm against my pelvis. Drags his lips over my cheek and down my neck. "Fuck, I've been dreaming about you coming on my hand."

I nod.

"I need you so much, baby. You drive me out of my fucking mind. You know that?"

I nod. He drives me out of my mind too.

Kit draws small circles over my skin with his fingertips. The touch is light, soft. Unbearably light. Unbearably soft.

I'm already at his mercy.

But I like it.

I arch my back, rubbing my ass against him.

Reveling in the feeling of his hard-on.

All that denim in the way.

I hate fabric. I hate clothes. I hate everything in the way of our bodies joining.

Like that noise.

That familiar noise.

A song.

Shit. That's my cell phone.

And that's the ring tone I sent for…

Oh my God.

Oh my fucking God.

"That's… that might be. I have to get that." Now,

where the hell is my phone? I move toward the sound of the ringing.

There.

It's sitting on the couch.

It's flashing. *Incoming call from Nexie Jones.*

There's no time to panic. I suck a deep breath through my teeth, reach for the phone, answer the call, bring the speaker to my ears.

Okay.

I'm calm.

I'm handling this.

I'm not going to freak out, no matter what the news is.

Grace.

I have grace.

"Hello." My exhale is heavy.

"Piper, hey." Nexie's voice is bright. Like this is good news. "Is this a good time?"

"Yes." If it's good news. If not…

God, I hope it's good news.

"We've been thinking a lot about the role of Elizabeth. And we can't see anyone but you."

My chest gets light. My stomach too. They can't see anyone but me.

"We want you. I wish I could offer you more money, but our budget is tight. And our timeline is fast. We just lost our August dates. We're going to need to start in two weeks."

"Two weeks?" That's a week after I finish school. That doesn't leave any time at all.

"It's a thirty-day shoot. I won't lie. We'll be working six days a week. Seven if we're not keeping pace. And the days will be long. Exhausting. We'll be in Toronto, so it won't be too hot. But it will be difficult. And you'll have to be there twenty-four seven. You're going to be in every scene."

I'm going to be in every scene.

Because I'm the lead.

There's no way I can turn this down. Even if it's going to be as difficult as it is amazing.

Even if it's going to take me away from Kit for the next month.

For the month I have him here.

Dangerous Noise is doing another one of those summer tours in Europe.

I'll be shooting through July.

He'll leave for Europe halfway through the shoot.

Where will we have time for us?

To just hang out, much less get married?

I take a deep breath and exhale slowly.

I want this part. But if I really do want us to make this official, I have to remember I'm half a team.

I have to at least run it by him.

"I want it, Nixie. Really. I have to check with my agent." It's an easier excuse than *I better make sure it won't further scare off my fiancé from making this official.*

"Good. I'm willing to move heaven and earth to get you in this film, Piper. If you have doubts, let me know. I'll make it work."

"Sure."

"I've got to make some other calls. Let me know by the end of the week. Okay?"

"I have finals." But it's not like I'm going to say no. Nixie's debut feature was a Sundance darling. And the script for this is amazeballs. It's sure to hit even harder at the festival. Which means it will launch my career. "But okay. By Friday."

"Good luck. I'll hear from you soon."

"You too."

She hangs up the phone.

Kit moves toward me. He wraps his arms around my waist. "That sounded like good news, baby."

I nod. "I got the part."

"Fuck." He leans in to press his lips to mine. "You deserve it. You nailed that scene."

I made him run lines with me for about a million years. I did nail the scene.

God, I really want this.

But—"Filming starts in two weeks and goes through July. I won't see you."

"We'll figure it out."

"Yeah, but… we kept saying." I swallow hard. My thumb traces the outline of my engagement ring. "We kept saying the summer after I graduate."

He arches a brow.

"That we'd get married the summer after I graduate."

He nods. "We can do that later."

"Yeah, but… well… Can we?"

He stares back at me.

"Do you actually want to get married?"

Chapter Thirty-Four

KIT

Of course I want to marry Piper.

What kind of question is that?

I stare back into my fiancée's expressive blue eyes.

They're filled with hurt.

Hurt I can't fix.

I press my palm against her lower back to pull her closer.

She lets out a soft sigh, but none of the frustration in her expression eases.

"I want to marry you." I draw circles over her lower back with my fingertips. "I want you forever."

Only, there's no conviction in my voice.

That doesn't make any sense.

I do want to marry Piper.

I do want her forever.

Every single piece of her.

So why is there this tension in my chest?

Why do I suddenly feel like a liar?

"You need to take this gig, baby. You've been talking

about it nonstop." Whatever fucked up shit is going on in my head, she's not going to throw away an opportunity for me. Not one she wants this badly. "We'll figure the rest out."

"When?" She presses her lips together. "We won't get to really be together until August."

"You can come to Europe with us. You know that."

"I know." Her eyes go to the ground. She doesn't buy this.

I don't buy it either.

Only I don't get why.

Everything I'm saying is true.

Piper is my beacon of hope.

My silver lining.

My fucking sun.

Every cheesy metaphor in the world—it applies to her. To what she does to me.

"We have time." There's no reason why we need to get married this summer.

But there's no reason why we shouldn't.

The thought of waking up next to her for the next sixty years makes my heart soar.

But my stomach is sinking like a stone.

Something isn't adding up.

"Okay." She presses her palm against my stomach. "I do want that job. I mean, did you see Nixie's first feature? It was amazing. She'll probably sweep Sundance with this one."

"You'll clinch it for her."

Piper smiles. "Maybe. I've never had a role this big."

"You've been lead in a dozen plays in the last three years."

"Half a dozen."

"I've barely seen you all year."

She nods. "That's true." Her expression softens. "I'm sick of missing you."

"Where are you shooting?"

"Toronto."

"I can be in Toronto."

"Really?" Her eyes light up. "We're not in the city. We're outside the city. In a shitty motel."

I chuckle. "You think I got this far objecting to shitty motels?"

"Maybe you're past that. Too famous for anything less than three stars."

"Am I?"

"You're an egomaniac."

"Sounds like me."

"I know. It's ridiculous. Why do I put up with you?" Her smile lights up her eyes.

She's teasing, but I feel the words in my gut.

Why does she put up with me?

She could find a guy who isn't a fuck up.

Who isn't at risk of slipping.

Who has his head on straight.

But she doesn't.

She stays with me.

Sometimes… a lot of the time…

No, I never doubt that Piper loves me. That she wants forever.

But how can I ask that of her when I'm still not sure I have a forever?

When I could easily become my mother?

God forbid, I become my father.

They're happy now. Happier, at least.

But…

"You really want to get married?" Her voice is soft. Vulnerable.

I need to choose my words carefully. I stare back into her eyes. "I want you, forever."

"Okay. But you're not exactly rushing to set a date."

"What's the rush?"

"Or offering up alternatives to this summer."

"I'm happy now. I don't feel like anything is missing." That's true. Every word of it. And it doesn't inspire any doubt or tension.

"Me too. But…"

"What do you think is missing?"

She takes my left hand and traces my ring finger.

"A man-gagement ring?"

"Haha. That's it. I need to mark you."

I bring her palm to my chest. "If you want to mark me, you can."

"Yeah?"

I nod. "But I get to mark you too."

Her lips curl into a smile. "I'm an actress."

“Somewhere people won't see it."

"I'm going to do nude scenes."

"You are?"

She nods.

"Ethan know about that?"

"You're more concerned about what Ethan is going to do?"

"You aren't?"

She laughs. "Fair." Her eyes meet mine. "Is that it? Is Ethan blackmailing you into delaying this."

"You wanted to wait until you graduated." I did too, but I can't exactly admit that. I need to figure out what my dysfunction is before I admit any of this shit.

"Yeah, I know, but now I don't. I guess I'm being a little bossy and demanding."

"You? Never."

She flips me off.

I grab her hand, bring it to my mouth, suck on her middle finger. "I'd like to get back to celebrating you getting this gig."

"What about?" She nods to the stove.

"It's supposed to simmer another hour."

"What about… well, if we're not getting married in June or July… Do you actually want to get married in August?"

"August is good."

"Yeah."

"What's wrong, baby?"

"You can tell me. If you don't want it. I… I'm not sure I can live with that, but I want to know."

"It's not that."

"But it's something."

"Nothing about you." I wish there was a way to convince her of that.

How do you tell your fiancée *I'm not sure about marrying you? Not because of you. Because I'm a fucking mess. Because I'm terrified of becoming my parents. Because I'm terrified of destroying you.*

But don't take it personally.

That's probably a good start.

Really.

I'm an adult.

I've been through eight million years of therapy.

I should be able to talk to the woman I love.

To have an honest conversation about my feelings.

Piper is the only person I can talk to.

But this…

I'll crush her.

I can't do that.

I ask so much of her.

I can't ask her to wait until I have my head together too.

I take her hand and pull her into the kitchen. "Let's finish prepping this."

"Okay." She moves to the fridge and pulls out ingredients one by one.

Lime. Garlic. Ginger. Cilantro.

She assembles everything on a cutting board and starts chopping cilantro.

She's turned away from me. Facing the other direction. But it's all over her posture.

Her shoulders are slumped. Her legs are shaky. Her grip is too tight.

Fuck, I'm hurting her again.

And I can't do shit about it.

Not if I want to be honest.

She sets up the cilantro in a bowl. Slices two limes into quarters. Brings one to her lips and sucks it dry.

"This recipe is turning out well." She tosses the peel into the trash.

I nod. "It is."

"It took forever. But it was worth it." She turns to me. Her eyes bore into mine. "I can be patient. I can wait for things. But I need to know that it's what you want too."

"Piper—"

"We don't need to get married this summer. But I need to know it's what you want."

"It is." It should be. I love Piper with every fiber of my being. I was fucking giddy when she said yes to my proposal. I do want forever with her.

"Then let's set a date. At least an approximate one."

"This minute?"

"Why not?"

"Okay." It's fair enough. "I'll pull up our schedule." I

find my phone on the coffee table and open up the band's calendar. "We have two weekends in August. Most of September. All of December, save that Christmas show."

"Okay."

"You still want to do the beach?"

Her smile is bright. Her voice too. "You remember?"

"You look at Lacey and Mal's wedding pictures every day."

"They're gorgeous."

"We could do it at that same spot on Malibu."

"We need to do our own thing."

"You still want to do Hawaii?"

Her eyes go wide. "Would I like to marry you in paradise? Is that really your question?"

I nod.

"That's a stupid question."

"It would be easier here. Friends are here. Family."

She sticks out her tongue. "I hope you mean Mal and Ethan."

"Your dad."

"No."

There's no arguing that point with her. I learned that lesson the hard way. "My parents."

"Are loaded and can fly anywhere."

"Still. A destination wedding is asking a lot of people. Bella and Joel have a two-month-old."

"That's true… We can run it by them."

"Yeah."

She looks up at me and arches a brow. "Do you somehow object to marriage in paradise?"

I guess I do. But it's not the tropical beaches that get my shoulders up at my ears.

Not that I really do beaches.

I certainly don't mind hitting the beach with Piper, watching her run around the waves in a tiny bikini.

But I'm not naturally a beach person.

It's sandy and sticky and messy. Why deal with that shit when there's air conditioning and private pools?

"The location doesn't matter to me." Every word of that is true.

"Okay. Hawaii is perfect. We can do December. Early December. Or… we could do it sooner. September. Or even next week."

"You really want that?"

"I don't know. I have my dress."

She does. She went crazy looking at dresses when she was helping Lacey pick hers out. She absolutely had to have this fancy silk dress—she describes it that way. I've never seen it. Tradition and shit.

Supposedly, it's perfection.

And necessary, in case we decide to do something last minute, the way Mal and Lacey did.

"If we're doing Hawaii, we can book a package. We won't need to spend a lot of time planning." I stare back into her eyes. "We can do it whenever you want."

She nods, but there's something in her expression—

She doesn't buy what I'm saying.

I try to muster up the enthusiasm to sell it better, but it won't come.

My brain can't seem to dissociate marriage from my parents.

And there's no fucking way I'll let us get like them.

I'd rather lose her than have her like that.

Chapter Thirty-Five

PIPER

Violet pulls me into a hug. "Did you get it? Tell me you got it."

My voice is meek. I can't seem to summon up any enthusiasm. "I did."

She squeals and claps her hands together. "I'm so proud of you. Oh my God. We have to celebrate. Cupcakes?"

Mmmm. Sugar. "Okay."

"Coffee first?"

"Yes, please."

"You have a problem," she teases.

I laugh. It's a full, hearty laugh. It makes me forget I'm here because something is fucked between me and Kit.

I follow her inside the apartment. It's as beautiful as always. Sleek. Clean. All black and purple and crimson.

Most of it is pure Violet. But there are touches of Ethan. The clock on the wall with guitars for numbers. The framed prints of musicians. The bookshelf overflowing with old CDs.

Her voice is soft. That classic Violet *are you okay* tone.

"You want fresh coffee or you okay with the half a pot that's been warming all day? Ethan always brews too much."

"That's fine." There's no problem coffee can't help.

Especially coffee this creamy and sweet and rich.

My mouth is already watering.

Violet leads me into the kitchen. She fills an electric kettle with water and turns it on.

I fix a cup of coffee with extra honey and lots of almond milk

Ethan drinks his coffee black and Violet is all almond milk, all the time.

They don't have any milk in the fridge.

But I'm used to that.

I'm used to them being together.

They belong together. And they're both sure. They've both been sure for a long time.

Why can't I… Why can't we…

"You're in the clouds today." Violet turns to me. Her expression is soft. Caring. "Are you okay?"

I'm tempted to say yes. It's habit. If it was anyone else, I would.

But Violet is the one person I trust.

"No. But coffee first." Okay, I do have a problem. But I need comfort.

Violet laughs. "Always coffee first. I know you that well."

I can't help but smile. Even if she's making fun of me.

I take a long sip. The warm drink soothes something deep inside me.

But it isn't making this any easier.

If Kit isn't sure, if he doesn't want to marry me…

I don't like my options.

The kettle whistles. Violet pulls it off its stand and fixes a cup of green tea. She nods to the table. "Shall we?"

I nod. "Where is Ethan?"

"Same place as always."

"Well, he's clearly not between your legs. So I'm not sure what you mean.

Violet blushes. "Okay, his third favorite place."

His second favorite place is with his guitar. So third favorite must be–"The gym?"

Violet nods. "He's due back in about half an hour. We can go somewhere else to talk if you want."

Maybe. I trust my brother, but he has a temper. Especially when it comes to men disappointing his baby sister. "Here is good for now."

"What's wrong, Piper? I can't remember the last time I saw you this defeated."

Is it really that bad? "I'm excited about the gig. It's going to be a lot of work, but it's a great opportunity. And the part is amazing. But it starts in two weeks. And it's through July. The next tour starts in July. Kit volunteered to go to Toronto with me. We'll get time together. But…"

"But?"

"I thought we'd get married this summer. We talked about it. We didn't have a plan, but we'd talked about it."

She nods.

"But when I talked about it." I pull my arm over my chest. It's not enough comfort. "He wasn't excited. No, it's more than that. He doesn't want to."

"Did he say that?"

"It was in his voice. In his eyes. Those dark eyes… they always betray his true feelings."

"Hmm." Violet's green eyes fix on me. She's studying me. Figuring out how to phrase this best.

Is it that awful?

Her voice is even. Matter of fact. "Guys aren't always big on commitment."

"You really think it's something that cliché?"

"No. He seems so happy to be with you. Happier than he's ever been."

"He is." That's why it doesn't make any sense.

"You're young. Do you really need to be married?"

"No. I can wait. But not if... Not if he's biding his time."

"Hmm." Violet tilts her head to one side. Her eyes get contemplative. "You know your relationship better than I do, but I can't see that. He looks at you like you're the stars in his sky."

"Yeah..."

I take another sip of my coffee. It's still sweet, creamy perfection but it isn't easing this. It isn't offering any insight.

Violet takes a long sip of her tea. She stares at the green liquid for a long moment then her eyes are on me. "Most people get cold feet. Most people need to think hard before they're sure they're going to legally bind themselves to someone for the rest of their life."

It makes sense. Marriage is a big deal. A binding legal contract. A meaningful symbol. A hell of an expensive day.

But—"I think it's more than that. It was in his eyes. In his posture. He doesn't want to marry me."

"Would that be the worst thing in the world?"

Of course it would. How am I supposed to deal with my fiancé not wanting to marry me?

Not wanting forever with me?

Not sure he wants to be with me?

"I *can* wait." Really, I can. "But how can he not be sure after three years?"

"Some people are never sure."

Maybe.

"It may not be about you."

"But it is. Even if it's about him. He's not talking to me. He's not sharing this with me. He's locking me out."

"You're right. There's no excuse for that. But..." Violet looks me in the eyes. "You're lucky you never hated yourself."

"You really think Kit hates himself?"

"A part of him, yeah." Her voice gets contemplative. "I blamed myself for what happened to Asher. I thought I didn't deserve to be happy. That I didn't deserve help. But I couldn't articulate those thoughts. It was like I was folding into this little box and throwing away the key... it felt like anything else was too hard."

"I'm sorry you went through that."

"I locked Ethan out, but it wasn't because of him. It was me... Maybe Kit can't help it."

I bit my lip.

She might be right.

I can give him some leeway.

But I can't live like this forever.

I can't constantly wonder what he's thinking and why he's locking me out, again. Not after three years.

Not with a rock on my ring finger.

Violet shouldn't know my fiancé better than I do.

She looks at me carefully, like she's not sure I'll take this well. "He's been sober for years, hasn't he?"

I nod. It's been three years now. Longer.

"It's been longer for me. Since Asher. But I still have that feeling sometimes. I still worry I'm not enough. That I'm toxic."

I want to do something to make this easier. But I know Violet, and I know I can't.

This is something in her head.

Nothing can fix it.

No amount of love or care or affection.

Ethan loves her more than any man has ever loved his wife.

He showers her with affection.

They're the cutest, happiest couple I've ever seen.

If that isn't enough…

Either Strongs are somehow unable to convince their paramours of their self-worth.

Or it's straight up impossible.

"He should be talking to you," Violet says. "I won't make excuses for him. But, I'd hate to see something happen to you too. You're good together."

"We are."

"And he's super hot."

"He is."

"And the tongue piercing." She raises a brow. "You don't have to share details, but…"

"Perv."

She laughs. "I blame your brother."

"Probably."

She smiles. "You set the terms of your relationship, Piper. If you need him to be sure, that's okay. But make sure it's what you need."

I nod.

"You'll be Miss Thing soon. You'll meet other hot guys. Other sweet guys. Even other guys with tongue piercings."

I laugh.

"But none of them will be Kit."

"Nobody is."

I take another sip of my coffee. It still fails to offer insight, but thoughts are starting to come together in my head. Sort of.

I look at Violet with a smile. "How did you two get so wise?"

She smiled back. "It's the matcha."

I stick my tongue out. "Not worth it."

She laughs. "Your choice."

Definitely, my choice. That stuff is gross.

Her expression brightens. "Do you want cupcakes?"

"Do I want cupcakes? Is that really your question?"

She laughs so hard her cheeks turn red. "You want to stay for dinner after?"

I nod. "If you promise to help me run lines. Drama final is tomorrow."

"Sure."

"And, maybe you could help me study for my chem final. It's Wednesday. And I'm helpless."

"Do I want a chance to show off my science prowess?" She copies my teasing tone. "Is that really your question?"

I move closer and wrap my arms around her.

"My favorite sister-in-law."

"You too. But don't tell Lacey."

I laugh. "My lips are sealed."

Chapter Thirty-Six

KIT

My jeans are buzzing.

That quick jolt.

A text.

Piper left in a huff after lunch, said something about needing to clear her head.

I still don't have a fucking clue where she is.

And my attempts to clear my head aren't going anywhere.

I set my controller aside and pull my cell from my pocket.

Piper: I'm going to get dinner with Ethan and Violet. I'll be home late. You don't need to wait up.

Fuck, I can hear the coldness in her voice.

See all that pain in her expression.

I deserve every ounce of it.

But I…

Fuck, I still don't know how to fix this.

"Lockhart, what the hell?" Joel groans as his character knocks my character off a ledge. "Are you trying to set a new record for most losses in a row?"

Playing video games with Joel is supposed to distract me.

But it's not working.

My thoughts are screaming *you can't fix this*.

"It's not like I'm putting up a fight. Damn, I have a headache." He pushes himself off the couch, moves into the kitchen, pours a cup of coffee. "I miss sleep."

A few years ago, Joel with a headache could only mean a hangover. Maybe a one-night stand with a particularly heavy drinking woman.

Now, he's getting up at the crack of dawn to change diapers.

He's a fucking father.

It's weird.

It's weirder how much it suits him.

He runs a hand through his sandy hair. It's longer than usual. Like he's been too busy to bother to get it cut.

Fuck, I don't care about Joel's hair.

Am I really that desperate to not think about this?

"You look tired," I tease.

"You look miserable." He takes a long sip of his coffee and lets out a heavy sigh. "It's been a while since that was your norm."

"Yeah."

"Fuck, I can't possibly understand why you'd look so miserable after staring at what must be a text from your fiancée with those communication skills."

"Fuck off."

"You invited yourself here."

I know. I just… "You would have insisted."

He shrugs *fair enough*. "What did she say?"

"She's having dinner with Ethan."

"Chose her brother over you? Harsh."

"And Violet."

Joel laughs. "More reasonable."

I nod. Piper adores Violet more than… well more than anybody adores anybody else. They're like sisters without the rivalry.

"What did you do to piss her off?" he asks.

"It's not like that."

"Course. It's not that cliché nagging wife shit. But she is a Strong. They're difficult."

"Tell me something I don't know."

He nods to the carafe. "You want some."

"Yeah."

He grabs a cup from the pantry, fills it with coffee, gets out the sugar and a spoon, and leaves them on the table. "Still going with that *I need the dopamine* bullshit?"

"It's bullshit?"

"It's been three years."

"And?"

"Just admit you like it that way?"

"What's it to you?"

He shrugs. "Fuck. You need to get laid. You're more pissy than I am, and I haven't slept in three nights."

"And I'm supposed to believe it's *just* 'cause of Hermoine?"

Joel's smile is bright. "Well, I hate to brag…"

I arch a brow. "Do you?"

"Why you trying to hurt me like that, Lockhart?" He laughs. "I might have spent half the night making my wife come. I gotta say. Having a soundproof room is fucking amazing for this shit."

"Yeah?"

"Yeah, we turn the baby monitor on, then we can make as much fucking noise as we want."

"And the walls bouncing?"

He laughs. "Kids like vibration."

"Poor girl is going to be scarred when she's older."

"Better she knows sex is a beautiful part of life than that she's scared of it."

"Kids always want the opposite of what their parents have."

He arches a brow. "Do they?"

Yeah, I guess they do.

That's what this whole thing is.

Someone should stamp *mommy issues* on my forehead.

"Why *are* you so pissy?" Joel takes another sip of his coffee. Lets out another deep sigh. "You're about to have a month with Piper."

I shake my head. "She got that gig. She'll be, well, we'll be in Toronto most of July."

"And you hate our neighbors to the north?"

"No."

"Hate Tim Horton's?"

I shrug.

"You want to be pissy, be pissy." He nods to my coffee. "But I've got shit to do today."

"Your wife?"

"Of course."

I stir sugar into my coffee and take a long sip. It's good. Sweet. Rich. Warm.

But it's not soothing.

It's not lessening my frustration.

"Are you two good?" Joel asks.

"Sort of."

"Sort of?" His face screws in frustration. "What the fuck do you mean *sort of*? That girl is crazy about you."

"Yeah."

"And?" He stares at me like I'm crazy.

Maybe I am.

"We're not on the road with ten hours to go until the next stop. Spit it out."

It's a fair point.

Joel nods to the TV. "Or we can play another round."

Fuck.

I'm here to say this.

It's just…

I don't want to hear Joel's response. I've got a feeling I won't like it.

"She thinks I don't want to marry her." I take a sip from my coffee like I'm relaying an argument that doesn't have the potential to end our relationship.

"Well, yeah." Joel's voice is utterly matter of fact.

"Well, yeah?"

"You've been engaged two and a half years."

"And?"

"And you haven't set a date. You always say *after she graduates*, but I don't see you making plans now that she's about to graduate."

"Yeah."

"Facts seem pretty clear."

They do.

"Don't tell me it's some bullshit about not wanting to settle down."

"It's not."

"Good." He takes another long sip. Lets out another heavy sigh. "You're settled." Joel tops off his coffee. "It's over. Your hers."

"I know."

"And?"

"We can't all be sure in six hours."

"Fuck." He sets his mug on the counter. Shakes his head. "It is that bullshit. Damn, Kit. You're better than that."

"It's not."

Joel mutters under his breath. "Sounds like it."

It does. But it's not. I try to find an explanation at the bottom of my mug, but it doesn't come.

Shit. I guess I better try to string a few words together.

"I've seen my dad with a dozen different women," I say. "And he tried to hide his affairs."

"Barely." Joel scoffs.

"Still. Must have been two dozen. And that's only over the five or six years where I was paying attention."

"And you were high as a kite half that time." Hurt seeps into his voice. He's still not over me keeping that from him.

He's never going to get over it.

But he's still my closest friend.

He still trusts me with his life.

That means something.

"I saw what it did to my mom." It destroyed her.

"You're not Keith."

"Still…"

Joel's expression gets dead serious. "You want to fuck other women?"

"No."

"Then what's the problem?"

"You think he was already desperate to stray when they got married?"

"This is bullshit, Lockhart. You've been with her three years. If you were gonna get the itch, you would have. And who fucking cares if you do? Put on some porn. Do a little role play. Make a fucking effort to keep things interesting."

"You're the expert on marriage now?"

Joel holds up his left ring finger. "Fuck yeah. Ask Bella when she gets home. I ace this shit."

He does. He's a great husband. A great father.

"When does she get back?" Joel grabs his cell and taps the screen a few times. His expression gets dreamy. "On her way back." He slides his phone into his jeans and looks to me. "You gonna stay for dinner?"

"I don't want to get in your way."

Joel raises a brow. "Still with that shit?"

"What shit?"

"You think I'd invite you if I didn't want you here?"

"Maybe. I'm pretty pathetic at the moment."

He laughs. "True. But I don't let shit get in the way of my two favorite girls unless it matters to me."

"Good to know I'm shit that matters to you."

He nods. "If it's not bull about you wanting to spread your seed—"

I cringe. "Never say that again."

He waves me away. "Then what is it?"

I press my lips together.

I fucking know the answer to this.

I just don't want to say it.

"Well?" Joel taps his coffee cup, impatient. "Some of us are used to the attention spans of two month olds."

"Is that different than normal for you?"

"Cute. Like you don't desperately need my help."

"I…"

"Yeah."

"My mom slipped so many times."

Joel's eyes flare with understanding. "You think you will?"

"Everyone does."

"Not Miles."

"Yeah. I guess."

"Not you. Not in three years."

"Yeah."

"He's got what? Six? Fuck, a lot. I don't know. You

should talk to him. He might have more patience for this moody, introspective, *I need your help but I won't talk to you* bullshit."

"Will he?" I arch a brow.

Joel shrugs. "Anything is possible."

"True."

"Is this 'cause your mom relapsed last year?"

"Maybe." That doesn't help.

"You're not your parents." Joel presses his ass against the kitchen counter. "But I get it. Your DNA is half philanderer, half junkie. It's hard to think you're husband material like that."

I nod.

"Hard to think you can ask someone as sweet as Piper to stick around."

"Yeah."

"But get over yourself. Figure out what it will take. Therapy. A fucking intervention. I don't know. Piper deserves better than your pity party."

"I fucking know that."

"Then why aren't you talking to her?"

The man has a point.

"You're a good guy, Kit. A good friend. A good boyfriend, as far as I can tell. You'll be a good husband."

"Thanks."

"If you get over this *woe is me* bullshit. How the fuck do you think she feels, you locking her out?"

Like shit, probably.

"You hurt, yeah. You've been through a lot of shit. You deserve a little leeway. But you're not the only person in the universe with problems. She hurts too."

"When did you get all insightful?"

He flashes his wedding ring. "I told you. I fucking ace this shit."

I have to chuckle. It's practically poetic.

Pure Joel.

There are footsteps outside the apartment. And voices. Bella's laugh. And another woman.

And a man.

"Oh fuck." Joel runs a hand through his hair. "I swear. It's every fucking day." He looks to me. "Just be polite."

"*You* are telling *me* to be polite."

He nods.

"Kids do change a person."

He flips me off.

The door pushes open. Bella steps inside. She's cradling Hermoine in her arms.

Poor kid is going to be mocked endlessly for that name.

They're two peas in a pod. They're practically in matching outfits. Bella is wearing a snug white blouse pink skirt combo. Hermoine is in a dress with a similar hue.

Only she's got tiny pink Converse on her feet.

She's half Mom, half Dad.

Bella isn't wearing her exhaustion the way Joel is. She looks sharp. Like she's about to head to work.

Or like she's on her tenth Earl Grey.

"I want to play." A small child runs into the room. Not any small child. Alexandria.

And there's Kara, running in after her. "Baby girl, your cousin is sleeping. You can play after she rests." She crouches on the ground and wraps her arms around her daughter. Her dark eyes are tired but happy. She shoots Bella an apologetic smile. "Sorry. She can't help it. She's in love."

And there's Drew, holding their other daughter, Margaret. She's still tiny.

Fuck, he looks so happy.

It's weird.

Drew was part of the original Dangerous Noise line up a long, long time ago. Back then, he was a moody asshole who made me look well adjusted.

And now… he's happy.

"I've got her." Drew crouches next to his wife and sets his daughter down. She crawls over to her sister and tugs at her skirt. "You going to play nice with Hermoine or are you going home with us?"

Alexandria pouts but nods.

"You gonna take care of your sister?" he asks.

Again, Alexandria pouts but nods.

"Good." Drew smiles as he looks to Bella. "You sure you don't mind?"

She nods. "Positive. I need to convince Joel one kid is all we can handle."

Kara smiles. "Two is easier. Really."

"Can I quote you on that?" Drew asks.

Kara shakes her head. "We better hurry. Margaret gets c-r-a-n-k-y fast when we leave her alone and I'm starving." She blows Bella a kiss. "Thank you forever."

"Sure." Bella nods goodbye to the happy couple.

Kara waves hello to me. "Sorry. I'd love to talk, but—"

"You're starving?" I offer.

"You buy that?" Joel laughs. "I think it's more s-e-x."

Kara blushes.

Drew shrugs.

He's happy.

Used to be the two of us were toe-to-toe in the moodiest mother fucker competition.

I wouldn't have wished a marriage to Drew on my worst enemy.

But he's smiling.

At ease.

Looking at his wife and daughters like the happiest person in the world.

They nod a final goodbye then pull the door closed.

I sink back into the couch.

Bella nods to the practice room turned nursery. "I'll put her down." She looks to Alexandria. "You want to help, Alexa?" She looks to Joel. "Can you watch Margaret?"

"Of course." Joel nods.

The kid follows Bella into the room.

Joel watches his wife wistfully.

It's about time for me to leave.

And figure out my shit.

Everybody else is moving on. Growing up.

And I'm asking the woman I love—

I'm not asking her shit. I'm not even talking to her.

I need to fix that.

Chapter Thirty-Seven

KIT

It's past midnight when the bedroom door creaks open.

Soft yellow light surrounds Piper in an angelic glow.

It's accurate.

She didn't save me. Not exactly.

I'm not saved.

But she…

Wanting to be the guy she thinks I am, wanting to prove I'm worth all her love and affection…

That's all the motivation in the world.

I turn toward her as she moves into the room. Her steps are quiet, soft. She's trying not to wake me.

"Hey." It's not exactly poetry, but it's all I've got. I still can't explain this. Not exactly.

"Hey." There's heaviness in her voice.

I'm still hurting her.

No matter what happens, I'm always going to be hurting her. I'm never going to be able to articulate my thoughts the way Mal does.

I can't write a song to save my life.

I can't use words to explain this.

But maybe…

"You coming to bed?" My voice is even. I'm not sure how I manage it. I'm going to tear at the seams if I can't figure this out.

She shimmies out of her jeans and leaves them on the floor. "Yeah. I already brushed my teeth."

I pull the covers back and pat the spot next to me.

She tosses her t-shirt over her head. Throws off her bra. Kicks off her panties.

I can only see some of her. A sliver of yellow light over the curve of her chest. The outline of her hips. That blond hair. It catches every bit of light in the room.

She pulls on her pajamas, presses the door closed, moves toward the bed with soft footsteps.

Climbs in without shifting the weight on the mattress.

She's close enough I can make out all the hurt in her expression.

"You all set for your final tomorrow?" I press my palm against her lower back.

She looks up at me and nods. "Yeah. Violet and Ethan ran lines with me all night."

"You need me to wake you up in the morning?"

She shakes her head. "The final isn't until three."

"I believe in you."

Her lips curl with a half smile. "That means a lot to me."

"I do what I can."

She moves a little closer. Her fingertips graze my shoulder. My bicep. My forearm. "Kit…"

The single word says everything. How can she do that? How can she pack so much meaning into a syllable?

I slide my hand up her back, and plant it between her

shoulder blades. The feel of her skin against my palm does something to me.

Centers me.

Convinces me I'm where I belong.

I need her. There's no doubt about that.

It's more her needing me that gets me all fucked up.

I stare into her gorgeous blue eyes. "I want to explain this to you, baby. I wish I could. I will. Once I figure it out."

Her eyes go to her hand. She watches herself doodle on my skin. "I don't know."

"I do want you forever. I never doubt that. I know it's cliché shit, but this has nothing to do with you. It's me. My head is a mess. When I think about my parents' marriage, how fucked up it was…" I run my fingers through her hair until she's purring. "I'm going to figure it out."

She looks up at me. Those blue eyes fill with something I can't place.

"I don't want to lock you out." I stare back into her eyes. I don't know what to say. I don't have anything else to say. It's rare I wish I was good with words. But right now…

I'd give anything to be as obnoxiously introspective as Mal.

Or to be as effervescent and charming as Ethan or Joel.

Is everyone this fucked up or is it just me?

Piper's voice is a whisper. I can barely hear it over the air conditioning. "I don't want you to lock me out either."

"You are the sun in my sky, Piper. You know that?"

"Really?"

I nod. "You're my silver lining. All that cheesy shit. I don't know what I'd do without you.

She nods. "I don't know what I'd do without you, either. You're not the only person who struggles with stuff. You know that?"

"Yeah. This shit… It gets me stuck in my head. Makes me selfish. I hate doing that to you."

"I don't want to lose you."

"You won't. I love you so much, baby."

"But… You still don't want to marry me?"

"No. I do. It's just all this shit is tangled in my brain. I can't say the word *wife* without thinking of my mom, staring out the window with a vacant expression, high as a kite. I can't stand the thought of that happening to you. To us. I *know* it won't. But I can't stop feeling it."

"I… I kind of understand. Violet helped explain it. But, Kit—"

"Yeah?"

"I don't want to go to Violet every time I'm not sure what you're thinking. I know it's not easy for you. It's not easy for me either. But I need you to talk to me."

I nod. "It's ugly."

"That's okay. We all think ugly stuff sometimes."

"I keep hearing my dad's voice. He was so matter of fact about all guys getting bored. All guys cheating."

"Do you… Do you think about other women?"

"No. Never."

"Never? Not even a little?" She arches a brow, incredulous.

"You have something to confess?" I try to keep my voice light, but it doesn't land. I never doubt Piper's faithfulness, but sometimes… Sometimes I wonder if she is on the same page as me.

She's better off with someone who isn't a mess.

"I have thoughts." Her voice is light. Teasing. "Passing thoughts. Everyone does."

"Should we do some role play?"

Her cheeks flush. "No. Well, maybe. I've never really thought about that. You have something in mind?"

She's giving me a rope. A way out of this conversation.

I need to take it.

I can't explain this. Not right now.

But I need to feel close to her.

I need her skin against mine.

I need to make her feel good. However I can.

I let my lips curl into a half smile. "I can be the dirty drama teacher."

Piper scrunches her nose. "God no."

"The filthy leading man?"

"Let me hear it."

I try my best pervert actor voice. "Baby, we should get to practicing these lines. But naked. So we actually get comfortable with each other. Clothing gets in the way of getting into character."

"I can imagine someone saying that."

"I know. I'm good."

"In a bad way."

"Still good."

"True." She looked up at me as she presses her palm against my stomach. "I… This doesn't mean I'm not mad. Well, more frustrated than mad but… it doesn't mean this is okay.

I nod. It's not okay. "Means I'm irresistible."

"You really are. It's not fair."

"You're not exactly easy to resist."

"Yeah?" She slides her hand over my head. My ass. Her palm presses against my flesh. She arches her back to rock her hips against mine. "You're naked."

"Always sleep naked."

"Still." She presses her palm against my ass, pulling my body against hers.

"You're dressed."

She nods.

"We should change that."

Her nod is heavier. Needier.

"Come here." I cup the back of her head with my hand and pull her into a deep, slow kiss.

She tastes good. Like spearmint and like Piper.

Like need and love and lust.

And every bit of trust in the universe.

More than I deserve.

I have to figure this shit out. For me. For her. For us.

Losing Piper… that's not a possibility I can consider.

Even if there's a huge fucking part of me that thinks I'm selfish for keeping her.

I slide my tongue into her mouth. I hold her head against mine.

I kiss her like I'll never get a chance to kiss her again.

If I fuck this up, I won't.

My body is as eager as my heart. Blood is rushing to my cock.

I bring my hand to her ass and pull her hips against mine.

She groans into my mouth as my hard-on presses against her stomach.

Her palm plants on my side. She shifts her hips enough to wrap her hand around me.

Fuck. That feels good.

Too good.

I need to make her come first.

I tug her t-shirt over her head. Push her shorts off her hips. Drag my hand over her shoulders.

Over her chest.

I draw circles around her nipples. I rub her tender bud with my thumb.

She groans, kissing me hard, stroking me harder.

I tease her as she teases me.

It's a beautiful fucking circle of pleasure, want, need.

But it's not enough.

I need her screaming my name.

This is the one time I never doubt my ability to make her feel good.

I drag my lips over her cheek, her chin, her neck. I stop to suck on one nipple.

Softly.

Then harder.

Then hard enough she digs her hands into my hair.

"Kit," she breathes.

Her hips shift.

Her leg swings over my side. Her heel taps my lower back. That *I want you so badly I can't control my limbs* motion.

I move to her other nipple and work it every way I can. Fuck, she tastes good, and the way she tugs at my hair…

I need more of it.

All of it.

I drag my lips down her stomach. Her pelvis.

I plant a kiss on her hip bone. Then the other.

On her inner thigh.

Higher.

Higher.

She squirms. She bucks her hips. She groans my name.

I pin her thighs to the bed, holding her in place.

Right now, she's mine. And there are no fucking doubts in my head.

Or hers.

Fuck, there's not much in my head but *need Piper now*.

I move to her other leg and plant a kiss on the inside of her knee.

Slowly, I work my way up her thigh.

Higher.

She tugs at my hair.

Higher.

She fights my hands.

Higher.

She groans my name.

I drag my lips up her thigh. One more hint of torture.

There.

She lets out a low, heavy sigh as I bring my mouth to her cunt. I take my sweet time tasting every inch of her.

I'm slow.

Mercilessly slow.

She tastes so fucking good.

And the way she's groaning and squirming and tugging at my hair—

This is poetry.

This is where I belong.

If only I was this good at everything else about being in a fucking relationship.

I lick her up and down. Left and right. With circles. Tiny fucking hearts.

She tugs at my hair, that *make me come now* plea in her groans.

I tease her until I can't take it anymore.

Then I bring my tongue to her clit.

And I lick her exactly how she needs me.

That spot that always gets her off.

That perfect speed, that perfect pressure.

"Kit, fuck." She tugs at my hair. She bucks her hips against my mouth.

She digs her heels into my back.

"Fuck." She tugs harder.

Harder.

I hold her in place as she squirms against me.

As she groans my name again and again.

Then I change my stroke so my piercing is tapping her clit.

"Fuck. Don't stop." She tugs harder.

Groans louder.

I lick her again and again.

Fuck, the way her groans echo around the room—

The way she presses her thighs against my cheeks—

She's mine.

And I'm hers.

And the fucking universe is right.

With the next flick of my tongue, she comes.

She tugs at my hair, holding me in place.

I lick her through her orgasm.

Then she's tugging at my shoulders.

"Fuck me," she breathes.

I drag my lips up her torso, stopping to suck on her nipples.

I don't have the patience to tease her properly.

Not right now.

Right now, I need our bodies locked together.

Us as one.

All that cheesy shit.

I plant a kiss on her lips.

And I shift my hips, to bring our bodies into position.

My tip strains against her.

Then it's one delicious inch at a time.

Fuck.

She groans against my lips.

Tugs at my hair.

I wrap my arms around her.

I keep my body pressed against hers.

And I drive into her with steady pumps.

She lifts her hips, meeting my movements, bringing us closer.

Kissing me harder.

The universe is us.

Our groans.

Our flesh.

Our pleasure.

Nothing in the way of us connecting.

Not my hang-ups or my inability to articulate my thoughts.

Not fucking anything.

We stay like that, locked together, groaning and panting and moving together.

Until she's there, nipping at my lips as she pulses around me.

It pushes me over the edge.

With my next thrust, I come.

Pleasure spreads through my pelvis. Calm overwhelms me.

I rock through my orgasm.

I give her every drop I have.

Then I collapse next to her.

And I hold her close.

And I kiss her like she's fucking everything.

Because she is.

And I can't fuck this up.

I won't survive without her.

Chapter Thirty-Eight

KIT

You can tell a recovering addict by an excessive need for dopamine.

Sugar addiction.

Coffee habit.

Motorcycle.

I enjoy the thrill of my bike, but fuck does Miles have me beat. This place is a paradise for someone who craves steep curves, winding roads, and rushing adrenaline.

It's a strange fucking thing. My heart is pounding. My breath is catching.

My hands are steady.

If I'd arrived in a fucking car, I'd be shaking.

Asking for help, for advice, from a guy I barely know…

A guy who only talks to me 'cause neither one of us wants to hit the bars…

Not looking forward to it.

I pack my helmet in my trunk and shift out of my leather jacket. It's a hot day, blue sky, big lemon sun, but there's a beach breeze blowing over the hill.

A soft sound calls my attention. Piano music. It gets louder the closer I get to the house.

Though house isn't the right word.

This place is a mansion. A several-million-dollar mansion. It must be half a dozen bedrooms and an equal amount of baths.

Despite all the powwows I've had with the Sinful Serenade singer, I've never been to his place.

It's not like we're friends.

Don't get me wrong. I don't have anything against Miles. He's no more annoying than Joel or Ethan. He sings like he's coming, but that's no more disturbing than the way Mal sings like he's in the middle of a fuck.

It's more…

We're both sober.

That's all we have in common.

And hanging out with someone as a sort of mutual sobriety companion situation is a reminder I'm a fucking mess.

A reminder I don't want.

Fuck. I need to get out of my head here.

He was receptive to my incredibly vague texts.

It's time to stop beating around the bush.

I need help.

Advice.

The secret to how he's happily married when his past is as fucked as mine.

Maybe he's not happy.

Maybe it's all bullshit.

We're in the image selling business.

And it's not like I know the guy.

I shake it off. Yeah, Miles probably doesn't have any sort of secret. His advice is probably only as good as Google's.

But it can't hurt.

I'm not talking myself out of this.

I knock on the door.

A voice calls out. "It's open."

That doesn't sound like Miles. But it's hard to tell with the piano going.

It's a beautiful wisp of a song. Sad, but beautiful.

Composing isn't my forte, but I can appreciate something artfully put together, even when it's not my taste.

Fuck, after playing Dangerous Noise songs for the last half a dozen years, I'm not even sure what my taste is anymore. I mostly default to what Piper wants to listen to at home or in the car.

I pull open the door and step inside.

That wasn't Miles.

It's Logan.

The Wicked Beat lead singer.

I'm not sure what Logan is doing here. Don't care to find out.

Logan puts the drunk in party and the whore in manwhore. I don't begrudge the man his lifestyle. Whatever makes him happy.

But I don't want to be anywhere near that shit.

He turns to me with a nod. His light eyes are bright. His smile is wide.

It's like he doesn't have a care in the world.

Bullshit? Or is he that shallow?

Hard to say.

Ahem. This isn't my place. I need to be polite.

"Hey." I nod back. "You collaborating?"

"If you could call it that." Logan nods to Miles, sitting on the piano bench. "I'm not sure my input qualifies."

"It doesn't." Miles nods hello to me then looks back to the keys. He plays another string of notes.

It's good.

Fucking amazing, actually.

"You normally compose?" I ask Logan.

He shrugs. "I sing."

"I'm more of a ghostwriter," Miles says.

"Ask him which Top 40 songs he's written." Logan winks at Miles then turns back to me. "He lives to brag."

Miles shrugs. "When you hit number one this many times, you get bored of it."

Logan adopts Miles's breezy indifference. He runs his hand through his air. "Ugh. It's so boring, being rich, talented, and successful. What will I do with myself?"

"Strong words for someone asking for help," Miles teases.

"This shit isn't my responsibility. You think Wicked Beat keeps me around for my brains?" Logan arches a brow.

"It's not for your charming personality." Miles winks to his friend.

Logan flips him off.

Miles laughs.

"I thought I was getting Pete's help," Logan says.

"He's indisposed," Miles says.

Logan laughs. "He always is."

"The man has his priorities." Miles plays another string of notes. Something changes in his posture. He shifts into that meditative state.

The one we all know.

Even Logan.

Even if he lives to drink and fuck.

Not like I can talk.

I was there once.

"After all this time?" Logan scrunches his nose. "I don't get it. One woman for, what's it been now—"

Miles holds up his left hand and wiggles his ring finger. "You want me on your side here?"

"Still…"

"He's coming. Just later." Miles pushes himself up from the piano. He looks to me. "You want to talk privately?"

"Hey!" Logan feigns offense.

Miles nods to the piano. "See what you can do."

"Can you play?" I ask.

Logan shrugs, effortlessly casual. Or effortless about appearing effortlessly casual. "Mom made me take lessons."

Miles nods to the kitchen. It's to our right. Everything is in this giant main room. A couch and TV to our right. The piano behind it.

The steel and glass kitchen and a glass dining table is to our left. And beyond that is the backyard. A huge, gorgeous pool reflecting every bit of sunlight.

Logan takes a seat at the piano bench as I follow Miles into the kitchen.

Soft notes flow through the air. They start as nonsense, but quickly turn to something melodic.

As good as what Miles was playing.

Better even.

So Logan does know something.

That effortless party boy thing is bull.

Maybe.

I don't know with this shit anymore.

Miles nods to the fridge. "You want a drink?"

I shake my head.

"Suit yourself." He pulls out a can of green tea and pops it open. "I can put on coffee."

"Am I shaking?"

"I know the drill."

"God grant me the serenity…" I offer.

He nods. "You go to NA? AA?"

I shake my head.

"See a shrink?"

"Haven't in a while. You?"

"Ditto." He leans against the counter and gives me a long once over. His blue eyes fill with some sort of understanding.

They're softer than Piper's. Greener.

Still makes me think of her.

A million things about her.

He takes a sip of his tea and sets the can on the counter. "I like you, Kit. You're less annoying than most people I know."

"Thanks."

"I won't bullshit you. We're not exactly like this." Miles presses his first two fingers together. "I figure, if you want to talk, it's about—" Miles pulls up his sleeve and mimes injecting heroin.

"You're perceptive."

"My curse." He shrugs. "It's not all it's cracked up to be."

"You seem happy."

"I am."

"Married."

He chuckles. "Glad you noticed."

"Happily married."

"Oh." He takes another sip. Gives me another once over. His gaze stops on my left hand. "It's been a while since I've seen Piper. Shit, I remember the first time I met her. She was a kid. Young. But she didn't take shit. She's the same now."

I nod.

"That's the kind of woman you need."

"She's fucking perfect."

Miles looks back to Logan, now lost at the piano. "Logan is so full of shit. Thinks he needs to convince everyone he's a shallow asshole."

I shrug. Logan's pleasant enough as a tour mate, but that's as far as our relationship goes. And I like it that way.

"Shit. I forgot."

"Forgot what."

"You're almost as moody as Drew. No offense."

I can't exactly argue.

"My girl's at rounds all day. You're welcome to stay and listen to us bullshit each other, but I figure you've got shit to do."

Like fixing this. "How do you do it?"

He arches a brow. "*It*? First, I throw her on the bed. Then…" He winks. "I can spell it out, step-by-step, if you need a refresher."

"How do you ask her for forever?"

"Oh." His voice is knowing. Like Piper's. That *oh* is packed with a novel's worth of meaning.

How does he do *that*?

I arch a brow. "Oh?"

"What is it, exactly, that's eating at you?"

"Easy questions, huh?"

"Yeah." He looks back to Logan, still lost in his world. "She's not gonna get it. Not unless you explain it to her. I have it easier. Or harder maybe. Meg's sister OD'd. She knows how precarious this shit is. But she never gets how it feels."

"Helps that you have a dozen songs about it."

His laugh is hearty. "It's not too late for you to pick up a pen."

"Over Mal's dead body."

"Doesn't have to be a song. You love Piper, right?"

"Of course."

"You want her to understand, explain it. And don't skip over the ugly parts."

"Yeah." I run my hand through my hair. "But how did you get okay with it? With asking her for a forever you might not have?"

"I didn't."

"You didn't?" Is the man being purposefully oblique? If his lyrics are any indication, the answer is yes.

"Every night, I fall asleep wondering if tomorrow's going to be the day I slip."

That sounds familiar.

"If I'm going to be the second person to OD on my wife. The second person to break her heart."

"How the fuck do you manage that?"

"You get used to it." His expression gets intense. Earnest. A rarity for him. "That voice, the one that tells you you're going to slip, that you're not good enough, that you're the worst thing that ever happened to her—it never goes away. But you get used to it."

"That works?"

He nods. "It gets easier, every day. You must know that. You've been sober forever now."

"Yeah."

"You still feel like you're walking on eggshells?"

"No." Not exactly.

"You still think about getting high every time something hurts?"

"No." I don't.

It seems impossible, but I don't.

When I hurt, I think of Piper.

She fills my heart.

She convinces me I'm not a fuck up.

That I deserve happiness.

That I can do this.

But… that voice.

I look back to Miles. "You were thinking it, when you got married?"

"That I could slip?"

"Yeah."

"Fuck yeah. We were in Vegas. I'd be an idiot not to. It never stops crossing your mind. But you get used to it. Trust me."

I do.

And I think I know how to fix this.

I better fucking be able to fix this.

Chapter Thirty-Nine

PIPER

I don't exactly need to spend the afternoon at Mal and Lacey's place.

I don't mind.

I love my brother.

I love his wife.

I love that she's his wife.

It's still hard to believe that Mal is actually happy, much less married.

It's fun watching *The Apartment* with my sister-in-law.

And even more fun mocking Mal's need for an obscenely healthy dinner.

But I'm not here because I love my family.

I'm here because I'm running away.

Not far away. Not even three miles away.

My drama final went well. I actually feel like I have a handle on my last two exams. Everything is good.

Everything except me and Kit.

I try to block that out.

To focus on my new gig.

Lacey spends most of an hour gushing about the director, especially about her first feature. It's amazing. Perfection. Exactly the kind of thing she wants to make as she moves into features.

Mal is more quiet with his encouragement. But it's there, brightening the air, lifting my mood.

It feels good, being surrounded by this much support.

The second I leave their place and step into my car…

Fuck.

I don't like my uncertainty.

But I can't run from it. Not for long. Sure, I can crash at Mal's place. At Ethan's place. Hell, I can even crash at Joel and Bella's place.

They'll put me to work as a babysitter, but I don't mind.

Hermione is adorable.

And babysitting is as close as I want to get to kids. I'm not one hundred percent on my lack of desire to procreate, but I'm leaning that way.

Kit and I have talked about it. He feels the same uncertainty.

But then Kit isn't sure of anything.

Ahem.

I need to do this like a Band-Aid.

Quick. Fast. So all that pain comes in one burst.

I let my mind wander on the drive back to our place in Venice Beach. There's no traffic this time of night. This sky is dark. The stars are dull, but the moon is big and silver and luminous.

It's beautiful.

Cool breeze. Warm air. White bubbles as deep blue waves crash to the pristine sands.

It doesn't get better than this.

Beautiful house. Nice car. Ocean view.

My life is a fucking fantasy.

Except for the part about my fiancé...

No, he's trying. I need to give him a chance to figure this out.

I park the car in the spot in front of the house and turn it off. My hand reaches for the door, but I don't pull it open.

I need my thoughts in order first.

I'm going to demand an answer at some point, but not tonight.

Not until after finals.

It's an excuse. I can admit that. But I think I'm willing to give myself an out.

I've been with Kit for three years.

For most of my adult life.

I'm not ready for that to be over.

I push the door open and step outside. Cool breeze blows my hair in every direction. Pushes my t-shirt into my skin.

It's nice. Refreshing.

I feel awake. Alive. Ready for whatever he's about to tell me.

Or maybe he's not about to tell me anything. The house is dark except for the light in the bedroom.

It's a dozen steps to the door. I unlock it and press it open.

Moonlight bounces off the big glass table and the shiny silver coffee maker.

Footsteps move down the hall.

"Kit?" I kick off my shoes and drop my purse and keys on the kitchen counter.

All my muscles ache at once. I'm not in the mood for conversation.

I want comfort.

His arms around me.

His lips on my neck.

His fingertips on my skin

His body pressed against mine.

"Hey." He steps off the bottom stair. "Do me a favor and get that light."

Okay… There's a brightness in his voice. I want to take it as a good sign, but I'm not ready to get my hopes up.

Still, I reach for the kitchen light.

A yellow glow falls over the room.

My eyes go wide.

My jaw drops.

Holy shit.

Is he really… Is this really…

"Okay. Explain." There…

There's a palm tree in our living room. Five actually. Only they're not real palm trees. They're cardboard cutouts.

And there's another cardboard cutout in front of them. An altar.

The coffee table is flush with flowers. Real ones. Soft pink roses. My favorite.

And Kit…

He's wearing a black suit and a lei around his neck.

A fresh one.

Fuck, he looks good in that suit.

But the lei…

It doesn't suit him.

At all.

He takes my hands and drops to one knee. "Piper Strong, will you marry me next week."

"Next week? In seven days?"

He nodded. "I have it booked. Technically, it's tentative right now. We have twenty-four hours to confirm."

"This… You." I'm speechless. I'm never speechless.

"You want to do this in Hawaii?"

My chest is light.

My entire body is light.

He really wants to do this.

It's in his eyes.

Those dark, soulful eyes.

They can't lie.

They give his intentions away.

And they're mine.

They're all mine.

Officially.

He nods. "We fly out the morning after your last final. The wedding is the next day, at sunset."

A wedding in Hawaii at sunset.

Marriage in paradise.

Is this really happening?

I barely manage to nod.

"I talked to everyone. They're on board. The hotel has someone who could do hair and makeup. Her portfolio is up on my laptop if you take a look. Everything is ready. I just need you to say yes."

I want to say yes. Of course, I'm going to say yes. But —"How did you get from *I don't know if I can do this* to *let's get married next week*?"

"I did something crazy."

"Yeah?"

"I asked for advice. For help. I never would have done that before. It's being with you, Piper. You... You're the best thing that ever happened to me. You know that?"

My lips press together. "Yeah?"

"Hands down. I wouldn't have figured this out for anyone else." He rubs his thumb over the back of my hand. My index finger. My middle finger my ring finger.

He traces my engagement ring.

He looks up at me, those dark eyes on fire. "I talked to Miles."

Of course. The Sinful Serenade singer is also a recovering addict. Only, he always seems happy.

Well, happy is relative with these guys. They're all moody and demanding.

"He told me shit I should already know. But it helps hearing someone else say it." His voice is strong, sure. "I love you, Piper. I never doubt that. But, I'll always wonder if I'm going to slip. If I'm going to drag you down with me. If I'm going to prove myself right, that I really am the worst thing that ever happened to you."

"You're not. You're the best thing that ever happened to me." He is. I wish I could convince him of that.

"Sometimes, I do believe that. But, other times… I don't know if it's my brain chemistry or my past. I guess it doesn't matter." He stares into my eyes. "There's always going to be a part of me that thinks you're better off without me. Most of me knows that's wrong. But, that voice never quiets. Not completely."

Words get stuck in my throat. There's nothing I can say to convince him he's wrong.

He's the best thing in my life.

But those doubts…

They're still there.

They creep into his mind.

I can see it in the way he gets quiet some days.

In the way he looks at me like I'm far away.

I can feel it in the way he locks me out sometimes.

I don't like it.

But I have to accept it.

I love Kit. Every part of him. The beautiful parts. The ugly parts. The ones that hurt. The ones that make him hate himself.

I stare back into his eyes and I nod. "Okay."

"Okay?"

"I don't know what it's like to hate myself. I don't know what it's like to wonder if I deserve you. Maybe I'm selfish. But it never crosses my mind. I love you. I want you. I need you. And, I understand why you're never going to be sure of yourself. I hate that I can't convince you. But I get it."

He looks up at me. "I do need something from you."

"Anything."

"I'm gonna need you to keep loving me the way you do. When I see myself through your eyes, I get it. I understand why you love me. I don't doubt I'm worth it. That we can really make this work forever."

"Of course."

He stares into my eyes, searching for something. He must find it. Because his smile spreads over his cheeks. "I love you so fucking much."

"I love you too."

He pushes himself to his feet, presses his palms against my lower back, and pulls me into a slow, deep kiss.

God, he tastes good. Like coffee and sugar and Kit.

I sigh as he pulls back.

He's still smiling ear to ear.

I am too.

He made plans.

He's ready to do this.

Fuck, am I actually ready to do this?

I am.

I'm nervous as hell, but I am.

He runs his fingers through my hair. "You ready to get married, baby?"

"I am." I lean into his touch. "But first, we need to celebrate properly."

Chapter Forty

PIPER

The next few days are a blur of finals and congratulations.

Kit picks me up from my last exam and whisks me to Newport Beach.

He even has our swimsuits.

He even jumps into the waves with me.

The water is fucking freezing, but with his arms around me, and his smile lighting up my insides…

I can manage the frigid water temperatures when every other part of me feels this warm.

We're leaving in the morning.

Then we're getting married.

Everything is set.

Tickets are bought.

Friends are on their way.

Bella and Joel managed to convince their nanny to stay overnight for an extra few days.

Lacey is arriving a few hours before the wedding. She has a gig she can't cancel.

Everyone is going to be there.

Celebrating us.

Our love.

Our happiness.

Our marriage.

It still feels like a dream.

We shower and change at the beach then climb back into the car.

Only we don't turn toward the 405.

We don't get on the freeway.

We go straight to Ethan and Violet's place, park in the underground lot, take the elevator to their floor.

Kit slides his arm around me as we knock on the door.

He's nervous.

Too nervous for this to be dinner with Ethan and Violet.

The door pulls open.

And someone yells *surprise.*

Everyone yells *surprise.*

It's a packed room. Everyone is here. Lacey, Mal, Joel, Bella, Violet, Ethan, a dozen other friends.

Violet is standing at the door, her short hair in a perfect straight line, her makeup that perfect mix of *gorgeous* and *don't fuck with me*.

She wraps her arms around me and leans in to whisper. "He looks happy."

"He is. I am. It's…"

"You two belong together. It's that simple." She pulls back with a smile and motions to the crowd gathered around the coffee table. "First things first." She smiles. "We have coffee."

"Yes." I press my palms together. It's been hours since my last cup. Too many hours.

"And cake," Ethan chimes in.

"Cake?" My voice is much too loud and bouncy.

I have a problem, a sugar and caffeine problem, but I don't care.

"It's chocolate with mocha frosting." Ethan nudges Violet. "And a few matcha cupcakes."

Kit squeezes my hand. "Go, baby. I understand your true love is sugar."

I flip him off as I bounce into the room.

Cake and coffee and all my friends.

It's a perfect party.

I follow Violet to the kitchen. She cuts an enormous slice of cake while I fix coffee. Extra sugar. Lots of almond milk.

She sets the slice on a plate and offers it to me.

"Someone else should take the first one." I do have manners.

Violet's smile lights up her green eyes. "Really?"

I nod. "I'm an honorable party, um, what would you call this?"

"Eat the cake, baby." Kit winks at me.

"Come on, Piper. You're looking at that thing the way I look at Bella's tits," Joel says.

Bella hipchecks him.

"What?" He feigns offense. His eyes go to his wife's chest. "You demand more appreciation?"

"It never hurts." She brushes a dark hair behind her ear and adjusts her thick frames. "You do have that look in your eyes, Piper."

"It can be better to delay gratification." He winks at her. Then at Mal and Lacey.

My oldest brother chuckles.

Lacey blushes. No. It's more of a *yes, no, please* flush.

Gross.

That's more details than I need about my brother's sex life.

Damn, everyone here is looking at me like they can't rest until I eat this cake.

I'm being mocked.

But lovingly.

God, it smells like heaven.

"Okay. But only because you insist," I say to no one in particular. I pick up the fork, scoop a bite, bring it to my mouth.

Mmm.

The frosting is a burst of sweet, rich mocha flavor. It melts on my tongue. And the cake itself…

It tastes like heaven too.

I scoop another bite. Another. I motion to Violet. "Well, isn't this a party? Let's hand these out."

"Are you sure?" Violet motions to the enormous cake. "You could save it all for yourself."

"I'm sure." If it was anyone else, I'd flip them off. But it's Violet.

And she's right.

I am tempted to take the cake home with me.

But it's best to turn that down. A sugar crash is not the way I want to spend the flight to Maui.

Or my wedding day.

Or night, for that matter.

I'll have to watch the cake at the reception.

Horrible.

But worth it.

I look to my fiancé, to all the joy in his dark eyes and I motion *come here*.

He does.

He leans in to brush his lips against mine.

"You taste like cake," he whispers.

"Good?" I ask

He nods.

I scoop another bite of the slice and bring it to his lips.

He licks every morsel.

I do the same with my finger, scooping a glob of frosting.

He locks eyes with me as he sucks it off my finger.

Sometimes I forget how intense he is.

And now my knees are knocking together in front of a dozen and a half friends.

And I'm getting tempted to drag Kit into the office for a…

Ahem.

Violet cuts Kit a slice and hands it over. She gets to work handing out cake.

Ethan gets to work handing out coffee. When he's done, he heads over to me and wraps his arms around me.

"You're actually okay with this?" I tease.

"I'm not a total caveman." His voice is bright. Classic Ethan.

"Are too."

"Am not."

"Damn. I can't argue with that logic."

"I know." He pulls back with a smile. "Really, Pipes. I'm happy you're happy." He looks to Kit. "Doesn't mean I won't kick your ass if you break her heart."

I clear my throat.

Ethan shrugs. "Okay. I'm a caveman. I'm still kicking his ass if he breaks your heart."

I struggle not to roll my eyes.

Kit looks to Mal and raises a brow. *That go for you too?*

Mal's voice is even. Steady. "You know how I feel." He

looks to me and raises his plate of cake. "Are you happy, Piper?"

I nod. I'm bursting.

My oldest brother smiles. "Then I'm happy." He looks to Kit. "Take care of her."

"Or he'll kill you. No intermediary ass-kicking," Joel offers.

Everyone nods.

Kit raises his plate. "Wouldn't expect anything less."

Mal chuckles. "I aim to please."

Lacey giggles. Mercifully, she doesn't press the issue further.

Joel looks to Kit and winks. His green eyes meet mine. "You sure you want to put up with Lockhart, Pipes? In three years you'll be a star—"

"Excuse me?" Bella clears her throat. "Are you suggesting I won't help lead you to super-stardom."

"You drop shit like *don't worry, I can get you those dates even if your single flops* every three minutes," he says.

She laughs. "I can."

He laughs back. "But that doesn't exactly suggest you believe in our super-stardom."

"Uh-uh."

"Yeah-huh." He wraps his arms around her. Brings his hands to her ass.

Ethan clears his throat. "Take it outside."

"They're cute." Violet takes his hand and rests her head on his shoulder. "But he's right. Clothes stay on here."

Joel throws them a middle finger without breaking from his kiss.

Bella is more polite. She pulls back with a demure smile. "We'll be good."

"Speak for yourself, angel." Joel winks. He turns to me. "Is anybody gonna say some words? 'Cause I got a few."

Oh God.

"Nothing bad, I promise." He winks at Kit.

Kit nods. "Is there any way to stop you?"

"Fuck no." Joel slides his arms around Bella's waist. He turns toward us. "I've known Lockhart since he was a kid. I've seen him through a lot of shit. But I've never seen him happy like this. You're good for him, Piper. Don't let him forget that."

I can't help but laugh. "I won't."

He looks to Kit. "Don't fuck it up."

Kit nods. "Sage advice."

Everyone laughs.

It may not be lyrical, but it is sage advice.

Joel's smile spreads over his cheeks. "Now, that I've got that shit out of the way." He nods to a giant pink gift bag in the corner of the room. "Three years with Lockhart. I know he's got the tongue piercing, but you must lust after a little variety."

"I must…" Oh… God help me.

"You two get to the whips and chains yet?" Joel asks.

"No." I bite my tongue. I will not react. I will not react. I won't.

This is what he wants.

Like a child throwing a tantrum.

It isn't working. I'm blushing.

And Joel is laughing. "You don't fool me with that shit, Pipes. I know you aren't as innocent as you let on."

"How innocent is that?" I take another bite of cake to swallow down my awkwardness. It's annoying being marked as the naïve one, but looking around this group—

They're a bunch of filthy perverts.

Maybe I *am* the innocent one.

It's bullshit.

But I can live with that.

"Baby, I'm not sure your idea of innocence is in step with most people's." Bella squeezes her husband's waist. "Do you have to torture Piper the night before her wedding?"

"It's two nights before her wedding and fuck yes." Joel turns to me. "You still have that sweet look. Like you don't know what to do with a—"

"Watch it." Kit throws Joel a faux *I'll kick your ass* look.

Or maybe he means it.

"Three years and you haven't tied her up. What the hell are you waiting for?" Joel shrugs. "Or would you rather she…" He raises a brow.

Kit rolls his eyes.

Joel looks to me. "What you think? You have a baby Domme inside you?"

"No, thank you." I fold my arms.

"But Kit tying you up." Joel arches a brow. "I know that shit runs in the family."

"Only—" I nod to Mal.

Joel shakes his head and nods to Ethan.

My brother's smile is wide, proud.

Violet hides behind her hand. "Do we need to discuss this here?"

"Dunno. Do you need Ethan to drop between your legs at four a.m. on the tour bus and wake all us up by screaming his name?" Joel asks.

Violet nods.

Ethan's smile gets wider.

"Baby, that's a stupid question." Bella runs her hands through her husband's hair. "What would you do if it was us?"

"You want a demonstration?" He palms her ass. "More than happy to oblige."

"Can we have a blanket rule?" Ethan asks. "Joel and Bella can't fuck in anyone else's house."

"Who said anything about fucking?" Joel asks. "I'm thinking more getting those gorgeous thighs pinned to my ears—"

Bella covers his mouth with her hand. "Sorry. We..."

"Are perverts," Mal offers.

Lacey nods. "It's charming."

"Takes one to know one." Joel winks at them.

Bella smiles.

"I can control myself." Joel turns back to me. "Let's just say you can have a very fucking exciting honeymoon if you want."

"Thank you." This really is Joel's way of showing he cares.

"The vibe in there is fucking crazy. You should hear the way Bella screams when I—"

Bella clears her throat. It's enough to get her blushing.

Which gets Joel beaming.

Mal leans in to whisper something to Lacey.

God, I can't even imagine what he's saying.

I don't want to imagine it.

So. Much. No.

Ethan shakes his head at Joel. He turns to me. "Have you thought about the ceremony?"

"Huh?" I ask.

"You're not inviting Dad." *So who's walking you down the aisle.*

Oh. I stare back at my middle brother. There's an obvious answer, but I don't want to hurt Ethan.

"I... I was thinking Mal could do it." I turn to him. "If you don't mind."

His poker face cracks.

He melts.

Not for Mal melts.

He actually fucking melts.

It's the happiest I've seen him since his wedding.

"You sure, Piper?" he asks.

I nod.

I'm sure.

I'm sure about forever.

Chapter Forty-One

PIPER

The next day is a blur of airports, jetlag, and long walks on the beach. It's beautiful here. Paradise. But I don't take in much of the crystal blue water, the sweet air, the bright sky.

My stomach is churning with nerves. My chest, my head, my entire body is light.

This is really happening.

Tomorrow.

The thought flits through my mind all night. Sleep comes late, obscenely late. Even though my alarm isn't set to go off until noon, it's a cruel awakening.

I'm alone. In my own room.

I insisted on tradition, the two of us apart all day until we come together.

Forever.

I'm too nervous for coffee. Or breakfast. Or anything but showering, dressing, and meeting Violet in her hotel room.

She throws her arms around me with a squeal. "It's really happening."

I nod. "It is."

She smiles. "I was wondering when you'd crack."

"Huh?"

"You're nervous." She pulls me inside the room and points to the vanity where the makeup artist is setting up.

Why does her room have a vanity?

No fair.

The makeup artist, a pretty woman with long, dark hair, smiles at me. "Are you ready?"

I am.

I really am.

I'VE NEVER BEEN SO NERVOUS I LOST MY APPETITE BEFORE.

It's strange, forcing myself to eat my room service lunch.

It doesn't taste like anything.

I've never been so nervous that food doesn't taste like anything.

I don't want coffee.

That's…

That's ridiculous.

The makeup artist is good. Slow, but good. She starts with Violet, and takes an eternity sculpting her features with soft makeup.

Somehow, Violet manages to own her bright turquoise dress and her natural makeup. She looks beautiful—she always does—but this is the opposite of her usual style.

Then it's my turn.

It takes forever. Or maybe, right now, every second feels like an eternity.

I want our ceremony to happen so badly.

But I'm also drowning in nervous energy.

I try to focus on my surroundings. Beautiful hotel room, breezy air conditioning, silly TV show playing in the background.

It helps. Sorta.

It takes three hours to finish my hair and makeup.

But it's worth it.

It's perfect.

My long blond hair is pinned in an elegant updo. It's adorned with flowers, white ones that perfectly match my dress.

I step into said dress.

And I lose every thought in my head.

I'm really a bride.

This is actually happening.

A knock on the door pulls me out of my thoughts.

"It's not too late to call this off." Ethan's bouncy voice flows through the door. "You know, if you want to commit to never growing up."

"I'm afraid not." My voice is shaky.

Shit. I can't banter with my brother.

I'm in over my head here.

"Sometimes, I worry about you." Violet pulls the door open.

Ethan raises a brow. "*You* worry about *me*?"

She nods. "God, you look so good in that suit." She presses her palm against Ethan's chest. "Were we talking about something?"

"My inability to accept Piper as an adult woman."

She looks back to me with a smile. "She knows you're kidding." She mouths, *right?*

I nod. Once upon a time, Ethan couldn't deal with the idea that I wasn't an innocent, naïve virgin.

But he's over that. Or used to it.

Or smart enough not to bring it up.

Ethan leans into murmur in her ear. "Fuck, Vi, you look good enough to eat."

She clears her throat. "Later."

Ethan presses his forehead against hers.

They manage to make dirty talk adorable.

I'd hate them if I didn't love them so much.

Violet turns back to me. "You look so beautiful. And happy."

"And nervous," Ethan adds.

I flip my brother off.

He smiles. "It happens to everyone, Pipes."

"You were nervous?" I ask.

He nods. "I thought I was going to throw up."

Violet squeezes Ethan's hand. "It's a big deal. Even when you're sure."

"You didn't have any doubts?" Ethan asks.

Violet presses her lips together. "That I wanted you to be mine forever? No. About everything else… Yeah. Weddings make you crazy. But the way you and Kit are doing it… It's going to be perfect."

"I was planning on tormenting her a lot more." Ethan winks at me. "Unless you can't handle it."

I'm not sure if I can. I flip him off anyway.

He smiles. "Really, I am happy for you two."

"You don't want me to die a spinster?" I ask.

"Spinster? Isn't that a little old fashioned, Pipes?" Ethan teases.

"Haha." I mean to sound mocking, but I don't sell it.

I sound more like I'm going to throw up.

Fuck, maybe I am.

I nod to the couch.

Somehow, I make my way there.

I swear, my legs go out from under me.

Violet whispers something to Ethan. He whispers back. The two of them look to me with knowing expressions.

Violet crosses the room and takes a seat next to me.

"Don't worry. You got this." She pulls me into a tight hug.

Do I have this? I'm not sure anymore.

She looks me in the eyes. "You okay?"

I nod. Nervous, but okay.

"You want to be with him forever?"

"Of course."

"You want him to be your husband?"

Kit. My husband. God, it's so romantic it makes me want to throw up. Which isn't exactly helping with my nausea.

Still, I nod.

There's another knock. "Hey." Mal's deep voice flows through the door. "Limo's ready. But you can take as long as you need."

Mal steps inside the room. He's wearing the same suit as Ethan.

God, they both look so strange. All cleaned up, like they're nice Orange County rich boys.

I turn to the Violet. "I'm ready. But I need help getting up."

She smiles. "That sounds about right." She stands and offers me her hands.

I take them.

She pulls me up and into another hug. Her voice is low, a whisper. "You need me to ask your brothers to get lost for a minute?"

I shake my head. I want them here. But—"Does Ethan mind that I asked Mal and not him?"

Violet shakes her head. "Mal is basically your dad. Makes sense. Ethan gets that. He's just… He can't believe you're this grown-up. Honestly, I can't believe it either. But when I look at you, I see it. You're an adult. A woman with a career, who knows what she wants. I'm so proud of you."

I hug her again.

"Hey, stop hogging my baby sister," Mal says.

I choke back a happy tear. Fuck. I'm already crying. By the time I get to the altar, I'm going to be a mess.

I release Violet and take my turn hugging Mal, then Ethan.

We all walk to the lobby together.

To the front entrance, where the limo is waiting.

The driver opens the door for us. "Congratulations."

I wipe another happy tear from my cheek. "Thank you."

I climb into the limo first.

Then Violet.

Then Ethan and Mal.

They take the bench seat opposite ours.

Violet stays next to me.

I rest my head on her shoulder and channel her strength.

Usually, I have plenty of my own.

Right now, my stomach is in my throat.

My heart is beating like it's about to burst out of my chest.

My brothers are merciful. They don't tease me.

They make conversation about *Gossip Girl*.

I don't have a fucking clue what I'm saying, but I manage to banter back.

I take a deep breath as the limo comes to a stop.

Violet squeezes my hand.

"You've got this, Piper." Ethan smiles, his blue eyes bright. "Just think about tonight." He winks.

If he is telling me to think about sleeping with Kit?

He is.

What the hell?

"You actually understand that I have sex?" I'm pretty sure my jaw is on the floor.

Mal chuckles. "Only took four years."

"Hey," Ethan says, "it's good advice. Trust me on that." He looks to Vi. "Back me up, honey."

She laughs. "It's amazing advice."

The driver pulls the door open and offers his hand to someone.

Ethan scoots to the edge of his seat. "I'm proud of you, Piper. You're going to ace that acting gig."

"Thanks." I'd rather not think about that at the moment. I don't need any more pressure.

"And you... you're going to be a happily married woman." Ethan leans in to hug me. He whispers in my ear. "But Mal and I will kill him if he hurts you."

I laugh. "I know."

"As long as we're on the same page." He pulls back with a smile and turns to Mal. "You got this?"

Mal nods.

"You do." Violet gives one of my flowers a last-minute adjustment. "You're going to be perfect."

She follows Ethan out of the limo.

It's just me and Mal.

He looks just as happy as Ethan and Violet.

As I feel.

Well, I'm equal parts nervous and happy.

But it's good nerves. I'm about to own this audition nerves.

He offers me his hand. "Are you ready?"

"I think so."

"Need any advice on married life?"

"Do you have any?"

His smile gets wicked. "Nothing you want to hear."

I can't help but laugh. "Really? All your advice is about sex?"

He chuckles as he takes my hand. "Be honest with him. Tell him when you need him. Don't let him get away with that brooding shit."

"Is that possible?"

"More or less." Mal helps me out of the limo.

Then he steps onto the concrete.

The sky is orange and pink. Sunset. It's soft and beautiful and the beach is the backdrop.

The waves crash with a low roar.

People walk by the ceremony site.

Fuck, that's the ceremony site.

It's a little white altar decked with pink flowers.

And there are a dozen little white chairs.

Mostly full little white chairs.

Someone walks up to us. A wedding coordinator in khakis and a Hawaiian print shirt.

He smiles. "You must be Piper." He holds up my bouquet—pink roses with a bright turquoise ribbon. "Are you ready?"

I nod.

"You must be, Mal." The coordinator smiles at my brother. "You're walking your sister down the aisle?"

Mal nods.

"How sweet." The coordinator nods to the ceremony site. Then to the hotel just to the left of it. "We're going to head from that direction. It's about as much of a reveal as we can manage."

"Okay." I hold the bouquet to my chest.

The coordinator nods to the hotel. "Whenever you're ready."

I take my first step. It's shaky. My grip around Mal's arm tightens.

He walks with steady footsteps. "You know, when I first realized you and Kit were dating, I threatened to kill him if he slipped and dragged you down with him."

My next step is more solid. "That sounds like you."

"I meant it. I still do." His voice is soft, contemplative. "But I don't worry about that being a possibility anymore."

"Never?" Okay, I'm managing an actual gait here. I can do this.

"Every so often. But I know he's all in. With his recovery. With making you happy."

We stop at the winding stone path on the side of the hotel. The ceremony site is just around the corner. I can see the very edge of it.

The coordinator murmurs something into his walkie talkie.

"You're good for each other." Mal looks me in the eyes. "I know you two are going to have a long, happy life together." He leans in to hug me. "I'm proud of you, Piper."

"Everyone is saying that."

"We are. It's overwhelming, seeing how grown up you are. How strong you are. I've always wanted the world for you. I'm just happy I got my wish."

"Mal." I blink back a tear. "Fuck. I'm crying."

"I'm not taking it back." He smiles. "You deserve every bit of happiness in the world."

I hug him again.

Fuck, I'm really crying now.

I suck a deep breath through my teeth and exhale slowly.

The coordinator looks to me with a nod. "They're ready for you." He motions to the path.

I…

I'm ready.

I take Mal's arm and I take my first step.

My next.

My feet move of their own accord. I feel more like I'm floating.

We turn the corner.

The ceremony site comes into view.

And there's Kit, at the altar.

All my friends, standing, smiling at me.

The second my eyes lock with Kit's, everyone else disappears.

The world is us.

His wide smile.

That black suit that brings out his dark eyes.

God, there's so much joy in his eyes.

My nerves fall away as I move closer.

Past the first row of chairs.

The next.

There.

Mal leans in to plant a kiss on my cheek then he takes his spot in the front row.

And there's Kit.

And the officiant behind him.

I take my place and take my fiancé's hands.

He smiles at me.

I smile back the widest smile I've ever smiled.

I must look silly.

Ridiculous, even.

But I don't care.

My heart is bursting with love, affection, pride, joy.

The officiant addresses our friends. He goes through a short story about us.

Then he's reading a poem.

Turning to Kit, saying his vows.

And Kit is repeating them.

Then he's reciting my vows.

And I'm staring into Kit's eyes, repeating them.

The officiant passes Kit a ring.

And he slides it onto my finger.

And my heart is bursting out of my chest.

I barely catch the officiant's words. "You may now kiss."

Kit leans down.

Presses his lips to mine.

Kisses me like he wants me to have every bit of happiness in the world.

He does.

I do.

We both do.

Chapter Forty-Two

PIPER

Kit pins me to the wall as the elevator doors slide together.

He traces the sloping low backline of my dress.

The brush of his fingertips sends a shiver back up my spine.

It wakes up all my nerves.

Pushes away my exhaustion.

We've been dancing and drinking (sparkling cider for him, champagne for me) all night.

Okay, and eating cake.

Delicious, sweet chocolate cake with rich cocoa icing.

He brings his other hand to my hair and pulls out a bobby pin. "Ready to collapse?"

"Not until I have my way with you."

He presses his hips against mine as he leans in to kiss me.

He tastes good. Like sugar and chocolate and Kit.

Like every bit of love and affection in the world.

I sigh as our kiss breaks.

He drags his lips to my neck. "Whatever my wife wants." He pulls out another bobby pin. Another. Another.

Flowers scatter on the floor as my hair falls over my shoulders.

Fuck, that feels good.

Like my head is finally free.

I stare into his dark eyes as he drags his fingers through my hair.

I still can't believe it.

He's my husband.

Mine.

Forever.

Fuck, it's romantic.

I rise to my tiptoes, and I slide my hand into his hair, and I kiss him hard.

Like he's everything.

He is.

His tongue slides into my mouth.

His fingertips slip under my dress.

He caresses me with an impossible soft touch.

It wakes up every tired part of my body.

It dissolves my desire for sleep.

The only thing I want is Kit.

My husband.

Fuck, I'm never going to get tired of thinking that.

I rock my hips against his.

I tug at his hair.

I kiss him harder.

I'm about to tear off his suit when the elevator doors slide open.

"Congratulations." A stranger's voice flows into the tiny space.

My cheeks flame as I pull back. "Thank you." I nod to the stranger, an older man with his wife.

They look happy.

Like they're celebrating their anniversary.

Like they've been in love for thirty years.

Kit nods his own *thank you* as he takes my hand and pulls me into the hallway.

I practically run to follow him.

I love this dress, but I want out of it.

Now.

He stops at the end of the hall, pulls a keycard from his pocket, unlocks the door. "You want to do this, right?"

"Huh?"

He smiles. "Come here." He kicks the door open.

Then he's sliding his arms around me, lifting me, holding me against his chest.

I squeal as he carries me over the threshold.

The door slams shut behind us.

The room comes into focus.

It's a huge suite, with a plush king bed, a soft teal sofa, a balcony with a view of the ocean and the stars.

The sky is beautiful.

But there's only one thing in the room I want.

"Bed. Now." I wrap my arm around Kit's neck and hold on tightly.

He looks down at me with a smile. "You that tired?"

"Sex. Now."

He leans down to set me on the bed.

I spread out on my back as I stare up at him. "I like this view."

He drops to his knees, wraps his hands around my ankles, and pulls me to the edge of the bed. "I like this view better."

He peels off my shoes, one at a time.

Then he's pressing my dress to my knees.

Up my thighs.

My husband pushes my legs apart and plants a kiss on my inner thigh. "Been thinking about this all day."

"Yeah?"

"Yeah." His fingers curl into the edges of my panties. Slowly, he pulls them all the way to my ankles. "I want my wife coming on my face."

Fuck. It's so romantic. "Say it again."

"I want—" He presses his lips to my inner thigh. "My wife—" He drags his lips higher, higher, higher. "Coming on my face."

"Kit." I reach for his hair.

"Yeah, baby?"

"I love you."

"I love you too." He presses his lips to my thigh. "And I need you. Fuck, I need you so badly, Piper."

His lips mover higher.

Higher.

There.

His tongue flicks against my clit.

It's quick.

Soft.

A tease.

He does it again.

Again.

Again.

Until my thighs are pinned to his cheeks.

Until I'm groaning his name like it's a curse.

Until I'm tugging at his hair.

His fingers curl into my thighs.

He pins me to the bed.

And he licks me harder.

Harder.

There.

Pleasure floods my pelvis.

It's exactly what I need.

He's exactly what I need.

My muscles relax as he works me. His tongue is soft and wet, and fuck, it's right where I need it.

The tension in my sex builds.

That piercing taps against my flesh.

"Fuck, Kit." I tug at his hair.

It's intense. Almost too intense.

He does it again.

Again.

Again.

I buck against his mouth.

I groan his name.

Every flick of his tongue pushes me closer to the edge. That tension winds tighter.

Tighter.

There.

With the next flick of his tongue, everything releases.

I scream his name as I come.

The world goes white. It's bliss, nothing but pure, sweet bliss.

That's my husband between my legs.

It's so fucking romantic.

But I need more.

I tug at his hair. "You need to be naked. Now."

"You too." He pushes himself to his feet, wipes his mouth with the back of his hand, undoes his tie.

My legs are still shaking with aftershocks.

Somehow, I get on my feet.

And I pull Kit's tie off.

He slides out of his suit jacket.

I undo every one of his buttons.

"You looked so good in your suit." I drag my fingers down his torso. "I almost hate to take it off."

"No, you don't."

"Okay, I don't." I cup him over his slacks. Fuck, I want that. Now.

"You look fucking amazing, baby." He traces the right strap of my dress. "You're a vision."

"Yeah?"

He nods. "Perfect." He leans in to press his lips against mine. "My wife is a fucking angel."

Every part of me gets warm at once. "My husband is irresistible."

He pushes his slacks to his feet and steps out of them.

He pushes my dress off one shoulder.

Then the other.

It falls to my waist, catching at my hips.

Kit helps me shimmy out of it.

He wraps his arms around me.

We tumble onto the bed together, lips locked, limbs a tangled mess.

I slide my tongue into his mouth.

Wrap my arms around him.

Tug at his hair.

He falls back onto his back.

I push myself up, on top of him.

There's so much in those soulful brown eyes.

Love. Need. Trust.

Desire.

I plant my hands on his shoulders, straddle him, bring my body onto his.

His tip strains against me.

Fuck.

I sigh as he slides inside me.

That's my husband inside me.

I'm whole.

Complete.

Exactly where I'm supposed to be.

He wraps his arms around my back, pulls me closer, kisses me harder.

We stay locked like that as we rock together.

My world is Kit. His soft lips, his calloused fingertips, his hard cock driving inside me.

His groans vibrating down my neck.

His hair, his eyes, his skin.

It's all mine.

And I'm all his.

I shift my hips a little faster. A little harder. I'm almost there, and I need to be there.

I need to come with my husband.

He brings his hand to my pelvis and strokes my clit with his thumb.

Fuck.

I lose track of everything but the pleasure coursing through me.

A few more rocks of my hips, a few more groans, a few more tugs at his hair and I'm there.

I groan his name as I come.

He rocks me through my orgasm, staring up at me like I'm the only thing he wants in the world.

Then he flips me over, pins me to the bed, drives into me hard and fast.

His eyelids flutter together.

His lips part with a sigh.

One more thrust, and he's there.

Spilling inside me.

Groaning my name as he comes.

Collapsing next to me and holding me close.

I nestle into his chest as I catch my breath. "I love you so much."

"I love you too."

I let my eyelids press together. "Tell me I can sleep forever."

"After I'm done with you."

"Compromise." I press my palm into his chest. "The cornerstone of any happy marriage."

He chuckles. "True. But you can only sleep until ten. We're meeting everyone for brunch."

"Uh-uh. More sleep."

He pulls me closer. "We can cancel."

I shake my head. "It's sweet, everyone wanting to celebrate with us a little more." I stare into my husband's eyes. "We're a family. All of us."

He nods.

"A crazy, weird, dysfunctional family."

Kit chuckles. "True."

"But I wouldn't have it any other way."

Tempting Teaser

BRENDON

Get *Tempting* Now

Kaylee plants her palms on the table. Her cheeks spread to her ears. They're pink. Then red. She's laughing so hard her tits are shaking.

Damn, that tight blue dress, the same blue as her glasses.

She looks amazing, like the sweet, innocent angel she is and like the sex goddess I'm desperate to unleash.

But I still hate that scrap of fabric with every fiber of my being.

I hate every ounce of air between us.

Every flint of wood in this table.

Every guy here looking at her the way I am.

Fuck, if I don't get ahold of myself, I'm going to break a few arms. And maybe my hand. And I can't exactly finish Alex's back piece at nine a.m. tomorrow with broken fingers.

Em wraps her arms around Kaylee.

Kaylee laughs, pushing her long blond hair behind her ears and gathering it at one shoulder.

Her eyes flit around the room.

They catch mine.

They scream *I'm about to wish for you to take me to your room*.

Or maybe that's in my head.

Today is the day.

She's no longer a temptation that can get me locked up. Just a temptation that can rip away everything that matters to me.

Em leans in to whisper in her ear. I know my sister. I know exactly what she's saying. *Wish for someone to fuck tonight.*

Not happening.

Not as long as I'm here.

I hate to be a cunt-blocker, really, I do, but there's no way Kaylee is taking home anyone on my watch.

I have no idea how she's managed to stay single this long.

She's beautiful. Smart. Funny. Kind. And innocent... fuck, the way her cheeks are blushing.

The way she's leaning over the table, letting her eyelids fall together, parting her lips...

I could teach her so many things.

I could teach her everything.

But I can't.

She's my sister's best friend.

And as much as Em is a brat, she's all the family I've got.

These two are the most important people in my life.

My cock is going to have to cool it.

It's not getting anywhere near Kaylee.

I plant on the Kelly green deck chair, the one under the old lamp with the too yellow bulb.

Even though we're in one of the most crowded cities in Southern California, the beach is empty. Still. All the voices and laughter are coming from the house. The roar of the ocean isn't enough to muffle the party.

I should head inside and kick out Emma's friends. Insist on driving Kaylee back to her place. Lecture both of them about drinking too much.

But I'm not in the mood to play Dad today. I'm tired of playing Dad, period. Emma and I never got along, not exactly, but we used to have a rapport. We were a team. A *you're annoying, but not quite as annoying as Mom or Dad* team, but we were still a fucking team.

Now, the majority of my relationship is lecturing her and yelling some equivalent of *go to your room.*

And her yelling back *you're not my dad.*

I force myself to look out at the ocean.

It's beautiful. Dark water. Soft sand. Stars bright enough to shine against the black sky but dulled by light pollution all the same.

None of it distracts me.

None of the eight million things going on in my life distract me.

I need a way to get Kaylee out of my head. I've tried everything—work, play, other women, fucking myself, not fucking myself.

Nothing helps.

I pull out my sketchbook and flick my pen a few times. A few more. My warm up sketch is a messy abstract shape. It means something, I'm sure, but I don't have a clue what that is.

I turn the page. Outline the octopus going on Will's bicep tomorrow afternoon. Attempt to fill in the shading.

The details don't come. The only image in my mind is Kaylee. The brightness in her green eyes, the smile spreading over her pink lips, that coy hip tilt. Like she knows how badly I want my hands on those hips.

Like she's going to roll that dress up her thighs, plant her palms on the table, and shoot me a *please, fuck me now* look.

I don't need a tattoo mockup.

I need her naked in my bed.

"Hey." The side door slides open and Kaylee steps outside. Her steps aren't soft the way they normally are.

They're messy. Quick.

Her eyes are brighter than normal.

Bolder.

She plants on the lounge chair, next to me. Her thigh presses against mine. Her fingers skim the edges of my sketchbook.

She leans over my shoulder, pressing her chest against my arm, looking up at me with those doe eyes. "Can I see?"

Not the sketchbook. The shit I have in here, of her, will terrify her. Kaylee is sweet. Innocent. I haven't asked, but I'd bet—I have bet Dean—she's a virgin.

My cock rouses at the thought of being the first inside her. Fuck, my lips, my tongue, my fingers—every part of me wants to be her first.

Not happening.

"You looking for a nautical tattoo?" I shoot back.

Her smile spreads over her cheeks. "Maybe. What do you suggest?"

I drag my fingertips over her shoulder, drawing the

shape that best suits her. It's a bad idea, touching her like this. It's doing shit to me.

And from the way her eyelids are pressing together and her lips are parting with a sigh, I'm pretty sure it's doing shit to her.

Fuck, I need a thousand cold showers.

Even if Kaylee wasn't Em's best friend, she's a sweet girl. Someone who deserves a nice guy. A guy who can give her a normal life. Not an asshole who destroys everything he touches.

Even so, I trace the outline of a would-be tattoo up to the tip of her shoulder. "A mermaid."

"I like it."

"I know. You've seen *The Little Mermaid* a thousand times."

"At least two thousand." She looks up at me. "What do you say? Right now? I'm finally old enough to sign the form."

"Okay." I take her hand and pull her to her feet. "Let's walk to the shop. One topless mermaid."

Her eyes go wide. She stammers, presses her toes together. The plastic of her heels clicks. Her teeth sink into her lip. "I, uh..."

"Hate having your bluff called?"

"No, I just... I need to think about it a little more."

"Bullshit." I can't help but smile. She's adorable flustered.

"No, just regular... uh... that isn't why I came out here."

I arch a brow.

She scoots toward me. It's a tiny movement. Soft. More like the Kaylee I know. The sober one.

"Well, it's my birthday." Her fingers curl around my wrist. "And I want a birthday kiss."

How about a birthday fuck? How about a birthday coming on my face until my lips are numb?

"I only give birthday spankings." My voice is steady even though my heart is pounding against my chest. Fuck, the thought of bending Kaylee over that table and—

"Okay." She presses her lips together. "Let's go. Right here, right now."

"You can handle eighteen?"

She nods.

She can't, but it's tempting anyway...

"Let's go, Brendon." She takes my hand and places it on her hip. Her eyes meet mine. They bore into mine. They demand every thought in my head. Or at least all the ones about stripping her naked. "Or did I call your bluff?"

"Bend over and plant your hands on the glass if you want to find out." She *is* calling my bluff. And now I'm calling hers.

Only this is one time—

My sister saves me from my filthy thoughts. She bounces out the door, throws her arms around Kaylee, and pulls her from her seat. "Stop hiding from all the guys at the party."

"Your brother is a guy."

Emma scoffs. Her nose scrunches. It lights up her dark eyes—the same deep brown as mine. She runs her fingers through her violet hair and just barely restrains herself from rolling her eyes.

Kaylee's fingers brush the back of my hand as she turns toward Emma. "Sorry, Em, but it's undeniable. Just look at him."

Emma sticks out her tongue and mouths *gross*. "Mr. Look What a Brooding Bad Boy I Am will be here tomorrow." She grabs Kaylee's hand and pulls her toward the door. "These other guys won't." Emma looks to me. "You don't have to stay and supervise."

"Nice try," I say.

Emma laughs. She blows me a kiss then turns back to her best friend. "Don't wait up."

Kaylee's eyes meet mine. "Did you mean it?"

One part of me did. The rest of me knows better. I play coy. Shrug.

"I'll collect eventually."

"Birthdays only."

"Even so."

I watch her round hips sway as she walks away.

Fuck, that dress...

Fuck me.

How the hell am I going to get this girl out of my head?

Get *Tempting* Now

Sing Your Heart Out Teaser

Between the throbbing house music and the dance floor full of beautiful people grinding, it's difficult to move. It's harder to think.

I need to pee. Now. Waiting in the line snaking around the corner is not an option.

How can there only be one bathroom downstairs? One hundred people plus one bathroom equals far too many tortured bladders.

Kara must know where the bathroom is. Wherever she is.

I push through the crowd, but there's no sign of my best friend.

Someone bumps into me, her hip pressing firmly against my pelvis. Dammit, my bladder is going to explode at this rate.

Screw upstairs being off-limits. This isn't a church. It's some up-and-coming band's Hollywood mansion. I'm not about to pee my pants respecting the sanctity of rock stars' bedrooms.

There's a couple making out on the curving staircase. I step past them and make my way to the second floor. The sounds of music and conversation fade to a murmur. I'm tempted to hang out here until Kara is ready to go home.

Parties are not my scene. Even my bladder hates them.

I scan the wall, trying to figure out which of the five doors is attached to the smallest room. There. Second on the left. That must be it.

I turn the knob and push the door open.

Not a bathroom.

Definitely not a bathroom.

There are two people on a bed. The woman is on all fours. The man is kneeling behind her.

They're naked.

They're having sex.

Then they're not. The grunting stops. Flesh ceases to smack together.

The man looks at me. There's no sign of embarrassment or awkwardness on his face. He's totally unmoved.

The woman shrieks. She scrambles off the bed, pulling a sheet over her chest. "Miles, you fucker. I told you I don't do threesomes!"

Miles. There's something familiar about him. I try to place him but my thinking abilities are back to zero.

He's tall, broad shoulders and chest, sculpted abs, and below his bellybutton...

He's hard.

He's hard and he's huge.

Save for the condom, he's completely and utterly naked.

A blush spreads across my cheeks. I stammer, attempting and failing to speak. I've never seen that before. Not in person. In movies, sure. Textbooks, of course.

But never in person.

I can't look away.

The guy, Miles, makes eye contact. His voice is even. Calm. "You mind?"

I take a step backwards. My foot sinks into the plush carpet. I only barely manage to hold my balance. "Excuse me. I thought this was the bathroom."

"Next door on the left."

I know I'm red. Beet red. "Thanks."

I pull the door closed so I'm alone in the hallway. Next door on the left.

I step into the bathroom, lock the door, and die of embarrassment.

It takes twenty minutes for my cheeks to return to a normal color. I slink back to the sprawling main room and do my best to blend in amongst the partygoers.

Every inch of the hardwood floor is packed with beautiful people talking, flirting, or making out.

It's like the up-and-coming models, actors, and musicians are attracted to each other. They have a certain glow that mere mortals lack. And here I thought this was a normal college-students-with-a-keg-and-cheap-vodka kind of shindig.

Kara's friend invited us. He's in a band. Are they really this popular? I can't remember their name, but then it's hard to think of anything but Miles naked on the bed, hard and ready for action.

The lines of his hips and torso are burned into my brain.

And his…

Dammit, I'm not going there.

I find the closest thing to an empty corner and try to clear my head. I fail. My mind keeps going back to that vivid mental image.

Miles. He was unfazed, like the sex meant nothing to him. Like the girl on his bed meant nothing to him.

The man is a player. He's not the kind of guy I need in my life. He doesn't deserve my thoughts.

This stops. Now.

I scan the room for some better way to stay occupied.

It's no use. He's here. Miles is still effortless and aloof. He's still unaffected.

The guy has already moved on from the blonde in the bedroom. He's flirting with a redhead in a designer dress and stilettos.

She's model gorgeous with perfect hair and makeup. I'm standing here in an H&M skirt and blouse, my brown hair its usual frizzy mess, my black eyeliner doing little to enhance my plain-Jane brown eyes. Liner, mascara, and under-eye concealer are the extent of my makeup knowledge. I think I'm the only woman here who isn't contoured. Hell, I know I'm the only one wearing canvas sneakers.

I don't belong here.

It doesn't make sense that Miles is looking at me instead of the pretty redhead.

But he is. His clear blue eyes are fixed on mine. They're gorgeous. I couldn't see them in the dark but out here, they're practically shining.

Heat spreads across my chest. I'm gawking.

He smiles, reveling in my attention.

I press my eyelids together to temper my out-of-control blushing. It's no help. My head fills with that beautiful image of him in nothing but a condom.

Why did I let Kara talk me into coming to this party?

I push my way through the crowd, trying to get as far from Miles's gaze as possible. A dozen steps and I'm standing in the clean, modern kitchen. It's dark and mostly empty.

"You're not big on respecting people's privacy, huh?"

It's the same voice I heard upstairs. Miles.

I could swear I've heard it before. A lot, even.

I turn so we're face to face. Why does Miles seem so familiar? I don't go to parties. Hell, I've been MIA the last few months.

I wouldn't forget his strong jaw, his messy brown hair, or his gorgeous blue eyes.

Those eyes are fixed on me. He's staring at me, picking me apart.

I don't like the scrutiny. Sure, I'm hiding. But I'm not admitting that to him.

I clear my throat. "No, I'm not big on alcohol. Can't find anything else to drink."

He reaches past me. His hand brushes against my shoulder as he pulls open the fridge. He nods to a row of water bottles on the middle shelf. "Help yourself."

"Thanks."

Miles looks so familiar. And his voice is familiar too. Almost like he...

No. That's not possible.

There's no way this guy is the singer of alternative rock band Sinful Serenade, the guy who sings *In Pieces*, the guy who's been haunting my thoughts for the last three months with his breathy, tortured voice. With all the pain in his soulful eyes.

I try to recall the song's music video but my damn brain goes right back to the image of Miles naked on the bed.

Damn. I watched that video a thousand times. It was a

massive hit. The song hit the top 40 for a week or two, a rarity for alternative rock in this day and age.

More importantly, the video and the song went right to my soul. The singer was whispering in my ear. He promised that I wasn't alone. He promised that I wasn't the only person who had ever felt this way.

I understood him and he understood me. We were the only two people in the world who knew how badly it hurt, losing everything that mattered.

The man who sings *In Pieces* is a tortured soul. He doesn't screw one woman, wash up, then move on to flirting with lay number two.

Kara keeps playing down how famous her friend is.

He lives here. I know that much.

This Miles guy seems to live here.

Fuck.

Why didn't Kara warn me her friend was in *that* band?

Miles clears his throat. "You okay?"

I nod a yes and attempt to hold his gaze. "Don't walk in on casual sex very often."

"Mhmm."

"I was looking for the bathroom."

He laughs. "Is that the best you can do?"

"I was." I take a half-step backwards. "Excuse me. I should go."

His voice drops an octave. "You're not going to let me formally introduce myself?"

"Okay." My stomach flutters. "I'm Meg Smart."

"Miles Webb." He takes my hand with a strong grip. His eyes pass over me like he's trying to place me. "How is it we haven't met before?"

"I don't go to parties."

"Guess that makes this my lucky day." His hand

brushes against my wrist. Then it's back at his side. He leans in a little closer, his eyes on mine. "Why'd you decide to come tonight?"

I should be the one asking him that. "My friend convinced me I wouldn't hate it."

"What's the verdict?"

"I still don't like parties." I take a deep breath. "Why'd you come tonight?"

"That was my bedroom you burst into."

Somehow, my cheeks burn hotter.

His eyes rake over me. "Can't blame you for looking. I'd do the same."

My knees go weak at the seductive tone to his voice. That's him, the guy who sings *In Pieces*, the man who has been haunting my dreams.

That song is the centerpiece of my *listen on repeat and fall apart* playlist.

I try to formulate some excuse for why I need to leave immediately, but nothing comes. "You're um… you're in the band? The one that is throwing this party?"

"Yeah. Sinful Serenade. I'm the vocalist." His eyes pass over me again. He takes his time, like he's sure I'll be in his bed in thirty minutes flat.

A pang of desire shoots straight to my core. My damn body isn't obeying my commands. It can't help wanting Miles Webb. There's something appealing about the tattoos poking out from under his t-shirt. About the confidence in his eyes.

It's not like me to fall for the bad boy.

Even when he's so tall. Two inches taller than me at least. I'm 5'11', a giant for a women. I tower over most of the men I know.

But not Miles.

I take a deep breath, trying to convince my body it doesn't want him.

He's bad news.

A player.

A rock star even.

But I can't stop staring.

I clear my throat. "I was looking for my friend, Kara. She's tight with some guy in your band. They go way back."

"Oh, yeah, Drew's friend. Heard a lot about her last tour."

"So, I should really find her." I step aside. "And go home. I have to study. You know how it is. Or maybe not, being a rock star and all. But I have a test tomorrow."

I turn and make my way out of the kitchen.

There are footsteps behind me. "Meg?"

I spin, eye to eye with Miles again. Once again, my mind flashes with the image of him kneeling on that bed, his cock hard, the muscles of his thighs and torso taut.

How is it possible that Miles is the guy who has been singing me to sleep? He's not a poet.

He's a manwhore.

"Yes?" I ask.

"Your friend isn't in a state to drive."

He points to Kara, curled up on the couch. Her dark eyes are filled with an expression of drunken excitement. She looks especially short and curvy next to her tall, muscular friend. That must be Drew. His black hair and intense brown eyes are appealing. No wonder she's staring at him like she wants to devour him.

She bounces to her feet and throws her arms around me. "Are you having fun? Please, tell me you aren't completely miserable."

I hug back. "Only partially."

She laughs. "That's a start!"

Good. She still happy. Kara is an endlessly patient friend. She's been dragging me out of mourning for months now. I'm not going to ruin her night.

"I'm about ready to go home," I say. "I'll take a cab."

"No. I can drive. It's getting late," she says.

The dark-haired guy, Drew, butts in. "Kendrick, you are way too drunk to drive. If you even think about getting in your car, I'll throw you over my shoulder, carry you to my room, and strap you to my bed."

Her eyes light up the second he calls her by her last name. "I didn't know you were into that. Do you have rope or handcuffs or what?"

"I'll call you a fucking cab." His voice is equal parts playful and protective.

She nudges him and points to me. "This is my friend Meg, who you are so rudely ignoring in favor of lecturing me."

He pushes off the couch and offers his hand. "Drew Denton. Nice to meet you."

I shake. "Meg Smart."

"Miles giving you a hard time?" Drew asks.

"I can handle myself," I say.

"If you won't listen to reason—" Drew turns back to Kara "—then I will drive you home."

Kara looks Drew in the eyes. "You were drinking too."

"I can." I bite my tongue. Dammit, Kara's car is a stick. I can't drive us home. "Never mind."

Miles butts in. "I'll drive you guys home."

Drew's eyes narrow. He shoots Miles an incredulous look.

"Not letting you drive tonight." Miles throws back a stern look. "You'd do the same."

Slowly, Drew's protective expression melts. He and Miles share a look of understanding.

The cocky singer turns to Kara. "Your keys."

"It's a manual." She digs through her purse.

"That's fine." He smirks. "I know how to handle my stick."

Author's Note

I didn't decide I was writing *Dangerous Encore* until the week I finished *Dangerous Fling*. I was nowhere near ready to let go of the characters. Or the series.

There's something intoxicating and overwhelming about writing a series. I've spent most of the last year living with the men of Dangerous Noise and the women they love. To me, the characters are as real and vibrant as anyone I know. Saying goodbye to them is like saying goodbye to a friend who's moving away. I know they'll be okay, wherever they are, but I hate that I don't get to hang out with them anymore.

I'm constantly humbled by how much readers love my characters. So many of you write me to ask for yet another glimpse at Sinful Serenade or Dangerous Noise. It's the most flattering thing an author can hear—that you can't get enough. Okay, "your books got me through chemo" is up there too. I'm not planning a *Sinful Ever After Again* or a *Dangerous Encore Two*, but I'm not going to say goodbye to these guys either. They'll be making appearances in the Inked Heart series, starting with *Tempting* (coming this

September, featuring tattoo artist Brendon and his kid sister's best friend Kaylee. Turn the page for a sneak peek).

I *can't* say goodbye. Not a forever goodbye. Not when I love the guys as much as I do.

But this is *a* goodbye, and it's bittersweet. I love the way this book turned out. I hate that it's the end.

Thank you so much for joining me on this journey. I hope you've fallen as in love with Ethan, Kit, Joel, and Mal as I have. And I hope you'll be back for *Tempting*.

If you loved this note, you'll probably dig my Facebook Group, Crystal's Groupies. It's packed with teasers, discussion, hot guys, giveaways, and personal notes like this.

Prefer more straight to business updates or not on Facebook? Join my mailing list. You'll get bonus scenes for every Dangerous Noise book and *Sing for Me*, the exclusive prequel to *Sing Your Heart Out*.

Need more tattooed bad boys? Check out *Tempting* and the rest of my Inked Hearts books.

As always, thanks for reading.

Love,

Crystal

Acknowledgments

My first thanks goes to my husband, for his support when I'm lost in bookland and for generally being the sun in my sky. Sweetheart, you're better than all the broken bad boys in the world. Even Jesse.

The second goes to my father, for insisting I go to the best film school in the country, everything else be damned. I wouldn't love movies, writing, or storytelling half as much if not for all our afternoon trips to the bookstore and weekends at the movies. You've always been supportive of my goals, and that means the world to me.

A big shout out to all my beta readers. You helped give me the confidence to put out a book a little more heartbreaking than usual. And also to my ARC readers for helping spread the word about Dangerous Noise to everyone else in the world.

A special thanks to my fellow pop-punk addict, Molle, for fangirling over music with me, for talking me through my business decisions, and for reminding me that loving my work matters as much as all the marketing money in the world.

Athena Wright, you are the best author BFF a girl could ask for. Thank you for your feedback, for being my chat buddy, and for always being there to give me the perspective I need.

To my cover designer Sara Hansen, thank you for your work in making my rock star series perfect. To my editor Marla, thank you for whipping the story and the prose into shape. And thanks to Give Me Books and The Rock Stars of Romance and to all the other book bloggers who helped get the word out.

As always, my biggest thanks goes to my readers. Thank you for picking up *Dangerous Encore.* I hope you'll be back for *Tempting.*

Also by Crystal Kaswell

Sinful Serenade

Sing Your Heart Out - Miles

Strum Your Heart Out - Drew

Rock Your Heart Out - Tom

Play Your Heart Out - Pete

Sinful Ever After – series sequel

Just a Taste - Miles's POV

Dangerous Noise

Dangerous Kiss - Ethan

Dangerous Crush – Kit

Dangerous Rock – Joel

Dangerous Fling – Mal

Dangerous Encore - series sequel

Inked Hearts

Tempting - Brendon

Hooking Up - Walker

Pretend You're Mine - Ryan

Hating You, Loving You - Dean

Breaking the Rules - Hunter

Losing It - Wes

Accidental Husband - Griffin

The Baby Bargain - Chase

Inked Love

The Best Friend Bargain - Forest

The First Taste - Holden

The Roomie Rulebook - Oliver

Dirty Rich

Dirty Deal - Blake

Dirty Boss - Nick

Dirty Husband - Shep

Dirty Desires - Ian

Dirty Wedding - Ty

Dirty Secret - Cam

Pierce Family

Broken Beast - Adam

Playboy Prince - Liam

Ruthless Rival - Simon - coming soon

Standalones

Broken - Trent & Delilah

Come Undone Trilogy

Come Undone

Come Apart

Come To Me

Sign up for the Crystal Kaswell mailing list

Printed in Great Britain
by Amazon

27093707R00239